Cyclone Racer

By

Doug Drummond

This book is a work of fiction. Places, events, and situations in this story are purely fictional. Any resemblance to actual persons, living or dead, is coincidental.

ISBN: 1-4107-0524-2 (e-book)
ISBN: 1-4107-0525-0 (Paperback)

Library of Congress Control Number: 2003093323

This book is printed on acid free paper.

Printed in the Unites States of America
Bloomington, IN

1stBooks - rev. 08/20/03

DEDICATION

I sometimes think of those that have given me a helping hand in the course of my life. They are people I will never forget. Yet, more than any, I appreciate my wife Linda.

Thanks. I love you.

PROLOGUE

Sixteen recruits had survived the six-week session of the Long Beach Police Academy. The stress and anxiety of intensive training had finally come to an end. Sixteen of twenty original candidates would graduate.

Announcement of the concluding ceremonies had been delivered. November 20, 1959 – a day all sixteen would remember.

* * *

The Long Beach Police Department requests your attendance to celebrate the

conclusion of its first six week

LONG BEACH POLICE ACADEMY

GRADUATION CEREMONY

November 20, 1959

4:00 PM

Place: Belmont Shore Fire Station (upstairs from the old police sub-station)

5365 East Second Street, Long Beach

Please join us as we honor these graduates of our new six-week police academy.

Dates attended: October 12, 1959 through November 20, 1959.

Space is limited, therefore only selected members of the Long Beach Police
Department and the immediate families of graduates are invited. All seating is by
reservation.

RSVP: telephone HE 69811, Personnel Division.

Cameras are welcome.

Please arrive early. The doors close and the program begins at 4:00 PM.

Members of the graduating police academy class sat facing west in the front row of the second floor classroom. Family members were seated in the four rows behind them. Coffee, punch and cookies waited on a folding table placed against the wall at the south end of the room. Selected Police Department officials sat in two short rows on the right side of the room.

The front of the room was prepared like a stage; the flag of the United States stood on the left of the podium and the California flag on the right. Between the flags, a uniformed Police Captain leaned forward, his left hand on the podium. A City of Long Beach seal emblazoned its front. A chalkboard stood to his rear.

The ceremony began with the pledge to the flag. A prayer followed and ranking officers were introduced. The recruits were asked to stand, raise their right hands and be sworn as police officers. They did. Family members were then called forward to participate as the new badges were pinned on the graduates. Smiling people followed and stood close with cameras and the flashes intermittently lit up the room. After that event, all returned to their seats.

The new officers, wearing shining gold badges, sat at a military brace. The badges made them in full uniform for the first time, guns on hips and hats in their laps. They looked toward the Captain in anticipation of his words – the keynote graduation address.

Captain Joseph O'Reilly had the flawless appearance of a military man. He stood a slender 6' 1" and radiated composure. Twinkling blue eyes put people at ease and his combed back impeccable gray hair gave him a mature experienced image. It was rumored that this man would be the next Chief of Police. If so, he would be the first college educated leader in the history of the Long Beach Police

Department. The new officers already knew his reputation and eagerly awaited his words.

Captain O'Reilly looked squarely at his audience, turned on his most charming smile, and began:

"I am truly pleased to see this class graduate. This first six-week academy is an important milestone in the history of our department. No group of officers has ever been given better preparation.

"That will not be enough," the Captain continued, "as this is one of the most punishing occupations in the world. Of these sixteen, several will quit, a few will be dismissed, some will retire disabled and one or more may die before age fifty. One may even be killed in the line of duty. That shouldn't be startling news. Still, many who come to work don't understand the difficulties they'll face. I started in 1933 and I've seen it all. I want to take this opportunity to share that experience, discuss problems that can be anticipated and provide some fatherly advice.

"Family members need to understand what these young men will encounter. You all need to listen.

"First: our business is to fight crime and promote order and that interferes with our personal lives. We have a twenty-four hour job. There'll be few weekends and holidays off. As a result, important family gatherings and religious holidays will be missed. To be fair, we assign working hours, days off and vacations in order of seniority. When someone gets promoted, they start over at the end of the line in that rank. These odd hours and days off can create marital problems. Cops need understanding at home.

"Second: city regulations must be followed. Anyone who violates our rules will be fired. They can't be forgotten. Employees must live within the City of Long Beach. Police officers are technically on duty twenty-four hours a day and have to carry a loaded firearm at all times; that means even at the beach. When an officer is sick, a sergeant will go to his home and assure there's no malingering. As you can see, we expect more from our own than from others.

"Third: it's important to say a few words about criminals. Examining criminality is simple. Those that are crazy, alcoholic or addicted to drugs are our most frequent customers. We deal with them because government has chosen to carry out those duties. They're our burden. Among those who are drunks, we don't count sailors; all men are fools when they're young. Remember the dumb things you've done. Alcoholics get sent to jail; thirty-day commitments help them regain their health and prolong their lives. After a while officers know drunks by their first names; when they're sober they like them. The Good Lord knows we can't solve their problems.

"One group I call the *Bare Bulb Society*. These are stupid people. Don't misunderstand; they're from every racial group. They're most often not educated, haven't been raised right, aren't influenced by religion or otherwise constrained from criminal activity. I call them the *Bare Bulb Society* because a light bulb hanging alone without a shade is symbolic of this group. These people are simply not concerned about a light without a shade. They don't care how they look or how their surroundings appear. They're dirty, sloppy and uncaring and they raise their children to be just like them. They're too dumb to understand that crime doesn't pay.

"Then there are real dangerous criminals. They think they're smarter than all of us and that laws really don't apply to them. They're the professionals. They might be murderers, rapists, armed robbers, dope dealers, pimps, burglars, bad check artists, auto thieves or anything else. They think they're too smart to get caught. When they're cornered they become dangerous. Sometimes I think these people are dumber than the uneducated folks. Crime doesn't pay.

"Fourth: when we arrest people we catch hell from their friends and families. You'll see. The public doesn't want the law enforced when it comes to them. They grab attorneys, march on city hall, and otherwise sling excuse-o-babble to the press and in the courtrooms. That spins it around and puts the police on trial. For example, from now on, those who know you're a cop will tell you stories about bad tickets from other officers.

"Fifth. One of our primary duties is that of assisting victims. Women are among those least protected by the law. They're often used, abused and battered. You'll see more domestic disputes than you can imagine and some of the memories will stay with you. I can only tell you to protect the women and children. It won't be fun.

"Sixth: you'll recognize the absurdity of plots by most mystery writers. You'll know that private detectives aren't allowed access to police information. You'll understand they spend ninety-nine percent of their time chasing divorce problems or other civil disputes and don't know a thing about murder. In fact, you'll seldom see private investigators. You'll see that investigation is largely the drudgery of contacting people and asking questions. We're not putting the Sputnik up; this is not rocket science. You'll discover that people just don't keep secrets. If two or more people know, eventually we'll all know. We just have to get close to those that know and persuade them to talk.

"Seventh: keep your religion to yourself and respect the religions of others. When you work, pay attention. You're going to meet clergy from every religion. You're going to see that people in all of the churches and temples are not the same people that we have in jail. It should be a clue to people that God, in all of His forms, is good.

"Eighth: you'll learn, first hand, of the weaknesses of cops. They often succumb to one of the *Three B's*. Remember that the *Three B's* are broads, bills and booze. In my time, I've seen women, debts, and alcohol ruin a slew of careers. You graduates think about that and try not to become another 'former cop'.

"Ninth: the reputation of each police officer is his bread and butter. You'll be evaluated according to your performance. In the course of duty, you'll be judged by your arrests, written reports and testimony. In this business, integrity is everything. Your work will not just make your reputation, but that of our entire Department. If you're not honest, you're worthless and you won't last. That's no threat; it's a promise.

"Tenth and last: police officers experience vast swings in emotion. I liken this to our Cyclone Racer, the frightening roller coaster in our Pike fun zone. Those emotion swings create a hell of a ride. Once in a while officers arrest those who have committed mean crimes and the satisfaction can be euphoric. Other times they see something that's just awful, like a dead sodomized five-year old boy, and consequently suffer tremendous depression. These wide swings in behavior, sometimes within short periods of time, can be overwhelming. Coping can become a struggle.

"In closing, I want to describe what happened the day I was hired. At that time, there was no academy. I received a letter, followed instructions, bought a uniform and a gun, put them on and reported for work. A crusty old sergeant greeted me and gave me a badge and a call box key. I told him I didn't know anything about law or police work. He asked if I knew the Ten Commandments. I said sure. Then he told me to go out to my walking beat, keep my eyes open, and when I saw someone violating one of those Commandments, drag him in to jail. He told me not to worry, that someone at the station would help sort it out. It worked; I'm still here.

"You're the new breed. You've received some of the finest training in the country. That's an incredible advantage. I want you all to go out there and show the public the value of this training and prove that you deserve their respect. That having been said, I want you to remember that I mean everybody's respect.

"Good luck, and may God keep you."

CHAPTER ONE

Saturday, November 22, 1959

At 11:15 P.M., following the squad meeting, Rookie Police Officer Jim Grant walked from the temporary bungalow behind the Police Department and City Hall toward the gas pumps. A former paratrooper, at 6' 2" and 200 pounds with brown hair and blue eyes, he felt nervous and capable, but wary of the unknown. The beautiful evening seemed a good omen for this first night of police work.

Fred "Red" Price followed. A grizzled veteran officer, he had red bushy hair, a square face and piercing brown eyes. He looked about 5' 10" tall, weighed over two hundred pounds, and was built like a brick. He'd been assigned as Grant's Training Officer. As any training officer, Red Price had the power to make or break a rookie during probation. The sober expression on Jim's face showed that he knew Price had that authority.

Red yelled, "Hey, Grant, you drive. I hope you know your way around this fucking city."

He threw a set of police car keys. Grant caught them and juggled a new brief case, flashlight, and nightstick as he walked toward rows of black and white Fords parked on the West side of Pacific Avenue.

The attached dog tag had the number 762. The ring held an ignition key, trunk key and a shotgun lock key. Each parked police car had a three-digit number in 3" block lettering on the left side of the trunk lid above the bumper. He saw the matching number on a '56 Ford four-door sedan, unlocked the doors, stowed his gear and got in.

Red sat down in the passenger seat, motioned for the keys and unlocked the shotgun lock, yanked the gun from the bracket. He stripped out three shells, racked back the

1

pump action of the Model 97' Winchester to assure it was in working order, reloaded and put it back.

He leaned toward Grant and said, "You check the lights all the way around – including those two red Mickey Mouse lights on top, see that the siren works and that the spring lock is pressed in. Make sure there are no dents or damage and check us in – let's get the fuck away from these sergeants NOW."

Price and Grant were assigned Unit Three, which included part of downtown and all of the adjacent beach, the Rainbow Pier and the municipal auditorium. It bordered the Pike amusement zone. Their beat included everything east of Pine Avenue, west of Junipero Avenue and north from the Ocean to Tenth Street.

Long Beach, twenty-five miles south of Los Angeles, had 250,000 people. Industries included the naval base, shipyards, the port, oil fields, Douglas Aircraft and other factories. Some called it a blue collar and Navy city. The downtown, though, was becoming seedy. The adjoining Pike fun zone showed its age, the Navy bars were grungy and retail businesses lost customers as new suburban housing and businesses sprung up in surrounding areas.

Grant fumbled with the microphone and checked in – just like the police academy had taught him.

"Unit Three 10-8, KA 4347."

The station radio replied. *"Unit Three 10-8, KMA-651."*

"Know where the Greyhound Station is?" asked Red.

"Yeah, west of Long Beach Boulevard on the south side of First Street."

"Take me to the 217 Club and double-park, it's right in front of the bus station."

Saturday night downtown with the fleet in, sailors could be seen everywhere. They stood in front of the locker-club at Pacific and Ocean, in line at the Roxy Theater, waiting at bus benches, coming and going from bars, in cars – everywhere. There were women too, and panhandlers, chicken hawks, an occasional pimp and street drunks. The country sounds of Hank Snow could be heard as they passed a bar.

At night, the nearby churches were closed and the large retired senior citizen population slept. The bars came alive and business boomed. Grant drove west on Ocean, a boulevard lined with palm trees illuminated by streetlights, turned north on Long Beach Boulevard, passed a rail line Red Car and turned west on First Street.

The bus station was busy and no parking places were open so Jim Grant dutifully followed instructions and double-parked in front of the 217. As Red Price unbuckled the seat belt, he brushed cigarette ashes from the front of his uniform shirt and tie, grabbed his aviator style police hat with the veteran's fifty mission crush, and pushed it to the back of his head.

"Wait here," Red said as he got out of the car and walked toward the bar.

The 217 had batwing double doors that were hooked back and opened the crowded bar to the street - an invitation to passers-by to step in.

Grant leaned toward the passenger side open window to keep an eye on his partner. Police academy instructors continually preached that cops had to look after each other. He saw Red push several sailors aside at the end of the bar and signal with two fingers held up.

And, he heard him clearly fifteen feet away and through the night air. "Hey, Charley, give me a double Jim Beam."

The bartender quickly provided a drink, and Red held it up in a silent toast to the crowd, gulped it down, smacked the glass back on the bar and wiped his mouth with the back of his hand.

"Thanks," Red said and returned to the police car.

A knot grew in Grant's stomach. What kind of a training officer had he been stuck with? He didn't seem to give a shit about rules or the department. He could get both

3

of them fired. Dealing with this would be like walking through a minefield.

Red dropped back into his seat, and grabbed the radio microphone. "Hey, they're calling us."

The radio dispatch sent Unit 3 to the south side of Ocean Boulevard for a flat drunk sailor. Red acknowledged the call and Grant drove around the corner on Locust to Ocean. Both officers saw the sailor prone on the sidewalk in a pool of vomit.

Jim was told to park close and leave the reds on. They walked over to the passed out drunk. He was big, white, probably 6' 4" and 220 pounds, and looked as if he would be hard to handle. Red went back to the police car, spoke to the dispatcher and asked for a Navy Shore Patrol Car. There wasn't one available.

Grumbling, he came back to the drunk. "We can't kiss him off to the Navy, so we'll have to take him to Shore Patrol. We don't book Navy people unless they're ass-holes or fighters or it's serious."

Red gestured toward the drunk, "Watch!"

He handcuffed the sailor and grabbed his legs, pulled his nightstick and began to beat on the soles of the sailor's shoes. The drunk awakened with a scream. Red dragged him to his feet and crammed him into the back seat of the police car. He went around to sit beside the prisoner and behind the driver. Red was a lot smaller than the sailor, but he made handling him look easy. The sailor kept screaming profanities.

"Shit, fuck. That hurt. Man, what did you do that for?" the sailor asked.

Jim rolled down the windows to vent the stench and Red yelled, "Fast, damn it, we don't want to breathe his shit all night."

Shore Patrol Headquarters was south of Ocean Boulevard on the beach at the end of Pacific Avenue. A

4

gravel parking lot adjoined the temporary wooden bungalow.

Jim Grant drove into the lot and skidded up against a telephone pole lying on the ground to prevent cars from striking the building. Red had the back door open before the car stopped, hurrying to escape the stink. He reached across and grabbed the sailor's blouse at the throat and dragged him out.

"Come on, you big puke," said Red. "You're home."

He yanked him erect and pushed him through the Shore Patrol door and against a wall to be searched. Red gestured toward the booking desk as he dug in the drunk's back pocket for a wallet and identification. "Grant, you fill out the protective custody form."

Jim turned to the desk and a Chief Petty Officer with thirty years of hash marks on his sleeve shoved a small pad of forms toward him. Red gave Grant the I.D. card of the prisoner.

While Jim filled out the form, Marine Shore Patrol Officers took the handcuffs off the drunk and gave them back. They put the drunk in a leaning position against the wall and systematically searched him for weapons.

Jim completed the form and passed it to the Navy Chief.

"You no good cop mother fuckers," yelled the drunk. "If I was out of here, I'd kick your ass."

Red figured that was enough. He reached across and snatched the completed form from the Chief's hand, spun the sailor around and slammed him to the floor.

"All right, prick," yelled Red. "Your motor mouth has just overloaded your asshole and you're going to jail."

Handcuffs were re-applied, the passive prisoner was jerked to his feet, and Red hollered instructions, "Open the passenger door, partner." With his left hand grasping the blouse at the back of the neck and the right hand lifting the sailor at the crotch, he threw him out the door toward the police car. Grant got to the car a second late and didn't get

5

the door opened in time. The sailor banged his head into the side of the car, and then Red crammed him into the car. Both officers took their places again and Jim drove toward the police station.

A new smell of feces augmented the stink of vomit. The drunk had filled his pants and urinated.

"God damned prick," Red cussed as they arrived at the rear of police headquarters. He yanked the sailor from the car. When the prisoner fell down, he grabbed both ankles and pulled him up the fourteen stairs to the booking desk door. The sailor hit his head on every step on the way up.

Inside the door, Red snatched him by the arms and put him into a seated position on the booking bench.

The prisoner howled. "You bastards, I'll get even, you can't fuck with me. I'll come back and kick your ass."

Red grabbed a blank copy of a short arrest report, pulled the Navy form from his pocket, and started writing.

Booking Sergeant Chuck White looked at Jim Grant and said, "He's a mouthy son-of-a-bitch. You ought to make him a Christian before you bring him in here."

Jim Grant tried to maintain a poker face. He couldn't think of a reply.

The prisoner continued to yell and curse. Red shoved the completed report over to Sgt. White and he initialed the approval blank. Red grabbed the prisoner by the arm and shoved him toward the elevator and pushed the UP button.

In a moment the door opened. A tall elderly Negro who probably weighed 250 pounds operated the elevator. Red propelled the drunk in, banging his head against the wall, and he slumped to the floor.

"Front please," said the elevator operator.

"Hi, Jonas," Red said.

"Good evening, Officer Price."

They went to the Fifth Floor Jail. Jim pulled the prisoner out onto the floor and Red handed paperwork to the receiving officers.

As the elevator doors closed one jail officer yelled, "Thanks, Red. We like the smelly ones."

Back in service, Red had Jim take him to the New Yorker at 210 West Ocean, another sailor bar, where he again ordered a double. Jim looked at his watch, realized it was fifteen minutes until 2:00 AM and gave thanks the bars would soon close. He hoped the drinking wouldn't lead to some incident that would ruin them both.

Ten minutes later, Red directed him to a liquor store at First Street and Long Beach Boulevard and stepped from the car. "Wait here," ordered Red. "What do you smoke?"

"Luckys," answered Jim. He wondered, what now?

Red returned and threw a package of Lucky's to him, opened his own Camels', lit one and tucked the pack in his right sock. Jim started to pass a quarter to Red for the cigarettes.

"Naw, they're free. All the liquor stores pop for smokes. Cigarettes, booze, and meals are usually free. The brass, our self-important fucking commanding officers, keep telling us to stop taking stuff. They call them gratuities. But that's bullshit; they take free crap too. But, remember, it's a DUTY to tip the help just like it's a full price meal, but that's all. This is just the beginning of your real training, it's time to forget all that shit they taught you in the police academy. You know, we do have some cops who BURN our pop-stops. They'll sneak into other beats and chisel smokes and other shit — even meals — and when too many cops hit a spot, they kill it, and we have to build it back up."

"Is there a pay-back for businesses that give us freebies?" asked Jim.

"Look at it this way," Red replied. "They want us to be seen in their places. It makes them feel safe and we're good for business. That ain't all though. We do look out for those who take care of us."

7

Red slapped his forehead. "Oh shit, we're supposed to be at the Stardust at First and Locust and standby the beat men as the bars close. Get us over there."

Grant drove in that direction, wondering what in hell he'd got himself into with Red.

"At 2:00 AM, the swab jockeys are full of hot pop and raise hell if we don't keep the lid on. We stay visible; they straighten up and those that don't go to Shore Patrol or get booked. We help and transport for the beat cops."

Red checked out on the radio when they rolled up to the intersection. A Shore Patrol unit, already parked on the corner, took several sailors into custody. Jim observed that they had everything under control.

Back in service, radio traffic slowed and they drove circles in the downtown area.

"You a veteran?" Red spoke up.

"Yeah, three years in the paratroopers – both 82nd and 11th Airborne Divisions. No combat though. I did a lot of hell raising and had good times in Germany with the 11th. How about you?"

Red leaned back. "Yeah, you look big enough and strong enough. I hope they taught you to fight. You'll need everything you can put on the line. We'll test your shit here. I was Marine Corps, did my time in Korea, walked damn near to the Yalu River and those Chinese came in. Then it was an ugly son-of-a-bitch and those of us that were lucky got our asses pulled aboard ship at Hungnam. That was one time those fucking sailors sure looked good. I left a lot of friends there and I'm damn lucky to be alive. Got a family now and I'll be damned if I'm going to let some slime-bag fucker kill this cop. You got to be ready in this business and I'm ready."

Suddenly Red pulled himself erect in his seat, looked at his watch. "Shit, it's near 2:30 AM. Take me to Tobo's at Fourteenth and Long Beach Boulevard. Park at the back door, turn up the radio so we can hear it and go in. I need to hit the john."

Jim followed instructions. He knew Tobo's as a bar just north of the downtown area. When they arrived, Red alighted from the car, beat on the back door with his nightstick, and an elderly Negro janitor unlocked and opened the door.

"Hi, Mister Red. Come on in."

Jim followed and saw Red go to the men's room. He waited by the rear door of the bar to hear the police radio. In a few minutes Red came out of the men's room, zipping up as he walked, went behind the bar, selected a glass, poured and belted down another double. Grant inwardly moaned, realizing that closing time meant nothing to his thirsty partner.

"Unit Three, Unit Three."

Jim hurried to the car, grabbed the microphone.

"Unit Three, at 14th and the Boulevard."

"Unit Three, 927, check the unknown trouble, woman screaming, at 1834 Locust Avenue, first floor, apartment 12, in the rear."

"10-4, we're rolling."

It only took a few minutes to get the address of the disturbance. They parked in front and entered the old two-story apartment building through an unlocked front door leading to a long corridor. The walls had peeling paint, a bare light bulb hung from the ceiling half way down a hallway covered with worn and stained carpet. Radios played behind closed apartment doors as they passed. As they approached, Jim heard an angry male voice yelling. Children cried somewhere. They heard a woman screaming. They ran down the hallway to the apartment and could now clearly hear a man cursing inside.

Red and Jim positioned themselves on each side of the door and listened. A male voice cursed drunkenly, a female voice cried and young children whimpered.

9

"No – no, Daddy, please."

Red beat on the door with the butt of his nightstick, and yelled, "Police, open up."

A skinny woman, about twenty-two years old, with long stringy hair opened the door. She wore no makeup, tears ran down her face, she had a black eye and bruises were on her arm and throat. Red pushed her aside and growled, "What's the problem?"

Jim followed through the door into the dingy apartment. He saw two small children, about 2 and 3 years old, that clutched at their mother's rumpled and stained dress. The youngest, a girl had a wad of shit hanging in her diaper. The single apartment had a small bathroom and kitchenette. A crib sat in the corner and two old overstuffed chairs with cigarette burns were pushed against the walls. A pile of dirty linen mixed with clothes covered the pull-down bed and spilled over on the floor. Half dozen empty beer bottles lay on the floor next to the kitchenette door.

The smells of old tobacco smoke, stale beer, body odor, and dirty diapers filled the small place. The bed stood between the cops and the man leaning against the wall next to the kitchenette entry.

He looked about 22 years old, and 5' 9", swayed slightly and like a drunk seemed to be using the wall for support. He wore no shirt, needed a shave, had bare feet and was dirty.

"You the man of the house?" Red asked.

Suddenly the drunk swung up a double-barreled shotgun from behind his Levi pants leg and pointed it at Red Price.

The drunk grinned. "Gotcha fuckers!"

Neither officer had a gun in hand and both separated slowly. The children ran crying from their mother to the shotgun wielder and each clung to a Levi leg. The shotgun barrels claimed each officer as they were swung from side to side. The cops were about eight feet away from death.

10

"Don't shoot, Joey. For Christ's sake, don't shoot," his woman pleaded.

Red held both of his hands up, palms forward and said, "Take it easy, cowboy. We ain't pointing no iron at you. We ain't here to do you no harm."

"Be easy to gut shoot you fucking cops," the man replied.

Jim thought their position impossible. The children were in harm's way and if guns were drawn it would be deadly. He couldn't see how they could beat the shotgun. Then he thought of the kids, seeing the little ones still whimpering, each clutching a leg as tears ran down their faces.

"Yeah," Red answered. "You kill a cop and it's the chair."

"That ain't no big thing," came the slurred reply.

The dirt bag with the gun swayed. Mean and drunk, he had no smarts and didn't seem much interested in consequences.

Red kept talking. "Where you from?"

"Virginia."

"I spent some time in the Marine Corps at Quantico."

"Shit, I'm from the mountains in the west. That's in the tidal country. It's hot, wet and you'all were living with all those fucking skeeters."

"Yeah, we had mosquitoes up the ass."

The drunk moved the barrels nervously back and forth. He kept his finger on a trigger and death remained a three-pound pull away. It seemed a half hour went by, but it could only have been a few minutes.

"You dust us," said Red, "and what happens to the kids? Ain't that like running out on them? They going to respect what you did?"

He looked confused and the booze didn't help him think. He suddenly grinned drunkenly, used his left hand and pushed back his dirty blonde hair from his brown eyes, lowered the barrels and said, "Aw, what the shit, I din't do nothing – no harm no foul." He took a step forward and held out the shotgun in his right hand.

Red looked strained. He took it and slowly looked it over; the safety was off. He opened the breach, withdrew two shells and closed the gun. He read the shell labels and looked up. "They're double-ought buck man killers," he told Jim.

The drunk replied, "Yeah, those were made to kill cops."

Red closed the breech and swung the barrels of the empty shotgun into the base of the drunk's jaw, then hit him repeatedly across the head, arms, and shoulders. Blood splattered about the room on the walls, on the furniture and on the children. The woman screamed and the children cried as Red hammered him to the carpet – until he was unconscious.

"Jim, cuff him and call an ambulance."

This one went to Seaside Hospital. They sutured him, gave him a bandage that looked like a turban and cleared him to be booked. Hurt, quiet, and scared, he never let out another peep. It took an hour to get the reports filed and back to the street.

When pulling off the station lot, Red looked at his watch. "It's time we had some chow. Let's check out Code Seven. It's Saturday night, Sunday morning and it's our turn to hit Joe Jost's. It's a bit out of our beat, but it's OK. I'll check us out when we roll up. Take us to Anaheim and Temple. You must know the joint."

Grant did know the spot. If you knew Long Beach, you knew Joe Jost's – the city's oldest and most famous beer bar. Also an eating spot, it served great sandwiches, pickled eggs and had a poolroom. They arrived at about 4:30 AM.

Red explained that, though the place was closed, a janitor would let them in and they could make sandwiches.

12

A liverwurst sandwich, a pickled egg and Coke at that time of night sounded good.

The face of the building had tall glass windows. Double doors with glass tops opened into the place. An old fashioned bar with a stainless steel top stood on the left with bar stools. The beer, beverages and food were served there. Wooden booths stood opposite on the right front. Old calendars, pictures and old bottles of beer decorated the walls. A corridor led directly through to the rear; a large room with pool tables, cue racks and old elk's heads on the walls. When out-houses were outlawed, the toilets were boxed into the rear corners. They put the men's room in the left rear and the ladies on the right.

One old elk's head had been draped with Christmas lights for years. The old wiring, cracked with age, couldn't be moved. Each year, bets were taken before Thanksgiving – questioning how many lights would still work for the new season. Then replacements would be gingerly inserted.

After arriving, Jim hurried to the men's room, relieved himself and walked out. Red walked by with a case of Budweiser on each shoulder and yelled, "One's for you, partner."

He went outside and put them in the police car trunk.

Grant thought, Oh God, not more of this shit.

They ate and returned to service.

The sun came up, traffic returned to the streets and Red urged that they write a moving violation ticket. "A ticket a day keeps the sergeant away. Some cops don't like to work traffic, but you do what you have to do."

They did.

Finally at about 7:30 AM, nearing the end of watch, they were northbound on Long Beach Boulevard passing Anaheim when a step van passed the slow black & white.

Red yelled. "Get him, pull him over!"

Quickly, Jim turned on the reds, siren, accelerated, and the van promptly pulled over.

Red grabbed his hat. "Wait here, I'll handle this." He hurried out to the van.

Several minutes later he came back with an apple pie in each hand. "One's for you, partner."

It was a Marie Callandar's Pie Van.

They were called out of service at 8:00 AM.

James "Jim" Grant had finished his first day of police work. Sleepy, exhausted, still loaded with adrenaline and emotionally drained, he went to his car, pulled a jacket on to cover his uniform shirt and drove away. He circled the Main Post Office at Third and Long Beach Boulevard, parked and walked to the front of the first floor U. S. Army Recruiting Office.

He thought about how tough his first night on the police department had been. In his opinion, Red Price was a capable veteran cop. But, he also considered Red a mean drunken bully. Jim also knew he had to keep his mouth shut and do whatever Red told him to do. Bad reports about rookies ended their careers quickly. His field duty started in the middle of the month so the assignment with Red would last until the end of December; all of six weeks together. He didn't know if he could stand it.

Jim looked at the recruiting posters in the window. This is where he'd enlisted over four years before. He compared his time in the paratroopers with his first night on duty as a cop.

He thought, maybe, just maybe, being in the paratroops was a good life after all.

Then he went home.

CHAPTER TWO

Wednesday, December 30, 1959

Jim Grant shook his head, pushed against the steering wheel to stay awake and looked at his watch. 3:00 AM, five hours to the end of the shift. This would end six weeks of field training under Red Price, two weeks in November and four in December. Since they were off duty Wednesday and Thursday nights, this was Jim's last day of the month. It had been the most difficult six weeks of his life. He couldn't stomach Red's alcoholic, and on occasion, sadistic, crude style. Still, he had to admit that few men could match Red for courage. A cop would never have to worry about help with Red at his elbow. He had balls.

How would Red evaluate his recruit performance? He didn't dare offend him. Red had made no mention of his progress. It worried him and made him wonder if he'd pass probation.

It'd feel good to have this night end. He looked forward to two days off. Then, there would be a new unit to work and a new training officer. It just couldn't be as tough as December.

This week was the worst. It started at 11:00 PM, Friday, Christmas, and continued until tonight. The holidays depressed those who were alone and it became their time to drink. So it had been five long nights with drunks, drunk drivers, family fights and Red. It finally slowed down at about 1:30 AM.

Jim didn't have any family nearby and hadn't been able to visit much with friends so there had been little of the traditional holiday spirit. He now believed that people who'd never worked tough schedules couldn't imagine the problems involved.

He turned the black and white patrol car south on Pine Avenue from Ocean Boulevard; Red leaned his head against the window, dozing. Jim drove west to the entry of The Pike amusement zone and through the arch past a bar called Hollywood On The Pike. There had been no radio traffic for an hour.

Few lights illuminated the deserted walkway on the Pike. Without carnival music, crowds, and noise of barkers yelling their scams to passers-by, it seemed like another world. The neon lights were out, the Ferris Wheel stood still, shadows darkened the ticket booth at the Reckless Ross Motorcycle Show and the police car headlights reached through the light fog and bounced crazily from the front of the House of Mirrors. The daytime odors of deep fried shrimp, hamburgers, popcorn and corn dogs were replaced by the smell of the fresh salty ocean breeze. The trash had been taken away and the cleanup crews had gone home. The police car slipped slowly past the elephant shaped waste cans in the center of the midway.

Suddenly the station radio squawked, startling both officers

"Unit Three, Unit Three."

Jim snatched the microphone. "10-4, this is Unit Three at Pike and Cedar."

Red, instantly awake, grabbed his clipboard and turned his flashlight toward the tablet with pen poised.

"DB at the Cyclone Racer, Code Two."

The enormous wooden roller coaster, the Cyclone Racer, was the greatest ride on the west coast. It rated among the most famous roller coasters in the world and had made the Pike famous.

"10-4, we're almost there," Jim replied.

"Most likely one of our drunks died," Red said. "We sure don't have many dead bodies down here."

He turned the car south to the front of the roller coaster, skidded to a halt, and announced their arrival.

"Unit Three is 10-97."

16

Both officers leaped out as a fun zone night watchman waved both arms from the entry.

The skinny watchman, named Buddy, was bald and about seventy years old and had worked this night job for twenty years. Nothing ever seemed to bother him, but now he trembled and cried as he choked out his discovery to the officers, "Aww...shit, Red, it's a young pussy and she's been dumped – it's awful."

Buddy led the way through the timbered structure by flashlight beam as he explained. "Hell, I was looking for bums under the coaster when I found her. At first I thought she was a sleeping drunk. Then, when I got closer I saw it was a young girl and she was dead. Christ, I've got a granddaughter. Looks just like her. I thought it was her. Oh shit! Oh shit!"

Red and Jim shined their flashlights ahead as they followed Buddy's winding path through the labyrinth of structural timbers. Then they saw her. Nude.

Jim choked up. He knew her and the recognition stunned him. He'd seen her a number of times in the downtown area and every time her beauty captured his attention. He didn't know her name, but he couldn't forget her.

She was the most beautiful girl he had ever seen in his life. She appeared young; maybe 16 or 17, about 5' 4", with a figure that could match any movie star. *What a body!* She could wear a rag and make it look like high style. Her stunning blue eyes and thick waist-length honey blond hair complemented a gorgeous face with a few tiny freckles and a perfect nose. Her unaffected smile put people at ease. The sight before him made him shudder. He'd been to funerals, but had never seen death up close. There she lay.

Jim tried to remember his academy training. He tried to shut out the girl and death and grasp details. He looked carefully at the scene.

17

On her stiffened back, she looked like a waxen art figurine. Her eyes wide open, transfixed – frozen forever. Her body lay turned slightly on her side showing what could have been slight bruises, and her hair spilled backward into a loose pile in the sand. He saw no blood or visible wounds. She couldn't have been cleaner if she'd been bathed.

The girl rested across a parallel eight-by-eight reinforcing timber ten inches above ground level. The maze of cross-timbers, fastened with huge steel bolts, ran from creosote pilings driven deep into the ground. Her body did not sag as it lay across the beam. Jim thought it must have been stiff when put there.

She lay about fifteen feet west of the east edge and just thirty feet south of the north corner of the roller coaster structure. The Cyclone Racer stood west of the Pine Avenue parking lot; a long stone's throw west of the Spit and Argue Club platform and Rainbow Pier.

Red looked at Jim and gave directions. He knew his work. "Partner, go back to the car and call for homicide and the coroner. Then move the black and white around on the parking lot side. Block the entry to the Pike. Light up the surface of the parking lot near the roller coaster and look for tire tracks or other shit that'll help find who dumped her. Don't let anyone approach across that lot, and I mean no one. When this goes out on the radio, a bunch of dumb fucking cops will come gallivanting down here sightseeing. Remember, fuck'em, they don't get in."

Jim did as he was told. After moving the car he got out and looked around. He saw nothing – not even tire tracks. He leaned against the police car, waiting to give directions to those who would soon arrive.

His thoughts turned to the stillness around him. What a difference in the early hours of the morning from the hustle and bustle of daytime when the nearby Spit and Argue Club platform, an open air public forum, was filled with people

18

of every political persuasion trying to sell their point of view. All day and into the evening, the parking lot served as an activity center. Automobiles arrived and departed and people came and went continuously. A few feet away on the Pike crowds walked past. To the rear, a never-ending stream of cars cruised down Linden Avenue and went around Rainbow Pier in a one-way stream and up Pine Avenue. Careening cars on the rickety Cyclone Racer roller coaster rattled past as they carried screaming adults, kids, sailors and girls around the huge wooden structure.

He remembered when Disneyland opened in the summer of '55 and Pike crowds had declined. Weekends and summers stayed busy. Like the rest of downtown Long Beach, it seemed to need to change or die.

Now the parking lot was empty and the roller coaster rested silently. Not a single person could be seen. The girl had been dumped thrown out like trash.

It was as if the Pike were shocked and grieving. Not a sound could be heard. No lights flickered. Fog wafted across the lot from the ocean, changing visibility from a few yards to a hundred yards and back again.

The dead girl's face kept coming into Jim's mind. He remembered the times he had seen her. She'd always been with sailors and young girls. In the six weeks he had worked downtown, he'd probably seen her a dozen times. She'd been at the Greyhound Station, at the Star Café, and at Bundy's Locker Club Café. He was sometimes close to her, but in each case the circumstances hadn't given him an opportunity to start a conversation.

Then he remembered Red's lecture about the Navy and "hamburger whores." Red said that many young girls followed seventeen and eighteen year old boyfriend sailors to Long Beach. They were hometown sweethearts. They were dumb shits, but in love. They'd share a cheap apartment with another navy couple, shack-up in a motel if they had a few bucks, or even live in a friend's car. The boyfriend would come and go on shore leave. They would party with friends and live on love and find meals where they could. When the boyfriend's ship went to sea, the girls often traded sex with other sailors for a hamburger.

Being destitute, some found their way into prostitution. If they were lucky, the cops picked them up for runaway, notified the parents and sent them back to Podunk or wherever. Sometimes their love prevailed and they had successful marriages. It was a military town problem.

Did that describe what happened to the Cyclone Racer blonde? How did she die?

Three black and whites roared across the parking lot from Pine Avenue and he waved them over. Two cops alighted from each car and approached. Then, a fourth black and white squealed up – this one driven by Sergeant Chuck White from the station.

White exited quickly and, hands-on-hips, yelled, "All right you prima-donnas, back into service. This ain't no fucking sideshow. Get back into service before I have your ass. You won't be screwing up this crime scene."

The cops got into their cars and went up Pine Avenue. Sergeant White turned to Jim, pushed the brimmed police soft cap back on his head, and told him how to handle new arrivals. "Do just what you're doing, but tell the next car that comes that prick Sergeant White is here and will fuck with them if they try to enter the crime scene. Then, tell the dicks and coroner to park here and walk in. Keep them away from that area in front of your headlights. Okay?"

"Yes, Sergeant."

He reached back into his car, pulled out and keyed the radio microphone, "This is Sergeant White. Advise all units to remain in their districts and stay away from the Pike."

"10-4, Sergeant White."

"Attention all units. Remain in your assigned areas. Do not...repeat...do not come to the Pike area."

Sergeant White listened and then walked toward the scene.

No more black and whites came by.

A few minutes passed and Homicide Detective Sergeant Bill Millard and Detective Carl Peele rolled up in their '56 Chevrolet four-door sedan, parked and stepped out. Jim personally didn't know them, but knew who they were.

"Is that Sergeant White's car?" asked burley Sergeant Millard.

"Yeah," Jim replied. "He's under the Cyclone Racer with Red Price."

"No gawking cops screwing up the scene?"

"No, Sergeant White chased them off."

"Good," said Millard. "Let's go, Carl."

Jim watched them walk toward the Cyclone Racer. It would be a long wait, he thought, like standing guard in the army.

Two hours later, much after dawn, the Los Angeles County Coroner's '52 Dodge van showed up and Deputy Coroner Karl Schultz and his younger partner got out and ambled over. Schultz, famous for his work, humor, and cigars, told everyone that the strong tobacco smell and taste made investigations, where bodies were ripe, more tolerable.

Plainly, even a good attitude couldn't make this work fun. Schultz lit a large cigar, said hello, and made the same inquiries as the homicide detectives, and with partner, kit in hand, walked toward the roller coaster.

It must have been an off night for the press. None came.

The detectives and the coroner's people completed their work. The body was taken to the coroner's office for further investigation and an autopsy, and Jim Grant and Red Price returned to the station to file reports.

21

Red told Jim that homicide investigators and the coroner's investigators couldn't readily recognize the cause of death. What looked like bruises may have only been blood settling in the body. The investigators also didn't know if she'd been raped or had intercourse. They guessed she'd been dead for about six hours.

Their reports finally filed, Red and Jim left the station at 11:00 AM, tired and off duty at last after a long night.

At home, exhausted and finally asleep, Jim dreamt about the girl from the Cyclone Racer. He saw her in a crowd of sailors and young girls. She kept smiling at him and he would try to move through the crowd and find her but couldn't. It happened over and over again in different crowds and places.

Finally, he rode in the back seat of the Cyclone Racer and she sat in the front with a sailor and turned to smile at him.

CHAPTER THREE

Wednesday, January 13, 1960

Jim sat at the breakfast table in his spacious one bedroom Hermosa Avenue apartment near Bixby Park. Most of the neighbors surrounding the older white two story wood framed four-plex were retired. A quiet area; he loved it.

The evening had passed rapidly and it was 9:00 PM. His January days off were Monday night and Tuesday night, so this would be the first day back to work. At 11:00 PM, the shift would start for Thursday's morning watch. A fresh pot of coffee sat on the stove and he held a steaming cup. His open scrapbook lay on the kitchen table.

In the police academy, instructors lectured recruits to take detailed notes on activity each workday and save the material. They said the notes would become an information gold mine for future work that they would identify people, incidents, locations, dates, and times. Jim started keeping notes when he began field service, then started an abbreviated daily journal, combining it with a work and court appearance calendar, and now worked on a scrapbook.

He had few close ties. His parents were dead. He had one brother in San Diego and an aunt that lived in the mid-west. Most of his high school friends were away in the armed forces, married, or tied to new jobs. Police work, with odd days off and working hours, had separated him from old friends.

Jim remembered poverty as well as the loss of loved ones. It had not been easy and time had gone by. He accepted the past, shrugged it all off and made a personal commitment to build a new and better life. The scrapbook became an extension of the other records. A collection of written records, articles, and pictures associated with his experiences.

The open page contained three newspaper clippings, the last one new. On top of each article, he wrote the name of the newspaper, date, and page number. Then he read them for about the tenth time. They were about his first dead body/homicide call.

The top article showed his name in newsprint for the first time in his life.

December 31, 1959, Press Telegram, A Sect., page 4.

BODY FOUND UNDER CYCLONE RACER
Early Wednesday morning the body of a young woman was found under the roller coaster by Pike Security Officer Eugene Jones. Long Beach Police Officers Fred Price and Jim Grant were first to arrive and called for Homicide. Sgt. Bill Millard and Detective Carl Peele are investigating. There were no obvious wounds. The victim's identity is not known. The body was removed to the Coroner's Office.

January 8, 1960, Press Telegram, A Sect. Page 1.

BODY UNDER CYCLONE RACER IDENTIFIED
Early Wednesday, December 30th, the nude body of a young woman was found under the roller coaster. Today Long Beach Police identified the female as Peggy Evans, 17 years old, missing from Burlington, Iowa. She is survived by her parents and two younger sisters. The parents will come to Long Beach to claim the remains and return her to Burlington for services. The Coroner's Office has yet to release information about the cause of death.

January 13, 1960, Press Telegram, A Sect., page 1.

CYCLONE RACER GIRL ABORTION DEATH
Coroner's Office spokesperson Mary Coates announced that the cause of death of Peggy Evans, 17 years old, was hemorrhaging resulting from an

24

abortion. She had been found under the roller coaster on the early morning of December 30th. The girl's parents came from Burlington, Iowa, identified the victim, and will take her home for burial in the family plot. Chief of Detectives, Captain James Green, urged that parents maintain close relationships with daughters who might become pregnant, saying "Those back alley abortion mills are killers". This young girl reportedly came to Long Beach to join her boyfriend stationed here in the Navy. He last saw her September 8th, when his ship, the submarine Segundo, went to sea. The vessel returned January 8th.

Jim's interests had focused on the event because of the many unanswered questions.

He wondered what events led this girl to have an abortion? Where did it happen? Who dumped the body at the Cyclone Racer?

He knew this case would get little interest from the Homicide Detail. It'd likely be treated as a self-inflicted death. The reasoning involved led from beliefs that such victims solicited the abortion, knowingly and willingly participated, knew the procedure to be unlawful and accepted the risks. The victim's family didn't live in Long Beach, so there wouldn't be much pressure to find out who did it.

He wondered about progress in the investigation.

After a time, he pushed himself up from the table, poured more coffee, and looked at his watch. It was 10:00 PM. He put on his police uniform, grabbed his belt with gun, handcuffs, and nightstick and rushed out.

At the curb, he unlocked the door of his white '58 Studebaker Golden Hawk, placed the leather gear and equipment behind the seat, and settled behind the steering wheel. The 275 horsepower engine started with a roar. With little traffic and the short distance, the trip to the police station took less than five minutes.

With gear on and soft hat in place, Jim sat in a one-piece oak school desk in the squad room bungalow. Lester Peabody, his new Training Officer for January, sat at his left. At 5' 10" and 160 pounds, he wasn't anything to admire. From Tennessee, he had a pock marked narrow face, a ruddy complexion, thinning sandy hair and a quarter inch gap between his two front teeth. He claimed that was an advantage and that he could spit a stream of tobacco juice thirty feet. He was not pretty, but nobody made fun of him. A country boy he might be, but he was also smart, hardworking, wiry, tough, sober, and honest. So honest, he wouldn't even take a free cup of coffee.

And he knew how to make police work fun. He could be relied upon to do the right thing, didn't lose his temper, wasn't brutal. He had horse sense. What a change from Red.

Lester Peabody ran Unit Two. They worked just west of Red Price's Unit Three. The area covered included the remainder of the downtown area, west to the Los Angeles River, and the largest part of the Pike, – more sailor country.

The watch briefing took just a few minutes. Sgt. Chuck White handed out hot sheets, gave a quick run down on city crime in the preceding twenty-four hours, and chewed ass.

"Aw right, you prima donnas. Word has come down that black and white cars are being seen in twos and threes in donut shops. The brass are pissed and asked that you be reminded no more than one car at a fucking time. Don't congregate. I don't care if you're meeting to conduct police business; do it somewhere else. Hide. Now, get in service."

Lester Peabody led the way to the parked police vehicles. They got into the assigned car, completed the equipment check and were away in quick time. Lester drove west on Third Street and south on Cedar to Ocean Boulevard. Then he turned east into the lane next to the sidewalk in front of a string of sailor bars and cruised slowly.

26

Bar business remained brisk. Everywhere they looked they saw sailors. Coming toward them on the sidewalk were two men on Shore Patrol duty; one, a Navy Chief Petty Officer, the other a Marine Corps Gunnery Sergeant. A male Caucasian, maybe 22 years old and about 6' tall, wearing a brown leather jacket and Levi's, casually walked toward them. He didn't realize the police car followed. When he came abreast of the two Shore Patrolmen, he Sunday punched the Navy Chief, dropping him like he had been hit in the head with a ball bat.

The police car stopped abruptly, Lester yelled into the radio microphone, "Unit Two, 242 now at Ocean and Pacific."

Both officers were out running toward the battery suspect. Jim in front leaped on the suspect's back and dragged him to the sidewalk. Lester put him in handcuffs. Both officers yanked him to his feet.

"You O.K., Chief?" asked Lester.

"Damn," said the Chief Petty Officer, holding his jaw. "Why'd he do that? I've never worked Shore Patrol before. I'm on temporary duty, waiting to catch my sub. I've never seen him in my life."

"Maybe he had a grudge about something," Lester replied.

Two more Shore Patrol Marines arrived with a paddy wagon and ran over. They explained they'd seen the assault while west bound on Ocean, made a U-turn, and came to help.

"Let's see who this ass-hole is," exclaimed Lester as he dug in the right rear Levi pocket for a wallet.

He held up the wallet, saying, "Watch, all I'm pulling out is I.D.". Then, reaching in he pulled out a U.S. Navy identification card, returned the wallet to the pocket and handed the I.D. card to the Navy Chief.

"It looks like this ass-hole belongs to Uncle Sam. He's Navy. You guys handle him," said Lester.

"No shit," exclaimed the Gunnery Sergeant as he grabbed the handcuffed suspect and threw him eastward on the sidewalk, and yelled, "He's escaping, get the son-of-a-bitch."

The three Marine Shore Patrolmen leaped upon the staggering suspect, nightsticks flailing. They gave the dumb shit his just dues.

When the thumping ended, Lester retrieved his handcuffs from the now prostrate suspect. Shore Patrol cuffed him. Lester waved goodbye, and Unit Two reported back in service.

"Unit Two 10-8, Shore Patrol handling," reported Lester.

As they checked 10-8, a call came right back to them.

"Unit Two. Woman dumped, nude, 46 South Neptune. Code 2."

"10-4," snapped Lester into the microphone, "Unit Two rolling."

The Code 2 dispatch meant that they proceed as fast as safety allowed, without siren.

"The address is in the Jungle, several blocks west of Magnolia," Lester said. "It's an area of old beach apartments that's turned into a toilet neighborhood."

He turned west on Ocean and down the hill on Neptune Place. People were standing on the front porch of the old three-story stucco building when they skidded to a stop. No one appeared excited and nothing appeared urgent.

Again, Lester snatched the microphone and snapped out, "Unit Two is 10-97. No other assistance needed." Only two minutes had elapsed.

They hurried from the car to the concrete porch. It was about 12 inches off the ground, four feet deep parallel to the street, and as wide as the apartment building. Jim thought the building fit into the Jungle. Filled with elderly folks, it sat right in the middle of all the wild activity. Retired people in the daytime – sailors at night.

A pale bald man, about 80 years old, stood with several elderly ladies wearing robes. He came forward.

"What's the problem?" Asked Lester.

"Officers, I'm Tim Sutton, the manager. About five minutes ago, a bunch of sailors drove up in a green 49' Chevie four-door. They were loud, sounded like an argument. I looked out the front window of my manager's unit to see what's going on. I can hear a woman cussing, then they pulled her out of the car. She's nude, screaming and fighting."

"It was shameful!" exclaimed one of the ladies.

He rapidly continued. "They carried her to the front porch and put her down. She couldn't stand up. She might have been raped. I've never seen such a thing. And, the sailors drove off."

"Good riddance," said the same lady.

"We carried her into my apartment and put her on the couch. She's there now. Come on, I'll show you." Just then, up rolled Sergeant White. He came directly from his black and white, and walked up on the porch. Lester beckoned to him and said, "The victim's in here, Sarge," and led the way into the hallway and to the apartment.

The woman lay on the couch covered with a blanket. Standing close, Jim could smell a strong odor of alcohol and a faint hint of bile. She appeared comatose and probably drunk.

It appeared that Sergeant White thought she was injured and a crime victim.

"Grant, call an ambulance," he instructed.

Jim ran back out to use the car radio, requested an ambulance and it arrived within minutes. He waited for them in front and guided the firemen into the apartment. They brought a Gurney.

Sergeant White asked that she be revived with smelling salts and knelt in front of the couch. The ampoule was

29

broken under her nose and she awoke with a start, jerked upright on the couch, and cursed.

"You motherfuckers. What the fuck are you doing to me?"

"Are you all right? Have you been raped?" asked Sergeant White.

"Nothing wrong with me, asshole. I've been partying. I love to fuck sailors. Want to fuck?" And, the blanket slipped to the floor.

Jim and Lester knew her; Tokay Rainforest, an Eskimo whore. She hung out in the Jungle area and her sex scapades were legendary. At 5' 2" and a 160 pounds, with black hair hanging to her shoulders, she sat on the couch, drunkenly, modeling her tatoos. *Sweet* adorned one breast. *Sour* decorated the other. Then on her protruding lower belly, in large letters *kiss me here*, an arrow pointed toward her pubic area.

Jim Grant thought, don't take this girl home to your mother.

At that choice moment, as she sat erect, with the Sergeant kneeling below and slightly to her front, she vomited. It splashed across White.

Sergeant White bellowed, "Book her. Get her out of here."

Lester quickly handcuffed her. He borrowed a city blanket from the firemen. This replaced the blanket loaned by witnesses. Jim hurried the now staggering girl outside and put her in the car. Lester again drove. Jim sat in the back seat with the smelly drunk.

Enroute to the station, Tokay groaned drunkenly and blurted, "The cocksucker killed Peggy. The poor dumb shit, she got raped. Then the abortion. Abortion my ass, it was murder. It was murder. That prick murdered her."

Jim stared at her, startled. It's about the dead kid under the Cyclone Racer, he thought and started asking questions.

"This is about Peggy Evans?"

"Yeah…yeah. Did you guys know Peggy?"

"Tell me about it."

"She's dead." Drunkenly, Tokay began to cry and then babbled incoherently.

As they arrived at the station, she passed out.

After she was booked and reports filed, Jim frowned, thinking about what she'd said. Her drunken exclamations captured his interest. He made notes of her comments. He had earlier described the puzzling case to Lester.

As they walked back to their car from the station, Jim said, "She knew that dead kid under the roller coaster."

"I caught that," replied Lester.

"Do you think I'd get in the grease with the department if I caught her sober and asked about it?"

"It'd be all right if you're fishing for information to pass to dicks. It's part of our job to develop snitches. Stay with that angle."

"Okay"

Then, as a Training Officer, Lester Peabody lectured, "Watch your ass on this, Jimbo. I'll give you some pointers, but you all be careful. You're sticking your nose into detective shit. Rookies don't do that. Whatever you do, don't ask any questions at the station. If dicks get onto your little private investigation, play innocent. Say you just blundered to help. Get it? If something solid develops, pass it to them. It's their barnyard."

Jim nodded. He thought again of Tokay's words. This might not be just an abortion gone wrong. They might be onto some bad shit.

CHAPTER FOUR

Friday, January 15, 1960

Tokay Rainforest arrived for arraignment in morning court. She couldn't remember what had happened, just knew she had been drunk on her ass, and pled guilty. Judge Martin DeVries appreciated that little court time would be spent on the case and gave her a ten-day sentence. He even gave her credit for the day already served.

The staff in Women's Jail knew Tokay. They liked her attitude because she presented no problems and worked hard. She cleaned cells.

Jim Grant casually visited the booking desk, read Tokay's index card, and saw her newly entered release date. He didn't think anyone would be suspicious, officers looked up information on persons in custody all the time. There was no way the dicks could get on him, and besides they didn't know he had a purpose – Peggy Evans.

He got the release date – Monday, January 25, 1960, and because it might be hard to find her later, he decided to meet Tokay when she was released from jail. He knew she moved from place to place downtown and hung out in the Jungle south of Ocean Boulevard and west of Magnolia. Here were scores of old two, three, and four story walkup apartment buildings. All were thrown up hurriedly on the west beach during the explosive growth of 1900 to 1920. The Jungle had a reputation as a hard place to find someone not wanting to be found. With the Navy Landing close by, it made a great nest for prostitutes.

Jim wanted to keep this search for information confidential. Rookies sure as hell didn't investigate homicides. If anyone asked about the contact with Tokay, he decided the snitch excuse was best. Cops cultivated informants.

While on patrol, he'd spoken with her on a number of occasions. A fun girl when sober, she liked to laugh and joke, seemed bright, and knew everybody. She really fit in a Navy town. In more ways than expected, she could be described as a nice girl. Tokay was honest, supportive of friends, genuinely sensitive, well meaning, clean and usually reliable. Booze and sex were her enemies. She loved the booze and she loved sailors.

The night of Sunday, January 24 started slowly, then turned into hell on wheels for Unit Two. At 11:45 PM, Lester and Jim were on the Pike when the radio dispatcher called the unit working east of them. The call went to Red Price's unit.

"Unit Three, 4th and Orange, man with a gun, possible 211 (armed robbery) at the liquor store now."

Jim heard Red Price's stoic response, "Unit Three, 10-4. From Seventh and Walnut."

Then Lester grabbed the mike, "Unit Two rolling for a back-up."

Jim drove north rapidly on Magnolia to Fourth Street and then east toward their destination.

Surrounding units couldn't hear other unit messages unless the station relayed them. A block from the call, the radio relayed a second message from Red. He reported that no immediate assistance was needed at the liquor store and that suspect information would follow.

A few moments later the station dispatcher triggered his microphone. beep. beep. beep.

"Attention all units. Unit Two reports a man with a gun, and a possible armed robbery suspect. Suspect was spooked by the arrival of four patrons. One saw the gun in his waistband. Suspect is a male white, late 50s, wearing a red plaid woolen shirt and khaki pants. He left in a '49 Hudson four door, brown, with North Dakota license plates, eastbound from Fourth and Orange".

"Unit Two 10-4, 10-8," Jim answered.

He started to make a U-turn to go back toward their assigned area in Unit Two when Lester spoke up. "Easy, old son, go south on Cerritos and park just north of Third Street and turn off our headlights."

"What are we doing?" Jim asked as he killed the lights.

"Just wait," said Lester.

Then the radio squawked. *"Attention all units, a 211 just occurred at United Liquor at Fourth and Tile. Same Hudson eastbound from the scene."*

"I knew it. Watch out. When they rob a place and drive away, expect the bastards to double back in the other direction," explained Lester.

"There he is," Jim said. The Hudson came barreling down Third Street, headed west.

"Get him."

Jim peeled out, turned on the headlights, hit the flashing reds, mashed the floor solenoid button, and the siren growled. The '56 Ford jumped forward and closed the distance to the brown Hudson. Lester hit the solenoid button on his side of the floor, again modulating the siren.

"Unit Two in pursuit. 211 Hudson. Westbound Third, turning north on Alamitos toward Fourth," Jim announced.

Attention all units. Unit Two in chase. The Hudson from Fourth and Tile armed robbery now north on Alamitos at Fourth."

The Hudson accelerated to about seventy miles per hour, careened when turning, but couldn't shake off the black and white. Jim held all the cards, he drove well, knew the city and the suspect's brake lights telegraphed his coming turns. The chase went north to Seventh Street, east to Orange, south to Fourth, turning in front of the store where patrons scared him off and then drove past the store that had been robbed.

"The idiot doesn't know Long Beach," yelled Lester.

A few seconds later, the Hudson turned south on Junipero, east into the Carroll Park neighborhood, lost

34

control and ran off the left side of the roadway into a tree. The crash could be heard for blocks.

Jim hit the brakes and the police car slid past, stopping twenty feet beyond the wreck. Lester leaped out first, racking the shotgun as he moved. He ran to the driver's door of the Hudson and aimed at the driver. The suspect, hands still on the steering wheel, looked shaken.

"Don't move, asshole, or you're dog meat. Jim, get off to my right side with your gun on this puke. Watch his hands. If the prick moves, blow him away."

"Don't shoot. You got me. I won't move a muscle," yelped the suspect.

"Put your hands in the air, way up in the air, and slowly step out to your left and then face the car," commanded Lester.

"Yes sir. Don't shoot." His voice shook.

Jim holstered his handgun while Lester held the suspect at shotgun point.

Remembering police academy instructions and the need for extreme caution, he took the crook's right hand and pulled it behind his back, then his left hand. Once the handcuffs were in place, Jim turned him around and made a search for weapons. He found a Smith & Wesson .44 magnum revolver tucked in his belt, hidden under the red plaid shirtfront. As Lester watched, he pulled it free and waved it under the guy's nose.

"This is a cannon. Where'd you get it?"

The suspect didn't reply.

"What's your name?"

Again, he made no reply.

"Partner," said Lester. "This here is a veteran, an ex-con. He won't tell us shit."

Still, he made no reply.

Jim took a hard look at the man.

Before them, handcuffed, stood a male white, late 50s, 5'11", 200 pounds, round faced with a three day stubble of gray beard and balding gray hair. An old timer as crime suspects went, he wore a faded wool red plaid shirt, rumpled khaki pants and brown high top work boots. He looked and smelled like he could use a bath and a haircut.

By this time, other units were sliding up. Sergeant White, their area field supervisor, directed Unit Three to take the accident report and impound the Hudson, told Jim to place the suspect in the back of his police car and shooed the remaining cars back into service.

Lester and Sergeant White took their time searching the Hudson.

Jim sat next to the prisoner. The suspect said nothing.

Clipboard balanced on his knees, Jim began to make report notes. He re-traced the route of the pursuit, the probable time initiated, time terminated and recorded events of the arrest.

Lester returned with three empty cloth bags labeled First National Bank, Williston, North Dakota. Seated behind the wheel, he turned and held the bags in front of the prisoner. "So, you've been in North Dakota?"

The suspect looked back and said nothing.

"Well, what's the story?" Lester prodded.

The suspect slowly lifted his head and looked directly at Lester. He took his time to speak and finally said, "I've been there and back, you'll find out when you get my F.B.I. rap sheet. Beat the shit out of me if you choose, but I'm not saying anything."

They went to the station, booked the crook as John Doe and took him to jail.

On their way to file reports, Jim asked, "Why wouldn't he answer your questions?"

"That's the experience of hard time," Lester said. "He won't say anything that can be used against him. No alibi's, no excuses, just take his arrest like a man. He's tough. We'll classify his fingerprints, tele-type the F.B.I. and they'll send us his rap sheet. That could take several days. Then we'll

36

have his history and find out if he's wanted somewhere. You finish up the reports. I'll go get permission from the watch commander to use long distance and call North Dakota."

Jim settled in a chair to dictate to Isabel Packman, a graveyard shift clerk typist. On the job since 1941, her advice on reports was worth its weight in gold. Maybe in her sixties, thin, graying hair in a bun, matronly dressed, with a cutting wit, she constantly picked at cops.

Isabel peeled seven copies of an arrest report from a booklet of prepared forms. She put all seven, with attached carbon papers, in a manual Remington typewriter. Only about the first three would be legible. Jim, happy to get her help, began to dictate.

Isabel gave periodic advice and the resulting report was outstanding.

Lester returned just as they finished, wearing a big grin, laughed and said, "I called Williams County, North Dakota. Their Sheriff's Department polices Williston. I told the night deputy we had this old timer in custody for armed robbery and he had bank bags from Williston. They said they'd wake up the Sheriff, now it's 2:30 AM in Williston, and have him call me back. He did. Never heard anybody so happy. It seems this old guy stuck up the same market in Williston the last two Saturdays in a row. Took the money in bank bags. Altogether he got about $2,000. They hadn't had a robbery in six years. The Sheriff says our arrest will re-elect him."

"Pretty hard to beat," replied Jim.

"Are we done filing?

"Yeah. Let's go back to work"

The rest of the night remained quiet, like Sunday night Monday mornings should be. Weather came fast and furious. Wind blew. It rained hard until about 4:00 AM. The short storm hit when streets were empty. There were no accident dispatches and the pavement was dry before dawn.

They stayed warm and dry. They considered it a lucky night for Unit Two.

The shift over, Jim waited outside the door of the squad room bungalow near the rear door of the City Hall – Police Station. White puffy clouds drifted past. The great visibility made Catalina Island and Palos Verdes look as if they were only a mile away. The San Bernardino Mountains surrounding the Los Angeles basin were snow capped and gorgeous. Long Beach is a glorious place to be on a winter morning, he thought. Who needed Palm Springs?

Jim couldn't change clothes and didn't want to look conspicuous. He wore an old Army paratrooper field jacket over his police uniform. Rookies weren't given lockers. The old City Hall - Police Station and adjacent squad room were crowded. These problems were supposed to be solved with completion of a new police building under construction at 400 West Broadway. He didn't seem out of place when Tokay came out the rear door and started down the steps.

This morning she looked fresh and clean. She wore jeans, a gray sweatshirt and navy blue canvas tennis shoes. Her shoulder length black hair was pulled back with a rubber band. At 5'2", and 160 pounds, Tokay was not a looker. But, now, she appeared a different girl, rested and presentable.

"Hi, Tokay," Jim said.

"You just get off shift?"

"Yeah. You got time for breakfast?"

"With you? Sure. I've had enough jail chow."

"How about bacon and eggs at the Americana?"

"Lets get it on."

In Jim's Studebaker, they drove east on Broadway to Atlantic. The Americana sat on the northeast corner. It enjoyed a good reputation as a new clean twenty-four hour café. Nothing appeared fancy about it; just good chow.

Once inside, service was rapid, coffee came, and a waitress got their order. When she stepped away, Tokay started talking. "What do you want, Jim? This is nice, but you're not taking me breakfast for the hell of it."

Jim messed with his coffee and tried to decide how to approach the subject of Peggy Evans. He'd thought about it a lot. Tokay was friendly, but she was also street smart and had a big mouth. If he didn't tread carefully his interest in the case would be all over Long Beach by sunset. Every cop in town would know he was poking his nose into a homicide investigation.

"Do you remember being arrested?" he asked.

"No, I went partying with a couple of other girls and about six sailors, drank too much, and woke up in the drunk tank. The matron said I was dumped buck naked in front of an apartment house in the Jungle. I don't remember shit."

"That's about the way it went down. That was me alongside you in the back seat of the black and white when you went to the station. You were talking about Peggy Evans before you passed out."

"I did? What did I say about Peggy?" Tokay's eyes darted nervously and she shifted in her seat.

"You said somebody raped her, then killed her. You said it wasn't abortion, it was murder."

"I got a big fucking mouth," sniffled Tokay. "What you doing in this shit?"

"Old Buddy Jones found her and called the station. Red and I rolled in. Buddy led us to her under the roller coaster. It was bad."

"Yeah," Tokay replied, her eyes tearing up, "I read about it. She was a neat girl, a friend of mine. Shit, did she ever get had!"

"What do you mean?"

"I don't know if I should tell you about it. People could come looking for me."

"So, who's going to tell them you said anything?"

"Yeah, and if I don't say something, the prick will probably skate."

39

"Just run the story out to me. I won't give you up."

"Promise, Jim?"

"It's a promise!"

"O.K. but I got to tell you from the beginning. She really got fucked."

"Sounds okay, lay it out."

Their food came and the waitress filled their coffee. Each attacked the bacon and eggs ravenously.

Tokay continued. "I met Peg maybe sometime in early August. She came from Iowa to be with her boyfriend, Roy. He'd just finished sub training at New London. He wrote asking her to come out. His sub, the Segundo, was at the Navy yard for re-fitting. He bullshitted her, saying it would be here for months. All he wanted was a piece of ass."

"Did you get to know her well?"

"Don't interrupt! Yeah, I did. We were all hanging out at the Star Café. Peggy was young, pretty as a picture, naïve as a fence post, nice as pie, and drew men like flies. We just hit it off. She was staying with Roy in a fleabag apartment. I showed her around when Roy was on base, you know, introduced her to people, and let her know what's happening. She was a kick!"

"Did they get along?"

"Who?" asked Tokay, slathering her toast with strawberry jam.

Jim said, "Peggy, Roy."

"Oh, yeah. Well at least until Roy's sub goes out for sea trials. Then they got in a hell of a fight. She found out he would be out for about sixteen weeks, return for final inspection and stores, and ship out to Japan. She knew she'd been had and she was pissed."

"Trouble in River City."

"Yeah! She was in a corner, stuck. She ran off Roy. So there was no boyfriend, no pad, no money. Wouldn't call her family in Iowa. She's my buddy though, and I have to

40

admit being around her sure attracted guys. From that day forward, we were together. I showed her the ropes."

"How did you make it?"

"Well, I got this little place at the Stillman Hotel. I do cleaning there and they gave me the room for free. We crapped out there."

"So, you at least had a roof over your head."

"It made do. Then the trouble started. I'd been partying at Ivan Slade's. You know, the dude with the engine-rebuilding place on Sante Fe. He has a big apartment above his office, a party room that has a righteous jukebox a real one with all country music. He has food, booze, and even a few joints. He's real secretive about the weed though."

"He's sure a big spender."

"It ain't the money he cares about. It's young pussy. He's got to be in his late fifties and loves to screw and get head. He doesn't pay for it though. It's done different."

"How's it work?" Jim asked.

"He gives every girl a ten-spot for just coming to the party. Word is out in the Jungle, and the runaways come. His idea of sex is a blowjob from a thirteen year old. The only men allowed at the parties are a few of his buddies. I fucked up bringing Peggy. He went dip shit for her, the asshole."

"How many times did Peggy go to the parties?"

"Peggy only went to Slade's twice," replied Tokay.

"How did the rape happen?"

"We came back a few days after her first party there. I got smashed and wound up in the rack with a buddy of Ivan's. I wanted to screw, but Peggy got raped."

"Just like that?" Jim looked doubtful.

"Naw! He slipped her a mickey. Once she passed out, Ivan carried her back to his bedroom and raped her. He fucked a limp unconscious broad. What a depraved asshole."

41

The waitress placed the bill next to Jim's left hand while passing the table. It was $2.19 for food and coffee.

"How did you find out?" Jim asked.

"I got up about eleven, tried to down a Bloody Mary to straighten out my head, and this racket breaks out. I guess Peggy woke up in his bed, nude. She knew she'd been fucked and mauled, and the shit hit the fan. I'd never heard her cuss. She did then, called him every name in the book. I got dressed while she screamed at him and we split."

"Then what?"

"Shit, she couldn't call the cops. They'd find out she'd runaway and ship her back to Iowa. She wasn't ready to face her folks after being bullshitted by Roy and she sure didn't want to face the hometown gossip."

"Yeah, I can see that," Jim said.

"A few weeks went by and Peggy started getting morning sickness. She told me she and Roy were always careful. And now all of a sudden she's pregnant. She knew it had to be from that night at Ivan's. So she called him. That must a scared the shit out of him. He's a big fucking wheel around town. He didn't need that."

"So?"

"So, he called his sleeze bag attorney friend from the Apple Valley Steak House where he hangs out. The prick, named Johnny Redden, hunts down Peggy and tells her he'll arrange an abortion with a real doctor. Imagine that. The real fucking doctor killed her. And, he said she'd get $500 to keep her mouth shut."

"Did Peggy agree?"

"Yep. Said if she blew the whistle, she'd be stuck with the pukes' kid. So she'd go along with it. Bad fucking call."

"Where did it go down?"

"I don't know. I got busted for co-habitation and got five days. When I got out it was all over. One of our friends, Geri Kaufman, told me that she got her sailor husband to give Peggy a ride. I checked. He took her to the Grass

Shack drive-in by Cherry and PCH. She said she was supposed to wait inside. Then, no more Peggy!"

"What day and time did that happen?"

"Some time Tuesday morning. You know. I read the newspaper article in jail. It said you guys found her early Wednesday morning. I guess that's the whole story."

Jim placed two one-dollar bills and three quarters on top of the bill for the waitress. They both stood as if on signal.

"There's a lot to think about. Tokay, let me drive you back to the Stillman."

At the curb in front of the hotel, as Tokay opened the passenger side door, Jim spoke. "Tokay, this is a secret. Our secret. It goes both ways. I won't tell about you giving me information. You don't tell about my asking. This is some dangerous shit. We're in it together. Remember the old navy saying, loose lips sink ships. Tell no one!"

"I hear!"

"Certain people would do anything to keep this secret. That includes doing us."

Jim drove home, tired and troubled, knowing more than maybe he should. He needed advice.

CHAPTER FIVE

Thursday, January 28, 1960

Jim loved old attractive buildings, parks and well planned cities. He liked to read about the evolution of construction materials, building design and city planning. He included the courthouse among his favorite Long Beach buildings.

The ornate white brick six-story Jergins Trust Building, built in 1920, included the municipal and superior courtrooms, law offices, the State Theater and several storefront airline travel offices. The surprising combination of uses made it a success from the day it opened. In earlier years a tunnel brought pedestrians from the north side of Ocean Boulevard under the street to a basement arcade with shops. Now with the tunnel and arcade closed most remaining business was in the courtrooms. Duty took him there for a court appearance. Jim pulled the subpoena from his suit pocket and read it again: Thursday, January 28th, 9:30 AM, *Be There,* Department 4. Long Beach Municipal Court, Jergins Trust Building, Ocean and Pine.

A drunk driver case, he got there on time and the waiting began. Jim had already learned that lawyers commonly requested continuances and the delays slowed down the process. Then judges with crowded dockets were ready to plea bargain to get work out of the way. A lesser sentence resulted in the trial averted. He saw that ninety-five percent of cases never came before a juror.

Jim and Lester talked quietly to avoid being overheard by others in the hallway.

Victims, witnesses, suspects, and attorneys stood apart in clusters, chatting.

He told Lester about his breakfast with Tokay and described the events, the party house, the rape, the aftermath and arrangements for an abortion.

"Jim, y'all got to be real careful. I was going to tell you to lay all this on Homicide," explained Lester. "But now, I don't think that's the way to go. I know this attorney, Johnny Redden. He's a nasty bastard. Lower than whale shit. They don't make 'em any worse. Don't tell anybody — even your new partner, what you're doing. Hear?"

"I hear you," replied Jim, "but why?"

"Cause Redden hangs out with the homicide dicks. I mean Bill Millard and Carl Peele. I've seen them at the Apple Valley a dozen times. They're thick as thieves and have been for years. I mean they're really close."

"Do you suppose it's just a coincidence?" Jim asked.

Deputy Coroner Karl Schultz, with a big smile on his face and cigar in hand, came over to them and interrupted their conversation.

"Hi, guys. What's up? Court time?" asked Karl.

"A drunk driver," Jim said. "Waiting for the plea bargain. That's all. What's with you?"

"Oh, I'm down the hall on a two year old homicide. They want autopsy testimony."

"I haven't seen you since the Cyclone Racer when you came out for the Peggy Evans case," Jim said.

"Boy, what a beautiful young thing she was. Those are the worst. Young, pretty, and everything to live for."

"The paper said it was a hemorrhage after an abortion. Is that the way it looked?" Jim asked.

"That's so," grunted Karl, "and professional medical work, even if it was botched up."

"How so, botched?"

"Perforated the uterus — a standard complication. Just a small hole. It probably went unnoticed. Hemorrhaging started and didn't get stopped. Had she been in a hospital, they would've monitored for the problem and corrected the work. Wherever it was done they could've watched her and still taken her to a hospital. Probably wouldn't want to, though, cause questions'd be asked. So, she bled out.

45

Otherwise, the surgical work was professional. This was no quack. Too bad it came out that way," said Karl.

"See many of those?" Lester asked.

"Way too many. Seen hundreds die over the past thirty years. Most are like her, just kids. Even had a happily married gal once with four children who couldn't handle a fifth. Most are performed by quacks. Abortion deaths are the shit side of this job. And this is a job without many good sides."

"Any chance we'll catch the guy that did the surgery?" Jim inquired.

"We catch one in a thousand. Victims won't talk – no reason to – don't want anyone to know. Thousands of abortions are successful every year. Those people are happy. Why would this be different? Those that wind up pissed off usually think twice before complaining, cause they're participants in the felony. They solicited it."

"They're in a corner," Jim said.

"Oops, they're waving at me. Time to go on stage. In this dead body business, I'm essential, like a guy running a cemetery. As Red Skelton's character Digger O'Dell used to say, 'I'll be shoveling off.'"

Jim Grant and Lester Peabody stood quietly for few moments as they thought about abortions and the Peggy Evans case.

Deputy City Prosecutor Bill Burns came out of the courtroom, waved at the two officers and called, "You're out of here. It's over."

An attorney came from the courtroom behind Burns. With briefcase in his left hand, and his client's elbow in his right hand, he was speaking to him softly as he passed the officers.

"Johnny Redden plea bargained the case and the judge rolled over like Santa Claus," growled Burns, a no-nonsense prosecutor.

Just then, Attorney Johnny Redden turned back, smiled and chortled, "Don't be so red assed, Bill. You always beat the guys that hire shitty lawyers."

Jim looked Redden over. He made him as male white, 45 to 50 years, 5' 9", 150 pounds, with brown eyes, a slender ferret-like face and thinning brown hair combed straight back. He didn't wear glasses. His suit was expensive and brown, with brown shoes and belt to match his saddle leather briefcase. He looked and smelled like money. His manner of speaking communicated arrogance and he radiated influence. Jim didn't like him.

Burns muttered and walked away.

Lester turned to Jim and quietly spoke, "Let's finish this talk at Hody's PCH before work. Make it at 7:00 PM. Meanwhile, take care. Really take care."

A quarter to eleven, court finished for the day, Jim drove toward his apartment. He thought about the case, and Peggy – always Peggy. Had to grab some shut-eye, get up at 6:00 PM, shower and shave, get some personal work done, meet Lester, and be back for squad meeting at 11:00 PM.

* * *

Jim rolled out of bed and rubbed his eyes. You never get used to morning at 6:00 PM, he thought, groggy and bleary eyed. He cleaned up and hit the road. Since the discussion with Tokay, Jim had wanted to go by the Sante Fe Avenue party pad. Now, with some time to kill he decided to have that look at Slade's party house.

He drove slowly south from Pacific Coast Highway past the engine re-building business. The front chain link gate stood open. Jim looked at his watch: 6:40 PM and the place was still busy. He drove down the street, made a U-turn and parked about fifty yards south, across the street, facing northbound. He watched, studied the activity and tried to figure out the operation.

47

The office, on the south side of the lot, had a staircase up to an apartment above. The machine shop, engine rebuilding area, and parts storage were in a large building straight back in the rear. On the right sat a small auto body and paint shop. Bright lights hung from the sides of the structures.

Twenty feet back from the fence stood a second chain link fence. A third fence stood in front of the machine shop. Security couldn't have been better.

Jim saw a burglar alarm box high on the side of the office. The door to the office and the stairs to the apartment were between the first and second fences. He noticed a light, not working, at the top of the stairs over the door. This must be the blue party light and it wasn't on.

Three men pushed a newly painted Volkswagen from the paint shop back into the rear and they all came back outside the fence. A guy closed and padlocked the gate and pulled a lever that opened a kennel door. Three German shepherds were released into the enclosed area and they looked mean. At 6:50 PM, everyone left.

Having seen enough, Jim drove to PCH (Pacific Coast Highway) and turned east. He was just in time to meet Lester, and even more interesting, to visit a new girlfriend. The destination: Hody's Drive In, at PCH and East Anaheim.

He arrived, parked on the front row, and a carhop quickly approached his rolled down window. This trim cute redhead with a ponytail smiled broadly as she walked to the car.

"Hi, Jim. You've been hiding from me?"

At about 5'2", Fran couldn't top 105 pounds. Just a touch of lipstick complimented the color of her hair. She had an hourglass figure, nice breasts, and a neat ass. Every guy that came in wanted to bed her. Jim believed his love life looked better every time he saw her.

"Just work and court, Fran. I came by to hit on you, and have a bite to eat. You still have time for me?"

Fran laughed. They'd gone to a drive-in movie last Tuesday, a first date, and both were still interested. They'd gotten real cozy, but Jim didn't push too fast. It could be a good thing. Carhops and cops worked crazy hours. They often dated.

"Fran, I still have Tuesday and Wednesday evenings off. How about dinner at Welch's Restaurant next week?"

"I didn't think you were still interested. You didn't call!"

"You know cops. Odd hours, weird people."

That brought a laugh. "O.K. Jim. Next Wednesday. Pick me up at my folks place again at seven."

"Good, then I'll have black coffee, a medium rare cheeseburger, and apple pie ala mode."

"You got it. Back in a jiffy."

Fran was hanging a tray with coffee on the driver's side door when Lester walked up.

"You two a spooning?" he asked.

"Give us a break," said Fran. "Mess with me and get your coffee in your lap".

"Okay, okay. Y'all just fetch some coffee and apple pie with ice cream. I won't fuss with you no more."

"Got it, Lester." Smiling, Fran wrote down the order and walked toward another car awaiting service.

"Jim, I'm worried about Millard and Peele. Those homicide guys are just too close to that attorney Johnny Redden," explained Lester. "Still, you need to fill in some gaps."

"What's wrong?" Jim frowned.

"One," Lester said. "Most of the stuff from Tokay is hearsay. She didn't see Peggy get drugged or raped. Peggy told her. Can't use that in court. It's not admissible."

"I understand," said Jim.

"Two. Remember the only time we can use hearsay is a dying declaration. Somebody knows they're dying and swears it's the truth."

"I remember."

"Three. She can testify about the argument. That was in her presence and it's a great foundation."

"Understood."

"All the rest is just information," said Lester. But, sure as hell, you can build on it. You need to talk to this Geri Kaufman. Her sailor husband took Peggy to the Grass Shack. You need to find out what she knows and maybe if her husband heard or saw something."

Fran returned with coffee for Lester, he took it, opened the glove compartment door, took a sip, and sat it down.

"A couple minutes," said Fran, "and your order will be up. Be right back."

The food came, they ate, talked shop, paid for their chow, and Jim lingered over his goodbye to Fran.

Lester walked back to his car parked on the back row.

Each car headed for the station to start another shift.

* * *

Lester and Jim walked into the squad room and were immediately directed to relieve an afternoon unit that was standing by on a dead body call. Jim had never handled a routine family death before.

They drove to the Wilmore Apartments, a beautifully kept ornate 1920s high rise, with individually owned units. The elevator carried them to a top floor suite, where they met Watch Three (afternoon shift) Officer Franklin Marsh.

Marsh apologetically explained he needed to meet his wife, in labor at St. Mary's Hospital. He said this was a routine death of a ninety-two year old man, Joshua Goldstein. The family had arrived, arrangements were being made with a mortuary, and he only awaited confirmation that a physician would sign the death certificate. If not, a complete report was required and the body had to go to the Coroner.

Marsh introduced Jim and Lester to Luke Morgenthal, the son-in-law, his wife Ruth, and Rabbi Samuel Stern. They seemed very pleasant educated people. Then Marsh excused himself, nervously, and ran out the door.

A moment later Dr. Samuel Stern, a close friend of the family, arrived and confirmed that he would sign the certificate.

All had been touched by the death.

"We won't intrude any longer," Lester replied. "We'll just be on our way."

"Gentlemen," Rabbi Stern said, "before you leave, could you take a moment and join us, while we hold hands and recite the Twenty-third Psalm?"

They did.

The incident made Jim think. Police work showed the similarities of religions, not the differences.

CHAPTER SIX

Thursday, February 11, 1960

February. Another two months and probation would be over. On April 12th probation would end. Walking on glass wasn't easy.

Jim drew another training officer, Leo Jefferson, a Negro. Some of the cops wondered if he could handle it. They forgot Jim soldiered in the 82nd and 11th Airborne Divisions, where men had to prove they belonged. He looked for performance, not color. Besides, as the rookie, he worked for the training officer assigned. It was just like the army.

Leo Jefferson performed. He walked the walk. A Long Beach kid, he'd gone to Poly High then graduated from Drake University with a degree in sociology. While at Drake, he lettered in four sports each of the four years: football, basketball, track, and baseball – no small achievement. Only 5' 11" and 165 pounds, he was made of spring steel. What a fun guy to work for - educated, smart, not brutal, strong as a bull, and quick as a cat.

They hit it off. The new area, Unit Seven, ran north from Tenth Street to Willow Street and between Cherry Avenue and the Los Angeles River flood control channel.

In the first week they made four felony arrests. Two of the arrests were from a stolen '58 Porsche they'd cornered in traffic. Then came a felony injury hit and run suspect that fled in an old '46 International pickup. A sailor that cracked up on a stolen motorcycle made the fourth. They were hot.

Things were going well with Fran, too. The wonderful seafood dinner at Welch's Restaurant at San Antonio Drive and Atlantic Avenue made it all work. Since then they had been inseparable. She attended day classes at Long Beach City College and would slip into his bed in the afternoon to wake him up. Hot!

Jim had a good partner, a good unit, and a terrific love life. He leaned back in the passenger seat of the black and white. He glowed, happy with his work, certain he was in love, and basking in self-satisfaction. He didn't want this bubble to burst.

They checked in just after squad meeting, Thursday, February 11th (after midnight, Friday the 12th), the first night of his second week in Unit Seven.

Leo started laying it on. "Hot diggity dawg! Jim done died and gone to heaven, found him a woman. Who'ee!"

"Aw, Leo. Haven't you ever been in love?"

"Jim, I don't know if you know the difference."

"What do you mean, know the difference?"

"Between being in love, and being in lust," guffawed Leo.

"Unit Seven."

"Unit Seven," Jim replied, "at PCH and the Boulevard."

"Unit Seven, check the unknown trouble in the rear of 1829 Pacific. Make it Code 2: fast, but no red lights or siren."

"10-4, rolling."

Leo turned their car west on PCH, accelerated to Pacific Avenue, turned north, crossed to the wrong side of the street, and parked about 50 feet south of the destination. He knew his beat.

"Unit Seven. Be advised, about eight people are fighting in the rear yard. Any unit to assist?"

"Unit Ten, from Sante Fe and PCH, enroute."

"Unit Two, from Tenth and Pine."

"Unit Seven. We read."

Jim grabbed his nightstick and had his hand on the door handle when Leo reached over, put his hand on his left arm and said, "Take it slow, partner."

"Aren't we going to run back there and break em up?" Jim asked.

"No," responded Leo, "let's walk back there. We'll be rested. Help will be here. Then, if we have to kick ass, we can."

Nightsticks in hand, they walked north to the address. Loud music and arguing voices could be heard from the area of the backyard. They walked up the driveway and through an open gate and stood in the shadows looking into the rear yard.

They observed a typical loud party with music and arguing drunks, not a fight. There were about a dozen couples. All looked college age. A record player sat on the porch at the end of an extension cord. A woman lounged alongside sorting through a stack of 45 RPM records. "Shake, Rattle and Roll" could be heard a block away.

Jim looked back toward the front of the house. Four fellow officers came up behind them.

Leo looked back, nodded toward them, pointed to his nightstick and slid it up his sleeve. Then he stepped into view and spoke. "Hi, folks. Sorry to bother you. We came because of the noise. You're so loud, people thought you were fighting."

A big white guy, wearing a UCLA sweatshirt, struggled to his feet. He swayed and belched. He was drunk. A giant compared to them, at about 6'6" and 260 pounds, he towered over Leo.

His big blue eyes squinting, a huge grin on his freckled face, he rubbed his ham sized hands together and challenged Leo in a slurred voice, "Who the fuck gave you permission to come in my back yard?"

"The calls, the loud music, the arguing and the time of night make this our business. You're disturbing the peace," replied Leo. "If you would please turn down the music and go inside, we can go back to work."

"Fuck you, nigger," said the big drunk as he telegraphed the swing of a powerful right toward Leo's head.

54

Effortlessly, Leo moved under the arm. His concealed nightstick came from below, moving less than ten inches as quick as a flash and smacked the assailant's crotch. A perfect strike, the big guy doubled up with a groan and dropped to both knees. Since Leo had moved so quickly and the short stroke of the stick came from below, Jim doubted anyone clearly saw the hit.

Jim quickly applied handcuffs. Others in the group murmured, but no one stepped forward. Their big leader out of action, no others were willing to fight.

"Everybody inside," said Leo. "You." He pointed to the woman with the records, "turn off the music. The party is over. This guy is going to jail. Any complaints?"

Without a word, all of them disappeared inside.

Jim pulled the big would-be assailant up, frisked him for weapons, and dragged him, stumbling, toward the police car. The other units went back into service.

In the car, Leo turned to the now subdued defendant, saying, "This is one time your alligator mouth overloaded your rabbit ass. Next time, shut up and listen. Then you won't be in a heap of shit."

After booking and filing, a fight call came from the Star Café. This time they were backup.

The fighting ended before units arrived and Jim and Leo were in the third car that reached the café. Leo left Jim standing outside in the line of police cars. Those inside, a typical group of sailors and girls, were filing out.

"Hey Jim!" someone yelled.

"Hi, Tokay." Jim replied.

Tokay came over with a washed-out blonde. She looked dumpy in worn jeans and an old navy turtleneck sweater. A skinny sailor at her elbow, both looked half in the bag.

Tokay introduced the girl and the sailor as Geri and Al Kaufman. The names rang a bell and Jim's senses went to instant alert. What a break, Jim thought. He shook hands and motioned them away from others. Al Kaufman's looked thin and tough, about 30, height at 5' 10" and couldn't weigh over 130, had a thin face, brown eyes and brown hair. Clearly smashed, it wouldn't be a good time to talk to him.

"I'm glad we ran into one another," Jim said, keeping his expression neutral.

"I told them this was secret shit," blurted Tokay.

Jim shook his head. "It's not good to talk here. Can we meet tomorrow evening at the Tom-Tom Drive In? Say 8:00 PM?"

Tokay, Jeri and Al looked at one another then all nodded.

"Tokay, you know my white Golden Hawk. I'll park on the back line. We'll talk in my car. We don't need eavesdroppers."

"Yeah," Tokay said.

"Jim. Let's roll," Leo called as he returned to the black and white.

Several routine calls followed. Then, at daylight, the radio blared, *"Unit Seven, Code 3, a 901T injury accident, at Willow and Long Beach Boulevard."*

"Unit Seven, 10-4, from PCH and the Boulevard."

"Unit Seven, be advised, Fire Department enroute. Bodies all over the street. One of the P.E. Red Cars hit a station wagon."

The Pacific Electric rail transit line crossed Willow Street on the route south on Long Beach Boulevard from Los Angeles.

"Oh shit," groaned Leo, "another idiot hammered by a Red Car! You know, they're talking about taking the system out. People just don't understand the longer slowing and stopping distances needed on a rail line. It should have been elevated to separate it from cars."

They soon learned what happened. The car going west turned in front of the southbound rail car. The driver calculated that the Red Car would slow down. It couldn't. The weight and inertia, on steel rails, couldn't be overcome

56

and it smashed the right rear of the turning International station wagon. The wagon spun and scattered three bodies across the intersection. A fire department gut wagon (ambulance) and fire truck were already there and another on the way. The firemen did good work. Nobody died.

Jim collected the driver's license from the station wagon driver as the ambulance hauled him away. Then he retrieved the locomotive engineers permit from a pissed off Red Car operator.

"Thirty years I've been driving these things," he said pointing to the huge rail car, "and I can't get over these dumb shits turning in front of me. What is it? The unconscious fucks want to commit suicide?"

It took three hours to complete the work. A backup unit directed traffic around the wreck. The scene was measured and statements taken. The shift ended, and still no tow truck came. Jim and Leo kicked the backup loose and took over traffic direction. The tow truck finally arrived and did its job. Then they went to the hospital for final information about the victims and finished at the station. At 10:00 AM, they went home.

Jim thought about the simple, stupid mistakes that people make. Those in the accident were damned lucky.

* * *

Tokay arrived with Geri and Al Kaufman right on time at 8:00 PM. Geri and Al climbed into the back seat and Tokay settled into the front passenger side. They all ordered coffee and the carhop left.

Jim looked back at Geri and Al, "Everything said here must be kept among us. It is all secret, understand?"

"We'll keep our mouths shut," said Geri.

Al and Tokay nodded.

"Jim, Ivan already has his people sniffing around to see if we're talking," Tokay reported.

"How so? Jim asked.

"One of his gophers, Ben Clarey, has been asking questions. He hit all of our spots. It's scary," said Tokay.

"Who is this Clarey?" Jim asked.

"He's a runner for Ivan. You know, one of those suck asses you see hanging around the boss. He's the turd that pimps for Slade, brings pussy to him. He always sets up the parties. When the big guy wants something he sends Clarey," said Tokay.

"What does he look like?"

"Just think of a brown nose, it's him. He's young, short and heavy. You know, pear shaped with his belly and ass hanging over. And he has a brown crew cut," replied Tokay.

"Sounds like you could call Clarey a blivet."

"What's a blivet, Jim?" Geri asked, snickering.

"In the paratroops, we called three pounds of shit in a two pound bag a blivet." They all laughed.

"Anyway," Tokay went on, "Clarey's trying to be sly. He's asking around about what's being said about Peggy dying. They haven't had a party since then."

"You're right," Jim said. "He must be asking for Slade."

"They won't find out what we're doing," Tokay said.

"Are you sure they won't find out we snitched them off? Geri asked.

"Not unless you tell them," Jim answered. "They can't have any idea you know anything."

"I have to tell you what Peggy told me," said Geri looking at Jim. "Cause somebody ought to pay."

"What'd she tell you?"

"About her being so down after it happened," replied Geri.

"Go on," said Jim.

"She thought she was at fault cause she shouldn't have gone there. She thought she did something to give him a come-on. And she blamed herself for being stupid enough to be drugged. I never saw any girl beat up on herself so much. It wasn't her fault," Geri anguished. "I told her so."

"Yeah," Tokay interjected, "she wouldn't eat and stayed in bed for a week, she was so bummed. I tried to get her to snap out of it."

"What else did she say?" asked Jim.

"She was angry with herself for not going to the hospital to get washed out," Geri said. "She thought if she had, she wouldn't be pregnant and she didn't want his kid. Over and over again, she blamed herself. But she didn't have any money. How could she pay a hospital?"

"Did she miss her period and think she was pregnant?"

"Aw shit," Geri replied breaking into tears, "it kills me to think about this. Peggy was really a sweet kid."

"Take it easy for a minute."

"She'd been sick ever since the rape," continued Geri wiping away tears. "She thought, at first, it was a reaction from the drugs they used to knock her out. Maybe so. But then she got sick every morning and she knew. That's when she got mad and called Slade."

"What did she say to him?"

"She threatened him, said she didn't want his bastard and would blow the whistle on his depraved fucking ass. She said he got scared and tried to get her to calm down. That's when he offered to have some attorney named Redden get her a real doctor and give her $500 for her trouble."

"What then?"

"He told her to think about it and call back," Jeri sobbed again. "She didn't want the kid, couldn't think of any other way. I know she called him, and told him to set it up. Anyway, it happened. She asked me if Al could give her a ride to the Grass Shack Drive-In. I got him to do it."

"Al, did she say anything to you," asked Jim, "or did you notice anything, when you took her there?"

"Naw," Al uncomfortably replied, "we left at noon. It only took ten minutes. Nothing happened. Hey, I just remembered. She told me it was Clarey she was supposed to meet."

"Did you see him?"

"No. Saw nobody. Just drove in, dropped her off and drove out."

All were silent for what seemed like minutes.

Jim thought about the importance of the information. It linked Slade and Redden and Clarey. He had to talk to Lester again.

He turned on the Studebaker's headlights, paid the carhop and she took away the tray.

"We've gone as far as we can for now," said Jim. "Let's keep an ear to the ground. I'll work from this end, but if something else is going on, I'll need to know. Tokay has my number and she can call me."

"Sure," replied Tokay.

"One thing though. Remember this is dangerous. I'm not kidding. Slade has to be scared. He'd face felonies and be humiliated in this town – ruined. He could try to eliminate any threat. Don't let it be you."

They sat grim faced, no one saying a word.

Jim went on, "I've got to go."

They all climbed out.

He left for work. He had a lot to think about.

CHAPTER SEVEN

Thursday, February 25, 1960

Gunshots echoed through the Police Pistol Range. No wonder people living in the area surrounding Palos Verde Avenue and Spring Street objected. The range used to be encircled by a huge sugar beet field. Recently subdivided, new stucco G.I. homes surrounded the range. Every police officer qualified with his revolver quarterly. Civilians shot, too. The range included a small coffee shop, a cartridge reloading facility, and a private pistol club building. Across the street stood the Long Beach Mounted Police Clubhouse.

Jim waited for the cease-fire announcement and retrieved his target for scoring. An expert score paid an extra $96.00 every six months. A few bucks were always welcome with a salary of $409.00 per month. Court overtime helped, too.

A Smith & Wesson Model 28 Highway Patrol .357 magnum revolver with a 4" barrel rested in his Jordan Holster. He believed he carried the best available sidearm.

He joined Lester Peabody in line after shooting and they watched the crusty range sergeant mark each target for a score. Jim's score of 98 invited comment.

"Good work. Do you shoot this well all the time?" asked Lester.

"Yeah, I come here a lot. If I have to shoot, I want to be ready."

"I'd say you're ready," countered Lester, "but, on another note, what's going on with your Peggy Evans puzzle?"

"I've turned up some stuff and I need some advice."

"Yeah, let's go to the coffee shop, grab a cup, and talk."

They entered the ramshackle building. A new range and pistol club was under construction east of the San Gabriel

61

River south of Carson. This coffee shop and range would soon be closed.

They sat and an inmate trustee took their order. It cost a nickel for coffee and fifty cents for bacon and eggs. The inmate labor made it cheap. They ordered coffee and service was prompt.

"Well," asked Lester, "what's happening?"

Jim reviewed the meeting with Tokay and Geri and Al Kaufman. He reported Peggy's depression after the rape, the pregnancy, the cash offer to abort, the involvement of attorney Johnny Redden, the promise of a real physician and the abortion appointment with Ben Clarey at the Grass Shack Drive In.

Lester took a sip of his coffee, looked Jim right in the eye, and stated, "You've uncovered some dangerous shit. I know the homicide dicks, Millard and Peele, are thick with Slade. This'd be something they could bury. You sure can't tell them what you've uncovered. We need reliable big guns. It's time to talk with Captain J. C. Green. He's Chief of Detectives."

"Shit. I can't talk to him. I'm a rookie. I'm on probation," blurted Jim.

Lester waved both hands in the air. "Hell, don't have a conniption fit. You ain't done nothing wrong. Just relax."

"How do I approach Captain Green?"

Lester thought a moment, and answered. "Let me handle that. I know him; he used to command our patrol watch and I worked for him. I'll set it up so you get a memo to see him. That way, you'll be called in and it'll appear you're being asked about some report you filed. It'll all be official, you'll see. Just don't talk about it and don't sweat it!"

Jim did worry. He pitched restlessly all night.

* * *

Leo Jefferson put his bulging heavy black leather briefcase on the squad room floor next to an oak chair in the front row. It contained a penal code book, a vehicle codebook, a moving vehicle citation book, a parking citation book, report forms, maps of the city, blank report forms, a flashlight and a Rolla-Tape measure. He dropped his police soft hat in the chair, stretched, groaned and said, "Jim, I must be getting old. Every day this week I've been in court. My ass is dragging."

Jim laughed and replied, "Well, the overtime will make you well."

Leo grinned broadly, straightened his tie, gestured for Jim to stand closer, and whispered, "The court time took care of my wallet, and that ain't all. In a few minutes they'll read a change of assignment for next Tuesday, March 1st. Wait 'til you hear, I'm out of here."

Jim, surprised, whispered back, "Where're you going to work?"

Leo smiled and murmured, "Just you listen."

Sergeant Frank Gonzales, new to the shift, towered over the room from behind the huge oak desk. At 6'5" and 235 pounds he cast quite a shadow. He hammered on the desk top with a wooden mallet, and yelled for attention. "All right, you assholes, listen up!"

Suddenly, the room went quiet.

"You all have hot sheets and the urgent shit's on the chalk board. Write it down. The brass wants more tickets – no guff, just do it. Remember, the grand theft autos are killing us. Find me some GTA's; a few rollen' stolens.

"Oh. There is one change of assignment. It came in this afternoon. It concerns this watch, so I'll read it as written.

"It's dated today, Friday, February 26, 1960 to be effective Tuesday, March 1, 1960. Attention All Officers:

Patrolman Leo Jefferson, from Patrol Division Watch I, is reassigned to Detective Division Watch II, days."

The entire squad room broke into hoots and cheers.

Lester Peabody threw in a jibe, "Gone, to be among the chosen people. But, tell me Leo, how did you do it?"

More laughter.

Red Price yelled, "Leo, I knew your nose was brown, I just didn't know where you were putting it."

Everyone roared.

Leo stood with a somber expression, raised his right hand over his head, and replied, "I have relatives in high places."

The room was in stitches.

The sergeant barked, "All right you assholes, that's enough. Out of here. There's work to be done. Go clean up Dodge City."

They were into a car and up Long Beach Boulevard in a couple of minutes.

Leo drove. Jim checked in on the radio, turned from the passenger seat, and asked, "How did this transfer come about?"

"Captain Green called me at home at about 2:30 this afternoon, woke me up, asked me to come in and see him. I thought what grease am I in now? It took me an hour to shower, dress and get there. His secretary told me I was expected. Damn it, Jim, I was scared."

"What did he say?"

"Just asked if I would work day dicks. I said sure. He said the change of assignment would be typed immediately and that because of changes in days off, this would be my last night on the graveyard shift. Let me tell you, I was happier than a pig in shit. Me, going to detectives. Wow!"

"What'll be your assignment in the detective bureau?"

Leo turned from the steering wheel, looked straight at him, and replied, "He said it was confidential, I'm to work directly for him. You'll know soon enough. Don't even say I've said this much. O.K.?"

"Yeah, yeah, sure." Replied Jim.

"Unit Seven," commanded the radio.

"Unit Seven, at PCH and Long Beach Boulevard," acknowledged Jim.

"Unit Seven, A 10851 just occurred. The GTA is a black '58 VW from Jamestown Motors at 14th and Long Beach Boulevard. It's being chased northbound on the Boulevard by a new blue Mercedes sedan.

"Unit Seven, 10-4"

Jim looked back and then blurted, "Shit, that's them, they're coming right by us."

"I'm on that VW's ass," said Leo, "light up the reds, and make the growler go."

Jim mashed the right-side floor mounted siren solenoid switch as the black and white careened in between the Mercedes and the VW. Then he snatched the radio microphone and broadcast the chase announcement, "Unit Seven, in chase, northbound the Boulevard from PCH, the 10851 black VW. Now approaching Hill Street."

"Attention all units. Unit Seven is in chase, northbound Long Beach Boulevard approaching Hill Street. A black VW 10851."

The VW just couldn't compete with the police car in a pursuit. They barreled up on the rear of the little car.

Leo yelled over the siren, "Pull out the shotgun and roll down your window. I'm going to pass the son-of-a-bitch. He's a fleeing felon; that makes him fair game. Blow his ass away."

Jim followed instructions, yanking the Winchester Model 97 twelve gauge pump from its upright position in the dash mounted shotgun lock. He shoved the shotgun barrel out of the passenger side window, racked a round into the chamber, hunched over to aim and fire. The VW driver looked back.

65

Suddenly, he pulled over to the curb and stopped. The police car skidded crazily in behind it. The driver, with hands up, screamed, "Don't shoot! Don't shoot! I give up!"

Both officers jumped from the police car, Jim with the shotgun and Leo with a .357 magnum. The car thief submissively followed orders and they took him from the VW.

Jim watched with the shotgun while Leo searched him, put on handcuffs, and placed him in the back of the black and white.

The Mercedes sedan following the car thief, parked behind the officers. Jim knew the driver, Bill Wright, the general manager of Jamestown Motors, a dealership that handled both Studebaker and Mercedes Benz automobiles. He had sold Jim the Studebaker.

"Jim, you got the son-of-a bitch," said Bill Wright.

"He's rolled up," Jim replied. "This is Officer Leo Jefferson. Leo, this is Bill Wright."

Leo shoved his hand out. "Pleased to meet you."

Bill grabbed it, pumped Leo's hand and blurted, "What great work. I took that little Volkswagen in trade a couple of hours ago. That fucker just walked onto the lot, saw the keys in it, jumped in and was gone. I yelled at my lot man to call the cops and went after him in the Mercedes."

"Your lot man got the message to our radio. We were lucky," replied Leo.

"No, it's lucky for me that I got it back," continued Bill. "Those bugs are really popular. They're such hot sellers that you have to get on a list and then wait a year to buy one."

"The Volkswagen ads are neat," said Jim. "Did you see the billboard on the Long Beach Freeway with two VWs on it? It says $1645.00 each. What a deal!"

"That may be," Leo interjected, "but they ain't no Cadillac. They're so underpowered that they couldn't pull a sick whore off of a piss pot."

Bill and Jim chuckled.

Leo got serious. "Bill, we'll take a signed stolen report from you, include the recovery, release the car directly and you take it back to the dealership. It'll only take a few minutes. Never saw one this easy. When we're finished with you, we'll book the puke."

"Give me back the keys," Bill said, "and I'll go get a lot boy and come back for it."

The keys were returned, the report finished and signed and they drove back to the station. The thief would not answer a single question; he wouldn't even tell them his name. At the booking desk Leo searched him, found no weapons, and pulled out his wallet with the booking sergeant and Jim as witnesses. Fishing through the wallet he produced a drivers license.

"Is this your license?" Leo asked.

The suspect still didn't reply.

The driver's license picture matched the suspect. The license named Ronald Albert Cole and the description: male Caucasian, 33 years old, 5' 9", 145 pounds, with brown hair and brown eyes; born March 9, 1926. The driver's license showed his address as 1923 Chestnut Avenue, Long Beach.

They booked him as Ronald Albert Cole. A fingerprint check would confirm or deny that identity.

Next, they went to file reports with Isabel Packman, the clerk typist.

As the reports were finished, Isabel commented, "I'm glad to see this arrest. I was talking to the auto theft guys in the detective bureau and they say VWs have really become a target. They think it's a professional chop shop. You know, steal them, break them down to sell the parts and make big money. Will this guy talk?"

"So far, not a word," replied Leo. "He came across like he'd done hard time. You know the type, Isabel."

"Sure," replied Isabel, "I know them. They think they're smart. Add up their income, total up their work with joint time included, and it averages at about a nickel an hour. Some smart guys!"

"Lets go, Jim, we've work to do," said Leo.

They walked past the booking desk on the way out. The station Sergeant Chuck White, waggled his finger, and called out, "Hey, come here. I've got something for you."

Approaching, Leo asked, "What's up Sarge?"

Sergeant White leaned forward and quietly stated, "Bail bondsman's already here with a writ to bail out for your car thief. How do you like that for fast service?"

"Ain't that the shits," said Leo. "The fucker hasn't been here forty minutes and they're springing him. How do you get a writ in the middle of the night, that fast, from a judge?"

The sergeant replied, "Simple. The bail bondsman makes friends with a judge, slips him a little cash or does a favor and has already signed blank writs in his desk. In this situation, the bondsman calls and wakes up the judge and gets verbal approval, fills in the empty blanks and it's done. Here he is with the writ and the bond and the guy's out. I've seen it happen even before the arrest reports were completed."

"Shit," Jim said, frowning, "this is really organized."

Sergeant White gave him a knowing look and muttered, "You're learning kid. Now get back into service and get me another one. Oh, and by the way, there's a memo here in the box. You're to see Captain Green when you get off shift Monday morning. Be there!"

"I will sergeant!" replied Jim, not daring to look at Leo.

"For a rookie, you're getting off to a good start," Sergeant White continued, "and I expect your reports are being noticed. That ain't too bad, kid!"

"I just hope I'm not in shit," said Jim.

"Nah," said White. "If you were in shit, I'd know it. Get out of here. Both of you. Go to work."

On the way to their beat, Leo turned in the passenger seat, looked at Jim and stated, "It's been fun working with you. You catch on fast and you've been right there when I needed you."

Drivers change every two hours. At 6:00 AM, Leo took the wheel, announced it was time to write a moving violation to keep the sergeants happy. He parked to watch the traffic signal at PCH and the Boulevard. It only took a few moments until a westbound Buick convertible, at least a hundred feet late, blew the signal.

Leo took off in pursuit, red lights activated, and the new convertible pulled over to the curb. He alighted and approached the driver as citing officer. As backup, Jim walked forward to stand adjacent to the right rear of the car.

The convertible top was down and Jim could see all occupants and hear everything said. Four naval officers, probably on their way to the Naval Base, sat in the vehicle.

"May I see your operators license please?" asked Leo.

The driver, an ensign, curtly responded, "What the fuck are y'all stopping me for?" And he passed his license over.

"Sir, you were about a hundred feet late for that red traffic signal."

The driver's curt voice became nasty, "Don't you realize you've stopped an officer and gentleman of the United States Navy on the way to his duty? Don't y'all realize you're dealing with your betters, nigger?"

Leo quietly replied, "I'm sorry, sir, please wait a moment while I step back to the police vehicle. I'll have to write a citation. This is a serious offense."

Seeing the situation as safe, Jim joined his partner back inside the car. Leo, saying nothing, wrote the ticket. Jim glanced at the Alabama driver's license attached to the clipboard. Leo appeared angry, yet controlled, and Jim believed he had every right. The work completed, the two officers returned to their positions by the convertible.

Leo passed the completed citation to the ensign and asked, "Sir, where did you attend college?"

The ensign angrily sputtered, "The University of Alabama, nigger. What the fuck does that have to do with this? And, I ain't signing this fucking ticket. No nigger gives me a ticket."

"Nothing really sir, I was just trying to make polite conversation."

Jim moved closer and saw the discomfort in the eyes of the other officers. They looked upset with the rude conduct of their driver.

"Sir, this is not an admission of guilt, it is only a promise to appear in court."

The ensign snarled, "I'm not signing no fucking ticket from a nigger."

"Sir, I am frankly embarrassed by your conduct. As a graduate of Drake University and a former naval officer myself, I am appalled by your display of bad manners. Apparently you have not been raised and schooled properly. Perhaps this should be a lesson to you about how to treat others. I may even report your misconduct to the base commander." Leo's smile changed to a frown. "Now, I'm going to ask you once more to sign the ticket. Again, it is only a promise to appear, not an admission of guilt." His voice turned mean, "If you don't sign, I'm going to pull your honkey ass out of that fucking car and drag you kicking and screaming to jail. And, believe me, cracker ass, I will be kicking and you will be screaming. Do you understand?"

Without a word, the ensign quickly signed the citation and passed it back.

Leo separated a copy from the citation book, handed it to the driver, and stated, "Remember this lesson. You will be an officer and a gentleman. You will treat all people respectfully. Thank you. Have a nice day, ass-hole!"

Jim liked Leo.

CHAPTER EIGHT

Monday, February 29, 1960

Jim stood in uniform in front of Captain J. C. Green's office at 8:00 AM. The Captain's secretary, Edna, led him into the inner office, stating the Captain would arrive momentarily.

As Chief of Detectives, J. C. Green wielded tremendous authority. His nickname told the story; the troops called him "the real J.C."

Jim remained standing, and glanced around the office. Family portraits, military pictures and certificates decorated the walls. He already knew the Green legend. A World War II veteran, Green, at that time a patrolman with two small children, volunteered from the Police Department on December 8th, 1941, the day after Pearl Harbor. At age 31, with four years of prior enlisted U. S. Army service, he was catapulted into Officers' Candidate School, then to the military police. The pictures told it all; the front in Europe, captured German POWs, the opening of death camps, military government and the apprehension and prosecution of Germans operating the camps.

J. C. Green ended the war a Major. A framed diploma from the F.B.I. National Academy hung behind the desk adding law enforcement credibility.

A personnel folder sat, neatly arranged, in the center of the desktop. The name on the folder was James D. Grant - Jim's folder. Suddenly a lump formed in his gut.

A tall man of military bearing entered. Captain Green, thought Jim. The man stood 6' 2", weighed about 220 pounds and wore his gray hair in a short crew cut. His eyes were a jail bar gray. His glance cut through to the bone.

"Jim Grant," the Captain said, as he extended his right hand.

"Yes, sir," blurted Jim, nervously, shaking his hand. He wasn't prepared for the gesture. He had expected military formality.

"Sit down," Green said. "The coffee will be here a minute."

"Yes, sir," Jim answered. "It's been a long night and I'm to be in court at 9:30AM. I think I need it to stay awake."

"How well I remember," replied the Captain.

Edna, re-entered with two large coffee mugs in one hand and a pot in the other. She put the mugs on the Captain's desk and poured the coffee.

"Officer Grant, the Captain takes his black. Would you like anything in yours?"

"No thank you," Jim replied.

She started from the room and Captain Grant spoke, "Edna, please pull the door shut as you go. I don't want to be disturbed."

"As you wish, Captain." She did as requested.

Captain Green sat down, gestured to the chair in front of the desk. "Take the weight off. I'm not someone to be afraid of."

Jim sat down, picked up his coffee cup and took a sip.

The Captain settled back in his chair, coffee in hand. "Last Friday I had a chat with Lester Peabody. He's a good cop and he says you're a good cop; that's a great reference. I also reviewed your personnel file and found it to be complimentary. Peabody told me quite a story about the Peggy Evans homicide. What he said sounds interesting. Now, I'd like to hear it from you – from the beginning."

Jim knew the subject and displayed confidence as he told of the discovery of the body, then the arrest of Tokay and her drunken remarks. Then he described the information collected. He reported the rape by Ivan Slade, Peggy's confrontation with Slade when she awoke, her depression, her pregnancy, the telephone call to Slade, his

72

offer to get Redden to arrange for a doctor, Peggy's agreement, Slade's promise of a $500.00 payoff and her travel to the Grass Shack Drive-in for the abortion.

Captain Green, did not interrupt, maintained eye contact, and listened intently. He kept a pencil poised over a yellow legal tablet and made short notations. He didn't even seem to look down when he wrote.

At this point in his explanation of events, Jim's confidence seemed to slip as he shifted uncomfortably in his chair and his voice faltered. He told of asking advice from Lester as information unfolded, knowing everything had to be given to homicide – it was their work. He reported becoming worried when Lester said Detective Sergeant Bill Millard and Detective Carl Peele were good friends of Slade and Redden. He grimaced, explaining that being friends didn't make them guilty of anything, but he didn't know what to do. Then Lester arranged for him to see Captain Green.

Concluding, Jim expressed worry about being a rookie and gathering the information. "Captain, I hope I haven't done the wrong thing here."

"Quite the contrary," Captain Green said. "I doubt a veteran could have done a better job. You've done it well and quietly. Those are two important demands of police work. And, in this case we have to make sure it stays confidential."

"Yes, sir,"

"Another thing. You were right when you said we don't know if Millard and Peele are dirty. It's troubling enough to take precautions. We'll just have to find out. That's the essential reason for absolute secrecy. Everyone in this building tells tales. Gossip can ruin an investigation. They can't know we're looking at them. Do you understand?"

"Yes, sir."

The Captain reached over to Jim's personnel jacket, opened it briefly, closed it, smiled and said, "Yeah. You were a paratrooper. The yes sir-ing made me think about the army. That's what good training does. It brings back memories."

"Thank you, sir."

"Now, all of this needs to go on paper. In a minute I'll call Edna and have her file this as a memorandum. It will be done in my presence in this closed room. No others need know. It will not be formalized as a follow-up to the existing homicide case. I've already discussed this with the Chief of Police. The investigation will continue. You will be advised of those working the case and of information only if your further involvement becomes necessary."

"Yes, sir,"

"Also, Jim, you'll be asked about our meeting. Men aren't called to my office for nothing. People are curious. Just explain that the Captain wanted additional information about the Red Car accident at Willow and Long Beach Boulevard. Tell them I'm on a committee, with the Captain of Traffic, looking at safety issues and trying to plan signal design changes for that intersection."

"Sure."

"Let me call Edna now and we'll get this finished," Captain Green said, "and then you can get on to court. Oh, another thought. I don't want you digging for any more information. As I said, this inquiry has to stay confidential. But, if something comes back to you from your sources, hand-write a memo and slip it under my office door. Got that?"

"Yes, sir."

The dictation completed, Jim hurried out of the station. He felt light headed, the worry gone. He admired "J. C." and felt confident that the investigation would be properly handled. Unloading the information made him feel good.

He hurried home, ran into the apartment and changed clothes. Instead of a uniform, a suit, white shirt and tie were the expected dress. Living nearby made this convenient. He

74

drove back to the station, parked, and hustled to court, barely arriving at 9:30 AM.

As usual, it was hurry up and wait - just like the Army. He didn't testify; a plea bargain finished the case and Jim left at 11:30 AM. He walked north on Pine Avenue from Ocean Boulevard on his way back to the station to get his car. A clear breezy day, few pedestrians walked the street.

At First Street Jim crossed to the west side and passed the old Bank of America with the clock tower and proceeded toward Buffum's Department Store. As he passed the alley he heard a scream.

Turning back, he saw a woman lying on the ground and young man running toward him, purse in hand. The woman yelled, "He stole my purse!"

Jim acted just like a businessman and stepped gingerly out of the way as if intimidated. The runner came right past him. Suddenly, he stuck out a leg and tripped him. The thief tumbled face first on the sidewalk. Jim leaped on top of him. With a knee on the back of his neck and an arm twisted up behind his back, he growled, "Police officer, stay still. You mess up my suit and I'll pull your fucking arm off."

The crook grunted, "Ow, that hurts. Go easy, will ya?"

About the same size as Jim, the thief smelled of alcohol, and appeared dirty and disheveled. Blood streamed from his nose and his skinned face.

Several passersby gathered and the victim ran over. Nearly forty and an attractive brunette, she looked fashionable in a navy blue woolen dress worn a foot above the ankle, a matching cardigan with a single strand of pearls and navy blue low heeled shoes. She adjusted her cardigan, torn at the shoulder.

"That was super," she said. "You did that like an expert."

"Thanks, I'm a police officer. Has anybody called for a car?" Jim asked.

"I did," a young man replied. "The cops will be here any minute. I'm a parking attendant from the garage. Mrs. McKenzie just left her car with us and started across the alley to Buffum's when he snatched her purse."

"Thanks, Fred," Mrs. McKenzie replied.

Two one-man police cars and a three wheeled parking control motorcycle slid up. Jim, who had only worked graveyard, didn't know any of these crusty day officers. The three patrolmen came running from their vehicles.

"Police officer," called Jim, holding up his badge. "This is a strong arm robbery suspect. He grabbed this lady's purse," Jim pointed at the victim, "knocked her down, ran and I got him."

"Who are you, kid?" the biggest cop asked.

"Jim Grant. I work Watch One (graveyard) and just left court. I came on in the last academy class."

"Well, good work. I'm Jeff Lewis. Glad you're on board. Let me cuff this turd, then we can all relax."

The officers handcuffed the suspect and placed him in the nearest black and white. The big cop, Jeff Lewis, now with cigar in hand, took charge. A natural leader, he sorted out witnesses and organized the report taking.

"Kid, we'll do all this for you. You worked all night. You need to get home."

Before Jim left, the victim introduced herself as Debra McKenzie, asked for his name, thanked him profusely, provided necessary report information, and hurried away.

Officer Jeff Lewis walked over to Jim and commented, "It really was good work. I'm not just bullshitting. You didn't even get your suit dirty."

"Thanks."

"Do you know who that lady is?" the old cop asked.

"No, is she somebody special?"

"Yeah," Officer Jeff Lewis said. "That's the Gray Wolf's wife."

"You mean the hot shot attorney, Craig McKenzie?"

76

"That's him," Lewis nodded. "They call him that because he stalks his adversaries, puts 'em in a corner, then rips them to pieces. There ain't no better. He finds out you did this and you got a friend for life."

Jim commented, "A cop just might need a lawyer friend like that."

"Well kid, it's nice meeting you. We've got all we need. Get home and get some sleep."

"Thanks, Jeff," Jim said. "Nice meeting you, too."

* * *

Jim hurried home. As he walked into his apartment, the phone rang.

"Hi, Jim. This is Captain Green."

"Yes, sir!"

"Nice arrest you made at Buffum's," Green stated.

"Thank you sir. Is something wrong?"

"No, as matter of fact everything is all right. Did you who the know the victim was?"

"Officer Lewis said it was Attorney Craig McKenzie's wife."

"That's right," said the Captain. "And he'd like your home number. He's a good friend of mine. Do you mind if I give it to him? He's on the other line."

"No, sir. That would be all right."

"Good. I'll talk to you later."

Not thirty seconds later, the phone rang again.

"Jim, my name is Craig McKenzie. Captain Green said it would be all right if I called."

"Yes, sir."

"Forget the formality, I'm Craig. I appreciate what you did for my wife, Debra."

"It's just my duty, sir."

"That may be so, but I want to get to know you. I understand you're off duty Wednesday. Would you please join Debra and me for dinner that evening?"

Jim looked in his pocket calendar. Fran Fox had told him she would be out with girlfriends that evening. She'd seemed distant and it made him uncomfortable. He wondered what he could have done to put her off. Maybe he'd try again for Wednesday, find out what bugged her. He asked, "Would the following Wednesday be okay?"

"Good," said McKenzie. "That's the March 9th. How about the Pacific Coast Club at 7:00 PM?"

"Sounds great, sir." Impressed, Jim grinned.

"Damn it Jim, it's not sir. It's Craig, okay?"

"You bet, Craig. See you at 7:00 PM, Wednesday, March 9th.

CHAPTER NINE

Monday, February 29, 1960

Roberto "Bob" Ortega became Jim's new partner on the evening of Monday, February 29th, March 1st. They worked Unit One, which included the Port of Long Beach and everything west of the Los Angeles River up to Pacific Coast Highway. That assignment let them slip into downtown, the Pike and the Jungle when backups were needed.

While born and raised in North Long Beach, Bob's parents were both from Mexico. They came to this country to work, gave it their best and prospered. They wanted their son to succeed. Bob attended Jordan High School, served in Korea as a Marine and brought home a Purple Heart and a Bronze Star. He attended Compton Junior College, received an AA Degree and came on the police department.

Bob Ortega loved to lift weights. At 28 years old, and barely 5'9" he weighed nearly 200 pounds. All muscle, he wasn't a cop to challenge. He liked to work and he seemed to know everybody on the west side. And Bob loved jokes.

In the field on their first night, they checked into service and Bob drove into the industrial area north of PCH and east of the River to 2453 Golden Avenue. He parked by the loading doors at Johnny Miller's Sandwiches next to a line of catering vans. The company made sandwiches and provided other food supplies for catering trucks to deliver to work sites all over the Southland.

"Wait here, partner," Bob said as he went inside.

Several minutes later he returned, opened the drivers' door, popped the hood release latch, and said, "Got to put these babies in the oven." He lifted the hood.

Curiosity got the best of Jim; he got out and went to watch. Bob took readymade packaged burritos from a bag and placed four alongside the exhaust manifolds. "Check

79

your watch," he told Jim. "These babies need forty minutes, and then we feast. I brought salsa, hot sauce, and chips. We'll get Cokes just before we eat."

The radio crackled as he closed the hood.

"Unit One, 901T, injury accident with a possible fatality at the Pontoon Bridge. Code Three."

Jim ran for the microphone, snatched it and answered, "Unit One, 10-4, from PCH and Oregon."

Bob got the car moving, the reds on, the siren going, turned back toward PCH and went south on the Long Beach Freeway and west across Ocean Boulevard to the Pontoon Bridge.

Terminal Island was home to the Navy Shipyard, the Navy Base, other shipyards, the Coast Guard Base and a Federal Prison, and rested between Long Beach and San Pedro.

About half is in the City of Long Beach and the remainder in the Port of Los Angeles. From the north, the Terminal Island Freeway Bridge crossed onto the island next to old Henry Ford Bridge (alongside of the closed auto assembly plant). On the west a ferry reached to San Pedro. The Pontoon Bridge crossed the deepwater channel from the Long Beach side.

The highway from Long Beach curved as it approached the bridge. When ships came through, a siren sounded, railroad style safety arms fell, and traffic stopped. The bridge separated in the center (each end withdrawing under its approach way) and the ship passed in the open channel. Then the action reversed and traffic resumed. The slippery steel bridge roadway from each direction (depending on the height of tide) could be steep and the speed limit restricted traffic to five miles per hour.

Fog frequently obscured the approach, unfamiliar drivers speeded and drunk drivers added to the continual risk. Drunken sailors regularly bounced their cars down the slippery steel deck and into the fifty-foot deep channel. If

80

they didn't get out quickly the mishap became fatal, divers were called, and the car and bodies retrieved.

Trucks and cars were backed up behind the safety arm when Unit One arrived. They announced their 10-97 arrival time with the radio, left their car at the side of the road behind the line of cars, and ran toward the pontoon bridge.

Only the top of what looked like a big '48 Buick Roadmaster could be seen floating in the channel. A man dog-paddled from the car toward the pontoon bridge. Bob and Jim hurried down the approach. A Chief Petty Officer and a Second Class Petty Officer, side by side, reached down, each grasped the swimmer by an arm, and pulled him over the edge. He lay gasping and spewing up saltwater. The car, windows open, sank.

Bob reached him first, kneeled at his side and asked, "Anyone else in the Buick?"

"Nah," choked the man. "Just me. Thank Christ I got out."

Jim turned toward the onlookers and asked, "Did anybody see this happen?" He suddenly realized he knew both of the men who helped the swimmer from the water. The Chief had been the one on Shore Patrol duty on Ocean Boulevard who was hit in the face. The other, Al Kaufman, sporting new Second Class Petty Officer chevrons, gave Peggy Evans a ride on the day of the abortion that ended her life. They both grinned.

Chief Petty Officer Adam Hertzburger said they saw the Buick speed by, use the wrong side of the road to pass cars, careen past the descending safety arm, and slide sideways down the slippery steel bridge approach and splash into the channel.

Al said it took the guy at least five minutes to figure out he had to roll down a window, crawl out and swim away; and that it was lucky the huge Buick continued to float.

About to ask for their duty station addresses, Jim started, as he looked at their shoulder tabs. They were from the *Segundo.* "Hey," exclaimed Jim. "You're both on the same sub as Peggy Evans' boyfriend, Roy."

"Yeah," Chief Hertzburger answered. "That's Roy Jensen."

Jim pulled them away from the bystanders and asked if they could meet, bring Roy, and see if he had any information about Peggy and what happened. They agreed to get together that evening, Tuesday March 1st, at Mari's Pizza at Broadway and Lime Avenue at 7:00 PM. The Chief assured Jim that Roy would be there. Al Kaufman, given Jim's home telephone number, said he'd call if there were problems.

Meanwhile, Bob worked with the driver. Once recovered from the water, it became obvious he was drunk. Off to booking they went. In less than forty minutes they finished the work and returned to service.

Patrol took them up Sante Fe and past the Ivan Slade's place. Jim looked it over every time they went by. This time, a guy unlocked the gate for a flatbed truck with a car that appeared a total wreck. No party light on, he observed, and 2:00 AM.

Bob flipped out yelling, "Pull over, pull over. The burritos are burning."

They parked, lifted the hood, and Bob fished out the overdone burritos with a pocketknife and a nightstick. They drove back to Pier J, then to Pierpoint Landing, parked at the all night coffee stand, sat at a picnic bench and polished off the burritos.

The salsa, hot sauce and chips made it a feast. Cokes washed them down. They watched as longshoremen and railroad workers tossed pieces of day old hot dogs to the timid feral cats. People dumped kittens and those that survived turned wild and lived in the rocks. They would only approach at night and even then stayed twenty feet back from the tables.

The lights were on in Pierpoint Landing businesses. Crews worked on the fishing boats readying them for departure and fisherman walked from the parking lot to the landing carrying tackle boxes and gear. Sportfishing boats would soon leave for waters off Catalina and San Clemente Islands and even off Baja California. Most of the restaurants were closed and seals slept in the tank in front of the landing. Workers remained busy at Dearden's Fish Market, a place that never seemed to close. Across the street, Pacific Sportfishing Landing did a similar business.

Dinner finished, they drove back across the Pontoon Bridge and into the dirt parking lot across from Gate One of the Navy Base. It contained hundreds of cars. Sailors needed automobile insurance and proof of ownership to park on base. Cars parked across the street were borrowed, uninsured, and sometimes stolen. Many were left for months as ships were at sea. During quiet times, Unit One looked for those that were stolen.

They drove through and around huge chuckholes at about three miles per hour and checked license numbers against the hot sheet.

Jim's nose twitched, he grimaced and turned toward Bob. "Did you fart?"

Bob hee-hawed. "The best kind. Pinto beans and Ortega peppers. Nothing's better."

Jim quickly rolled down the window, exclaiming, "Smells worse than shit. The fucking air is turning green." It was the worst fart he ever smelled in his life.

Bob leaned over the steering wheel as he laughed.

The cold damp sea air rolled in.

"Stop the car." Jim ordered.

Bob slammed on the brakes. "What do you see?"

Jim, hot sheet in hand, got out saying, "I'll just walk and check the hot sheet with my flashlight."

Bob roared with laughter.

83

Jim walked in front of the police car, which followed him slowly. He went about a hundred yards and stopped. "This Healey is hot." He pointed toward the license plate on a blue '56 Austin Healey convertible. Clean as a pin, the top down, it looked out of place.

Bob advised radio of the license number and asked for confirmation. Jim got back into the car. It took a half hour to confirm the San Diego stolen. A tow truck called, they waited. A typical navy thing, San Diego ships came to the Long Beach Navy Shipyard for repairs. Sailors stole cars in Long Beach to go to San Diego and then stole cars in San Diego to make it back to their ship in time for duty.

Finally, at dawn, the tow truck did its duty. The report completed long before, they headed for the station then checked out.

The black and white parked, good byes said; Jim walked to his car. He saw an envelope stuck under his windshield wiper. He tore it open and read the typed message.

It said:

Jim,

> *Sorry to have to tell you. Fran Fox's*
> *screwing another guy. He's an attorney.*
> *While you work nights, they're hanging out*
> *at The Trap.*
> *A Friend*

Tired and angered by the information, Jim instantly went into denial. They were in love. There must be some mistake. He thought, shit, what is this? Who would leave such a note? Do I call her and tell her about the note? Do I swing by the bar? Maybe she went in The Trap, a bar at Ocean and Termino in Belmont, from time to time. So what.

His mind in turmoil, dead tired, he drove home. It could wait.

In bed, he dreamed about Peggy's death, not Fran. There were so many questions. Where did they take her to do the abortion? Who did the work? Why didn't they discover the hemorrhage? Who dumped her?

* * *

He woke with a start, the phone ringing, and grabbed it. The alarm clock, set to go off at 4:30PM, read 4:00 PM.

Sleepily, he spoke, "Jim Grant here."

"Jim, this is Al Kaufman. Roy Jensen got arrested leaving the sub."

"What'd he do?"

"He had shore leave and came off the submarine carrying a laundry bag. The Officer of the Day asked to see the laundry bag and Roy got shitty. The Master-at-arms grabbed him and they looked in the bag and found $10,000 in twenty dollar bills. They threw him in irons, then searched his sea bag and found another $10,000."

"Where did he get that kind of cash? That's enough money to buy a new house."

"Beats me! He won't say," Al replied. "But, he's in a world of trouble. There's the money to explain and you can't give the OD shit. The Commanding Officer will put him where the Sun don't shine."

"Where was he going with the money?" questioned Jim.

"You won't believe this," Al continued. "He told the old man he was going to hire a hit man and kill Al Slade."

"No shit," Jim blurted. "What does he know about Slade?"

"I don't know, he didn't get anything from me."

"We have to do some thinking."

"Should we still meet at Mari's Pizza?"

"You bet," Jim replied. "Can you guys make it?"

"Yeah, we'll be there."

85

"Okay," Jim said. "Then were still on. I'll see you there."

* * *

Mari's Pizza, at the northwest corner of Broadway and Lime, catered to a young crowd of college students from Long Beach State, sailors, and couples on dates. Raffia covered Chianti wine bottles hung from the ceiling and from the tops of booths. Walls were covered with foreign newspapers with handwriting, scribbling, and graffiti everywhere. Many messages were like *Joe Loves Sally*. Sawdust covered the floor. Lively Italian music blared from speakers high on the walls. An odor of spaghetti and meatballs laden with garlic hung in the air.

They sold some of the best American style Italian food in town. Melted goat cheese topped with chunks of pepperoni or Italian sausage covered the tasty hot baked pizzas. Salads, loaded with huge olives and onions and tomatoes and peppers and smothered with their special sour cream dressing were delivered in large wooden bowls. The spaghetti dripped with meat sauce and came with meatballs or sausage. Ceramic jars filled with foot long breadsticks adorned each table. The food, wine, music and people combined to make it a great place.

At 7:00 PM, Jim walked through the front door, gave his name to a hostess, and she led him past those waiting and down the narrow corridor between booths toward the rear of the restaurant. Al Kaufman and Adam Hertzburger, already in the corner booth, waved him into the opposite seat.

Adam, clutching a huge menu, smiled and said, "Let's order some pizza and beer before we start."

Orders made, beer delivered, all munched on breadsticks and serious conversation started.

"Chief, what's the deal with Roy Jensen?" Jim inquired.

Chief Petty Officer Hertzburger, one hand on his beer, pointed at Jim with the breadstick in the other hand. "We have a lot more information now. Roy will get out of this okay, but he needs a lesson. His only problem left is getting in the OD's face. You can't do that in this man's Navy."

"What about the money?" Jim asked.

"No problem," said Adam, "it all came out. He inherited it from his grandmother about four months ago. This week, he pulled the whole $20,000 out of the bank in twenties and hid it in his sea bag. In the submarine service, nobody fucks with your sea bag."

"What about the hit man story?" Jim asked.

"It's true," Adam continued. "Roy said a letter from Peggy waited for him when the Segundo docked. She wrote about Ivan Slade, what happened and that some Attorney named Johnny Redden arranged for an abortion. Then, when they told him she was dead, he said his head got all fucked up. He figured the cops wouldn't do shit cause it was an abortion. That's when he got the money out of the bank, hid it in his sea bag, and decided to hire a hit man. He said he didn't know how to find a hit man, but knew he could."

"Yeah," interjected Al, "and he still has Peggy's letter."

"Great," Jim said. "Do you think they'd let me see Roy?"

"Shit," Adam said. "I'm the Chief. I'll talk to the old man and get his permission. Everybody on board knows Peggy's dead. This is important. Are you off tomorrow?"

"Yeah, I am."

"Then," Adam said, "can you be at Gate One at 0800 hours?"

"Sure."

"I'll meet you there," Adam concluded.

The pizza came. It didn't last long.

CHAPTER TEN

Wednesday, March 2, 1960

Just out of bed, early Wednesday morning, Jim shaved, showered and put on a business suit as if he were going to court. He wanted to look professional for the meeting at the Navy Base to interview Roy Jensen. Jim was ready to leave at 7:15 AM and the phone rang. Fran Fox told him that she couldn't make the dinner date for that evening or for Thursday, sweetly apologized and explained that out of town family members had unexpectedly arrived. Before he could reply she hung up.

Jim felt rotten and thought the call confirmed the warning in the note. Since he now had no plans for the evening, he considered dropping in at The Trap. Would he see Fran there with someone else? How about the attorney? He hoped not.

He felt crappy. He hoped a night out would do him some good. When you work all night you're not really awake until midnight. He didn't want to just stay up and read. He couldn't adjust his sleeping patterns on days off.

Too bad, thought Jim, Fran didn't know it but he would be off Wednesday, Thursday and Friday nights. Police officers worked all of the national holidays so they received an extra day off each month. Like a three-day pass in the Army, he felt rich. Having a Friday evening off made it extra special. Real people were out there on Friday nights.

Jim left a few minutes early. The paratroops taught punctuality and so did the Long Beach Police Department. Those late for duty and the squad meeting were simply sent home *no work*. In other words the penalty became a day without pay. Those who did that several times found they had no job.

He drove to Gate One, parked outside in a marked visitors spot and waited at reception where visitors passes were issued. Promptly at 8:00AM, Chief Petty Officer Adam Hertzburger, in dress uniform, came through the door from the base side of the building, grinned at Jim, and waved him over to the counter.

An official pass awaited his arrival, recognized his police status and even permitted possession of a concealed weapon. Chief Hertzburger clipped it to the left breast of Jim's suit. They walked out through the door that entered the base and a car waited to take them to the submarine *Segundo*.

Proper U. S. Navy protocol followed; a boatswain piped them aboard, Chief Hertzburger led Jim to an opened watertight door, down a ladder into the vessel, and to the Commanding Officer's wardroom. Jim thought submarines offered little breathing space. The room looked similar to a 6′ by 6′ dining booth in a travel trailer. The Chief Petty Officer introduced Commander Richard Flynn who explained he had been briefed on the death of Peggy Evans, understood the seriousness of the matter and directed Seaman Roy Jensen be brought immediately to the wardroom.

Seaman Apprentice Roy Jensen entered the small room and the door closed. A handsome muscular young man, Jim guessed he was about 19 years old, stood 6' tall, weighed 190 pounds and sported wavy blonde hair. Jim immediately understood Peggy's attraction to him. Broad shoulders and narrow waist, he looked like the All American Navy recruiting poster boy.

Commander Flynn sat on one side of the table beside Jim. Chief Hertzberger placed Roy across on the inside and sat next to him.

"This is Long Beach Police Officer Jim Grant," said Commander Flynn. "When Peggy was found under the roller coaster, he was in the first police unit that arrived. If you're willing to cooperate, he'd like to ask some questions." The Commander gestured with his left hand toward Jim, alongside him, and continued, "The Chief and I are here to protect your rights. You certainly don't have to cooperate unless you want to."

A moment of silence followed. The young sailor trembled, a tear ran down his check, and he wiped perspiration from his brow and the tear off his cheek with his right hand.

Roy's voice shook in reply. "Do you mean the police are really going to investigate this?"

"That's right," Jim replied. "It is being investigated. For reasons I am not permitted to reveal, it's being handled in a very confidential manner. What's discussed here must not be passed on to others. It all stays in this room. Do you understand?"

"Yes sir."

"Now Seaman Jensen," the Commander interjected, "are you willing to speak with Officer Grant?"

"Yes sir."

"Then, carry on, Grant," Commander Flynn directed.

"Roy, it is my understanding that you may have received a letter from Peggy Evans that may contain valuable evidence. Is that true?"

"Yes sir."

"Would you please tell us about it?" Jim asked.

"Yes sir," Roy replied, still trembling. Obviously emotional, he remained silent for a moment and then continued. "We went to sea on September 8th, and that was the last time I saw Peggy." His voice breaking, it took another moment for him to regain composure and continue. "We came back into port on January 8th at about 0800 hours and I went ashore. That's when I saw our friends Al and Geri Kaufman and they told me Peggy was dead." A pause again and tears came to both eyes. "God, it was awful. It still is. I just don't know how to deal with it."

The commander passed Roy a paper towel and he wiped his face.

"What happened then?" Jim asked gently.

"I read the articles in the paper. There was one from right after she died and one the day I went ashore. Geri showed them both to me. Then I saw the article about a week later that said her folks came out." Tears came. "Shit, I just couldn't face them. I brought her out here."

"What about the letter?" Jim prodded gently.

"I didn't even know it was here," Roy replied. "When I went ashore that day I missed mail call. I just wanted to see Peggy. Then, I stayed in Long Beach on my three- day pass. I got shit-faced drunk. Lucky for me Al made sure I was back on duty on time.

The day after I came back I thought about mail from home, went to get it and found the letter."

"Do you mind my asking what's in it?" asked Jim.

"Its like, like, she was scared and that wasn't her at all. Peggy told how this Ivan Slade drugged her and raped her. He's a real asshole. Pardon the expression, Commander."

Commander Flynn gently waved a hand and shrugged as if to indicate it was not important.

"And then," Roy continued gaining composure, "that she got pregnant and didn't want the kid. She wrote how she threatened Slade and he offered to arrange an abortion with a doctor. Then she got a call from some attorney named Johnny Redden and she met with him and he set it all up. It's all in the letter. I bet I've read it a hundred times. Then my grandmother's estate settled and I got a cashier's check for $20,000. I went to Farmers and Merchants Bank and got it all in twenties and brought it aboard. I really wanted to get Slade. I knew it was wrong, but I wanted to find a hit-man and take him out. Then, the OD stopped me to check my sea bag. You know all the rest."

"Think for a moment," said Jim. "Is there anything else at all you'd like to say?"

Roy thought, sniffled, wiped his nose and replied, "Yeah, when I last saw Peggy she really chewed my ass.

She nailed me for bringing her out knowing I was going to sea. She was right. I was selfish and needed to grow up. I left knowing she had cut it off; it was over between us. She was the best thing that ever happened to me and I blew it. I'd like to make it good."

"That letter is really important," Jim said. "It's evidence from Peggy about Slade's involvement and ties Redden to the abortion. Would you be willing to give me the letter for evidence?"

"Yes sir, that's what Peggy wanted," Roy replied.

"I have to tell you though, there's no telling when you'll get it back or if you'll get it back. It's real evidence and the court will hold it."

"That's okay," replied Roy. "I can't fly off the handle and do it the way I wanted. That was dumb. I know now it has to be this way."

"Thanks, you don't know how much help this will be," said Jim.

Roy spoke to Commander Flynn, "Sir, permission to go to my sea bag and retrieve the letter?"

"Permission granted," answered Flynn.

Roy stood, opened the door, and left.

"Commander Flynn," said Jim. "I have to explain that there may be an internal leak on this case. That's the purpose for the secrecy. I can't have any information leave this room."

"Sure," replied the Commander, "everything said here will stay in this room. Right, Chief?"

"Yes sir," answered Hertzburger.

Roy Jensen returned and passed an envelope to Jim.

Jim opened it, counted four hand-written pages, and then stated, "Roy has given me this letter containing four pages. I'll initial the lower left hand corner of the envelope and each page for identification in your presence. That's in case you have to testify that this was done."

"Seaman Jensen," Commander Flynn said. "I'm proud of the cooperation just rendered to the police. If one condition is satisfied, your disciplinary problems can be eliminated."

"Sir," asked Jensen. "What might that be?"

"I want that $20,000 properly deposited in the bank of your choice. Do you understand that?"

"Yes sir."

"Then, the Chief will help you get that accomplished. The problems with the O.D. are over and you're out of irons and restriction is lifted. Am I understood?"

"Yes sir."

And Officer Grant," continued the Commander, "Chief Hertzburger can drop you at the gate on the way to the bank."

"Thank you, sir."

* * *

Back in his apartment, Jim took out the letter and studied the envelope:

――――

Post Office
Long Beach, CA

Miss Peggy Evans
Stillman Hotel
Long Beach, Cal.

12/30/59
Seaman/Apprentice. Roy Jensen
U.S.S. Segundo,
Long Beach Naval Shipyard,
Long Beach, Cal.
3/2/60 J.G.

Then, he opened the envelope, removed the letter and carefully read it:

――――

Page One:

December 29, 1959

> *Dear Roy,*
>
> *I know this letter is not expected. I was terribly angry with you when the Segundo went to sea. You knew when I came out from Burlington that you wouldn't stay in port long. I expected to be*

with you for months, not weeks. I was in love and you left me stranded.

Maybe it was for the best. You are still my friend. God knows I need one now.

I'm writing because I'm in trouble. I couldn't think of anyone else that I could tell. In fact, it's big trouble. This is a pickle I got myself into and I'm going to have to be grown up and take the consequences.

This letter is an explanation. If anything happens to me, it is record of what occurred. So help me God, this is what happened. That probably seems pretty sinister. I think it is. I've never been so scared in my life.

3/2/60 J.G.

———

Page Two:

When you went away I moved in with a girl that had a room in the Stillman Hotel. We do cleaning in exchange for the place. It works.

We partied a bit and that's how trouble came. This guy, Ivan Slade, has an engine rebuilding shop on Santa Fe. He has parties upstairs. I went, somebody drugged me and I was out like a

95

light. I woke up in bed with Slade – nude and screwed. I sure didn't cooperate and didn't even know when it happened.

I cussed him out and left. I'm still a runaway. I couldn't go to the police. I didn't want to make a report.

Slade is a bald old guy with a big belly and a mustache. What a pig.

Well, that was on September 21st. I figure I passed out at about 11:00 PM and came to at 7:00 AM the next day. Now I'm pregnant.

I called the son-of-a-bitch (well he is ONE) and he promised to get me a doctor for a proper abortion and the bum wants to pay me $500 for my trouble (as he calls it). I said I didn't know what I'd do.

3/2/60 J.G.

———

Page Three:

Then I got a call from this lawyer, Johnny Redden. What a slick shyster he is. I met him day before yesterday (the 27th) at the Olympia Café for lunch. He had a brown suit on that must have cost $200 with a matching briefcase, belt and shoes. Is he dapper. He's thin, smaller than you, has

96

glasses, and combs his hair back. He sure thinks he's a big shot.

He assured me they'll have a real doctor. Said he's been through two divorces and has to do abortions to make his alimony payments. He said it would be clean, safe and simple. He also offered me $500 in cash when it's over. Promised me he would give it to me himself. I was real reluctant so, to convince me, he told me the doctors name. It's Auggie French. So I said I'd do it.

I'm supposed to meet a guy named Ben Clarey. He's a pear shaped guy that hangs around Slade. Whatever Slade wants Clarey does. We're supposed to go to his apartment to have it done. That will be the 29th.

3/2/60 J.G.

Page Four:

So you know all of my darkest secrets. I wish it had not happened this way.

I did want to be with you always. I hope you will give this to someone who can help if this goes wrong. I hope you'll still think well of me. I feel trapped.

LOVE,

> *Peggy*

3/2/60 J.G.

Jim slowly placed the letter on his dining table. A vacant feeling in his stomach and weakness in his legs, he thought of Peggy. She was a young mid-western girl that was wooed to the city and destroyed. It just wasn't right. Those fuckers just had to pay the piper. He would do his best to have justice done. He believed the letter was dynamite evidence. It had to be given to the Captain.

Away at an investigators conference, Detective Captain J. C. Green would not be back until Monday, March 7th. The letter could not be left under his door. Preservation of the chain of evidence required testimony that control over the letter was maintained at all times. That proved no one else touched or tampered with the evidence.

Jim decided to write the Captain a note, explain the presence of the letter and its importance and slip it under the door. He would keep the letter until Monday. Today might be a day off, but he would deliver the message immediately. He wrote:

Date: March 2, 1960

To: Captain J. C. Green, Chief of Detectives

From: Officer James R. Grant, Patrol

> *Watch 1*

> *Subject: Peggy Evans Homicide*

> *A letter from the deceased, written the day of the abortion, has been found. It names those involved.*

> *It is in my possession and will be properly conserved.*

James R. Grant

The note written and sealed, Jim drove to the Police Department, parked and hurried into the building. He looked at his watch, almost noon, and arrived in front of the Captain's office. The door to the outer office stood open and Edna sat working at her desk.

She looked up, smiled and spoke, "Officer Grant, can I help you?"

"Yes Ma'am," Jim replied. "I know the Captain is out of town, but I have an urgent note for him. Could I please leave it with you?"

"Sure, and don't worry. I'll give it to him first thing Monday morning."

"Thank you!"

Jim walked out of the building and went straight to Farmers and Merchants Bank at 3rd and Pine. He kept a safe deposit box there. He couldn't wait to get Peggy's letter out of his pocket and into a secure place. Apartment burglaries or even fires were all too common. As a police officer, Jim had learned it's always wise to take precautions.

Constructed in the early 1920s, the F & M Bank had salmon colored stone on the floor, ornate bronze work and bars around teller cages and high walls with a skylight that brightened the huge room. Salmon colored marble pillars, ornate bronze lamps and elaborate Italianate frescoes completed the decor. An old stuffed mountain lion looked down from one wall and an old stuffed golden eagle from another. The American flag hung off the balcony. And, finally, large bronze doors completed the atmosphere of security.

Jim crossed to the rear of the bank, took an elevator down one floor, signed in, and waited his turn to be taken to the safety deposit vault. Soon summoned, an escort took him to the room, departed and he opened his box. With the original copies of his Army records and birth certificate, it contained a single percussion revolver. The Remington New

Model Army .44 caliber revolver, made in 1864, had been carried by Jim's great-grandfather in the last year of the Civil War. He lovingly removed it from the box, wiped it with a soft cloth, admired the condition and excellent bluing, and put it back. He carefully placed Peggy's letter beside the gun, closed the box, and left the vault.

CHAPTER ELEVEN

Wednesday, March 2, 1960. 5:00 PM

Up after a four-hour nap then a shower and shave, Jim looked in the mirror, rubbed his closely shaven face and combed his hair.

He'd dreamed about Peggy. They were at Pierpoint Landing. There were crowds of people, like on a Sunday afternoon. Holding hands, they walked through the crowds, past families with children, fisherman, tourists and other young people on dates. They stopped at Dearden's Fish Market, ordered smoked salmon on sourdough rolls, strolled, munched and chased it down with Cokes. They walked by the restaurants, out on the boat piers, watched seagulls and boats, and then stood by the seal tanks and looked at the happy children watching the seals. What a pleasant dream and a nice date, he reflected.

Feeling clean and refreshed, he put on a pair of charcoal colored wool flannel trousers, a maroon cardigan and black wing tip shoes and Argyle socks. Off duty on a Wednesday evening, Jim thought, and time to get out and find a woman. Who needed Fran? She didn't care for his police work. His last partner, Leo Jefferson, laughed at him and said he was "in lust, not in love." Good grief, was that true? Was he just a just horny guy?

Hungry, Jim jumped into his Studebaker Golden Hawk and drove toward Belmont Shore. He parked on 2nd Street in front of Hof's Hut, a single story small twenty-four hour burger and pie restaurant. A narrow place, there were booths down the left side of the room and stools against a counter on the right side. A grill rested against the wall behind the counter. A small homey place with good food, it thrived.

The menu announced that strawberries had just arrived. That sounded great. He ordered a medium rare cheeseburger and Coke. A discarded newspaper lay on the counter. His Coke arrived as he glanced at articles. The "C Section" of the local paper, it contained society news. The front page showed a picture of a man being presented with an award from a women's group that championed assistance for disabled children. The caption, beneath the picture identified Dr. Augustus French as the recipient of the award. Good grief, thought Jim, what a break. There couldn't be two physicians in Long Beach with names that similar. He believed this had to be the abortionist. Jim folded the paper and put it by his right hand as his order arrived.

The burger looked great, the thick meat resting on lettuce, and covered with cheese, a huge slice of onion and a slice of tomato. It dripped with house made Russian dressing. He went though it in just a few minutes, and ordered fresh strawberry pie and vanilla ice cream for dessert. That finished he leaned back, full and contented.

Jim added a generous thirty-five cent tip to the $1.95 bill and walked out. With plenty of time and the newspaper tucked under his arm, he stepped next door and browsed the shelves in Dodd's Bookstore. At 7:30 PM, he went to his car, threw the newspaper behind the front seat and left to see if Fran Fox might be with her new friend at The Trap.

Only a few minutes away, he parked on Termino Avenue, in front of the place. The Trap, at the west end of Belmont Shore, did a fair business with locals. A typical bar serving beer and mixed drinks, there were several game machines, including shuffle-board, and a mastic tile floor. This is just a joint, thought Jim.

The redhead with a ponytail at the south end of the bar looked like Fran. There were probably forty patrons in the place, so Jim stayed a distance away, took a bar stool in the corner and bought a mug of Budweiser. On or off duty, cops moved carefully, and Jim remained cautious and curious.

He watched Fran play shuffleboard with a guy in his mid-30s, about 5'8" and 135 pounds. Prematurely balding and wearing horn rimmed glasses, he looked like a pencil neck. Still, Jim felt shitty.

After a half hour, Jim casually walked toward the shuffleboard game. He acted surprised and exclaimed, "Fran, nice to see you. Is this the family member from out of town?"

Fran stammered, "Er... ah... no. This is Eric Abrams. Eric, this is Jim Grant."

The two shook hands.

Eric appeared confused and asked, "Fran, should I know him?"

Jim quickly replied, "Fran and I are dating. She hasn't told you?"

"No," Eric said.

Fran broke into tears and said, "Jim, I'm dating Eric now. He doesn't know about you. I just haven't had an opportunity to break it to you."

The conversation attracted the attention of a nearby couple standing next to the shuffleboard table.

Eric puffed himself up, became authoritative and spoke, "I guess she's told you. Now I'm telling you, I'm an attorney. Buzz off!"

Jim leaned close to Eric and spoke softly so that others could not hear, "Counselor, I'm a police officer. I guess she hasn't told you about me. So far I haven't done anything to offend you. This is a public place. You don't have any authority to tell me to go anywhere. Now be nice before I stomp a mud hole in your ass and walk it dry."

"Ah... ah... okay. Thank you," Eric replied. "Fran, we'd better go now."

Fran looked at Jim through teary eyes. They hurried out.

Jim, uncomfortable, went back to his barstool, finished his beer and left.

He drove west on Ocean Boulevard and then north on Atlantic without a destination in particular. Funny, he thought, I'm angry and disappointed, but don't feel so bad. No, he said to himself, be honest. It's a bummer. Still, maybe it was lust; it surely was fun for a while. Does that make me a bad guy? Too bad she snuck around on me. Better to find out now than later. He felt sorry for himself and decided another beer would be nice, but not in some toilet bar. Then he thought of the Chandelier, a fine French restaurant with a stylish bar on Atlantic Avenue next to the Crest Theater in Bixby Knolls.

Jim entered through the side parking lot door and took a seat at the end of the long bar. The remainder of the large room contained dining tables. All were covered with white tablecloths and were properly set with silver, crystal and linen napkins. A beautiful large chandelier hung in the center of the room. A night scene of Paris, illuminated with black light, sparkled behind the bar. The headwaiter commanded his reception podium at the entrance.

Jim came here once or twice a month for polite conversation and friendliness. There were no drunks. Tonight it would give him a chance to think about what to do with three nights off.

Cal, the bartender, approached and spoke, "Hi, Jim, your usual Heineken?"

"Yeah, Cal. Thanks."

The beer delivered, Jim paid, and took a sip.

"Jim Grant, what in the world are you doing here? Are you all alone on a night off?"

He turned to see Isabel Packman, the late night police department clerk typist.

"Hi, Isabel. You celebrating?"

"Sure am! This is my only niece – from Boston. We're here for dinner. Donna Stephano, this is Officer Jim Grant. Jim, this is Donna."

Donna was about 28 years old, tall and slender, about 5' 11", 135 pounds, with long legs, a narrow waist, a nicely shaped fanny and probably a 44D bust. Wow! She wore her dark brown hair in the Jackie Kennedy bouffant style. Green eyes and a slight smile brightened her pretty face. Her dress included a white angora sweater, navy skirt and matching navy belt. Her every move displayed sophistication. When she turned her head just right, he caught a glimpse of a single pearl earring.

"It's a pleasure to meet you," Jim said.

"You waiting for someone?" asked Isabel.

"No, I just stopped in for a quiet beer."

"Great. Then you can join us for dinner."

"I've already eaten," Jim replied.

"Bullshit," laughed Isabel. "You're with us. I won't take no for an answer. This is my chance show off my niece. I've helped you Jim, you're beholden to me."

"All right," grinned Jim. "You got me, but I'll pay for my own share. Okay?"

"Sure, let's sit down," said Isabel smiling.

They were seated at a corner table. Jim, already with police officer habits, took a position with his back to the wall facing Isabel. Donna sat on his right. Jim noted her perfectly manicured blood red nails. Drinks arrived and she stroked her screwdriver with her thumb and forefinger.

"Donna's a successful career woman," said Isabel. "She went to Bryn Mawr, then majored in interior design at Harvard. Now she's a renowned interior decorator. Many of her clients are famous."

"You're painting a perfect picture," interjected Donna. "You've left out the painful parts, like the long hours, hard work and a messy divorce."

"No," Isabel replied. "That was just a bad experience. You have no children to quarrel about, and you escaped with a handsome settlement."

105

Jim couldn't read Donna's expression. He thought she could be a hell of a poker player. Boy, thought Jim, this broad is great looking, superbly educated, high class, high maintenance, and out of my league – in fact, with that poker face, a real iceberg. In terms of sex he believed this an impossible dream. She looked like she belonged on the cover of *Vogue*.

A waiter took their orders.

Conversation resumed and their meals were delivered.

Isabel talked of family, growing up, college, friends and fun. Donna talked about her formative years, school and college experiences, then of her bad marriage.

They ordered after dinner drinks and the conversation went on.

Jim nearly jumped out of his chair when Donna tickled the side of his leg with her left hand and then rubbed the top of his thigh. Then he became hard and her hand stroked his erection. No one could tell. Isabel didn't know.

Left handed, Donna opened his zipper and had him in her hand.

My God, Jim thought, it feels so good, I've never been so swollen and I'm going to come all over my pants. It almost happened, but not quite.

She patted him, put it back in his fly, and zipped him up.

Whew, thought Jim, what a wild woman.

The meals almost finished, Donna excused herself to freshen up. Isabel followed.

When they returned Donna slipped him a note. He put it in his pocket, excused himself and went to the men's room. He washed up and then read the note. It said:

Jim,

> *I'm staying at Rochelle's Motel at the airport. Room 424. Let's play.*

He returned, made small talk as they divided the check, nodded to Donna, said goodbye, and left.

He waited forty minutes and went to Rochelle's Motel.

* * *

Jim drove home at 6:00 PM, Saturday afternoon, happy, exhausted and sexually spent after the wildest time of his life. It wouldn't be a relationship, but it was a hell of an experience.

What a woman. She'd opened the motel door for him wearing a towel and had him disrobed and in bed in less than a minute. They didn't get out again until dinnertime Thursday evening. Food came via room service. The whole program consisted of sex, talk, sex, showers, sex, naps and more sex.

Evenings, they went to nice dinner houses and enjoyed fine food. Every time she just threw down a Diner's Club credit card and told him it was a write off. Jim didn't know anyone with a credit card like that. Besides Donna said she wanted to make him a *kept man.*

In town on business, she planned to buy art in West Los Angeles for a client. So, on Friday they drove to Jim's apartment and he picked up a sport-jacket, shirt and tie. Then they toured several very exclusive art galleries, the Los Angeles County Museum of Art and the Museum of Natural History. Afterward they had dinner at the Pacific Dining Car. Then it was back to the motel for more sex and then more sex.

Her legs were long and gorgeous. She had put them behind her neck and helped drive the action. Her big breasts had made him wild.

Since he had to go to work Saturday evening, she insisted they spend the day in at play.

Whew! Jim thought, six years older and more capacity than I could ever handle. I sure couldn't keep up with her on a daily basis. I'd run out of steam. Still, this is one fun broad.

They parted cordially and she kept his telephone number, frankly admitting she had a boyfriend, but saying she would like to visit Jim again. Her parting words were memorable, "Jim," murmured Donna after the last kiss, "you are not in my league, but you're the best sport fuck in the world."

Not a bad compliment, thought Jim. It certainly had been good for his ego after the breakup with Fran. He parked in front of his apartment, stepped out and locked the Studebaker, walked toward the front door and stopped. The front doors to the apartment building, built in about 1905, were made of hardwood frames with eight 12″ by 12″ glass panes. He saw a broken pane near the doorknob, instantly drew his Smith & Wesson Military and Police off duty two-inch revolver from his shoulder holster, stepped to the side of the door and approached.

From outside he carefully examined the door. Someone had broken the glass, reached in and unlocked the door. It appeared that there were no latent fingerprints, still he took a handkerchief from his pocket, carefully opened the door and looked in before entering. Drawers had been dumped, belongings were scattered about and everything ransacked.

He walked slowly checking the bedroom, bath and then the kitchen. The rear door appeared undisturbed. The burglars were long gone. He holstered the two-inch revolver.

He called to have a report taken, and then returned to the bedroom to see if his service revolver had been taken. His four inch Smith & Wesson Highway Patrolman was gone. He went to his bookcase, pulled out a dictionary, and retrieved a handwritten page. It contained the serial numbers of his service revolver and his off duty gun. At least the loss could be properly reported.

The unit car arrived in just a few minutes. Two afternoon officers took the report. They all agreed there were no prints. They were gone in twenty minutes.

Jim spent the remainder of the evening putting things away. Even his clothes had been tossed about. Then, he retreated for another shower and changed into his uniform. He at least had a uniform. At work he knew he could check out a department .38 four-inch Smith & Wesson and work the shift. Monday morning he would go by Long Beach Uniform Company and buy a new gun.

Shit, he thought, that's an expensive loss.

CHAPTER TWELVE

Saturday, March 5, 1960.

Jim arrived a half hour early to check out a department gun. The Afternoon Watch Sergeant, unlocked the armory closet (the old City Hall-Police Station was short of space and every room seemed like a closet) and retrieved a loaner. He gave it to Jim.

"Watch your ass tonight, kid," Sergeant Merle Brown said. "We don't even know if that thing works."

"Thanks, Sarge," Jim replied. "Okay if I keep it until Monday and go get a new one?"

"Sure, kid. Fucking burglars, they ain't got no respect. That was tough luck."

Bob Ortega walked up. "Hey, partner, you can't even take three days off and do it right. I hear you got ripped off."

"Yeah," Jim said. "They sacked the place and took my service weapon. I just borrowed a spare and I don't know if it works or how it's sighted in." He put it in his Jordan Holster and being a smaller gun, it wobbled around.

"Well," Bob replied, "use the shotgun. Then you don't have to worry about accuracy. It's hard to miss with double ought buck."

Yeah, he thought, but how do you take a shotgun everywhere you're sent?

Saturday night's squad meeting was short and they were soon in service, with Bob driving, northbound on Pacific Avenue from City Hall. The radio squawked urgently.

"Unit Seven."

Bob grabbed the microphone to respond and Jim snatched his clipboard and a pen to write.

"Unit Seven, from 6th and Pacific."

"Unit Seven, check the unknown trouble. Woman screaming. Complaining Party thinks it's the second or

110

*third house on the north side of Alhambra Court and west of
Alamitos. The front door is standing open."*

"Unit Seven, 10-4," Bob replied.

"Unit Three is rolling to backup Unit Seven."

"10-4 Unit Three."

Jim thought it best to carry the shotgun on this call,
pulled it from the lock and held it, barrel up, against his leg.
With Bob at his side, and Red Price and his partner coming,
whatever the problem they would kick ass. Red might be a
drunk, but he feared nothing.

Already past Seventh Street, they turned east on Tenth,
north on Alamitos, and west on Alhambra Court squealing
to a halt on the north curb. Out of the car with the shotgun
at port arms, Jim saw the open door and heard
bloodcurdling screams coming from the house. A streetlight
lit up the front yard. Ignoring any risks, he ran straight
across the yard toward the front door and flattened himself
on the side of the jamb. He looked in, and time seemed to
slow down, then pass away. It was eerily silent. Nothing
moved, like an opening scene in a horror film. What was
here? Who had screamed?

An old poorly designed frame house, the door opened to
a living room furnished with throwaway junk. He peeked
around the edge of the door, shotgun muzzle shoved
forward, looked over the gun-sight at the dining room to the
right rear, then moved his head forward and saw a door in
the left rear of the living room. The screaming, as loud as
humans can scream, came again - from there.

Oblivious of his partner to the rear and all else, shotgun
aimed, he saw the door swing slowly open. He looked
directly toward the bathroom and saw a young naked
teenage colored female sitting on the toilet. Tears streamed
down her face as she screamed.

Jim yelled, "What's wrong?"

She stood from the toilet, stepped forward and pointed
down. A fetus, about six inches long, covered with

111

streaming blood, hung from her vagina by the umbilical cord. Her screams were incessant.

Jim ran forward, spoke softly and helped her to the floor, put down the shotgun and put an arm around her shivering body. He yelled at Bob.

"Call an ambulance. Quick. She's hemorrhaging. Run!"

Bob bolted out the door past Red and his partner, standing outside with guns drawn.

"I think she's going into shock. Red, find me a blanket," Jim ordered.

He continued to speak softly and slowly to the girl. Almost a child, her screams turned to sobs, and she clutched him, groaned and began to speak haltingly.

"I'm sorry. I'm sorry. Forgive me. God help me. Forgive me. Tell my Momma I'm sorry."

"My name is Jim," he softly said, "what's your name?"

She moaned and replied, "Flora. Flora Lewis."

"How old are you, Flora?"

Tears still coming, she answered, "I… I turned fourteen yester-yesterday."

"Where do you live?"

"With my Momma and my Daddy on Lime Avenue."

Red passed Jim a blanket and he pressed it over her shaking body.

"What happened?" Jim asked.

"Oh, I'm so sorry… so sorry. I didn't know it hurt so bad. I did it with a coat hanger … I did it with a coat hanger. I don't want no baby of his."

Jim softly asked, "Whose baby?"

"Sweetpea. It belongs to Sweetpea. You know Sweetpea. He be a pimp. My Momma told me not to take up with him. I wouldn't listen."

"You mean Sweetpea Jackson?" The only Sweetpea Jim knew was a pimp that ran girls out of the Lay Back Hotel on Anaheim.

"Yes," blubbered the young girl. "He followed me home from school, he put all that sweet talk on me and all he wanted was my pussy. Before him, I never had no man.

Then he made love to me every day after school. I knew we did wrong. I'm a church girl. He made me pregnant. I thought we'd get ... get ... get married." She gasped and sniffled a moment. "He wanted me to make him money, to turn tricks and suck dicks. I wouldn't do that. I'm a good girl."

The gut wagon arrived.

Jim stepped back to make way.

"Don't leave me. Don't leave me," she called, reaching a hand toward him, still crying.

Bob stepped close to Jim and spoke quietly, "We got lucky, the ambulance was at St. Mary's Hospital and came right here. Ride with her on the way to the hospital. Get all you can about Sweetpea. I've had enough of that fucker turning young girls into whores. Let's roll his ass up."

Bob told the firemen he thought the girl's condition was serious and they moved swiftly to put her on a Gurney and take her away. They beckoned to Jim and he picked up his shotgun from the floor and handed it to Bob. He saw a lot of blood on the floor where she had been. A lot of blood to lose in a short time, he thought, she's in real trouble.

"See you at St. Mary's," Jim said in reply.

In the ambulance, Jim rode at her side. She clutched his hand and cried quietly.

"Lean back and rest, Flora," Jim instructed. "We'll be at the hospital in a minute."

"Oh Lord," she replied. "It hurts, Jim, it hurts."

The ambulance backed to the doors of St. Mary's Hospital Emergency Room and the firemen came around quickly to open the rear door. The older of the two motioned for Jim to get out, turned and whispered, "Run for a nurse. We need a physician right now and a gynecologist

113

as quickly as possible. Tell them this kid is probably a goner."

Jim ran for help and delivered the message, then watched as the action started.

The small staff at St. Mary's dropped everything they were working on to help. They placed the girl on an emergency room operating table, put her in stirrups, and the doctor gave her a pelvic examination. He directed staff to get the on call gynecologist.

They hooked up an I. V., gave her plasma, fluids, red blood cells and antibiotics. The hemorrhaging continued.

The Mother Superior brought in a priest and he stood at the head of the table speaking quietly to Flora. Then he spoke with the doctors and motioned for the Mother Superior, whispered to her, and returned to Flora.

The Mother Superior walked over to Jim and asked, "Officer, is your name Jim?"

"Yes."

"The doctors are doing everything possible and they're worried. She's lost too much blood and her condition is critical. She asked for you. Would you please help her?"

"Sister, how can I help?" Jim asked.

"Go hold her hand, comfort her and do anything you can."

Jim went to the head of the emergency room table, took her hand and spoke softly, "Flora, it's Jim. Just hang in there, I'm with you."

"Jim, oh Jim, I'm glad you came back." The tears continued to flow. "It still hurts so much."

She squeezed his hand and held on tight.

Sobbing, she told Jim her Grandma died and her folks went to the funeral in Alabama, would be back in a week and thought she was staying with a family friend. Then she choked back her tears, became very serious, "I know I didn't do right, but I want you to put Sweetpea in jail for this. He's a lot older. He's thirty-three and he knows he did me wrong."

"I'll do my best for you, Flora."

The priest conferred with one of the doctors and then motioned Jim away from the table.

He patted Flora's hand saying, "Flora, excuse me for just a minute, I'll be right back."

She nodded through tears and he went to the doctor and the priest. His partner, Bob, walked across the room and joined them.

The priest quietly spoke in an Irish brogue, "I'm Father O'Reilly. The good doctor here thinks she's in rough shape and may slip away to the Lord."

The doctor nodded, "Her uterus was perforated in several places. That coat hanger took a terrible toll. One torn spot is awful. A gynecologist is coming from home. The damage compels an emergency hysterectomy. It's so bad we'll be lucky if we save her. What uneducated frightened young girls do to themselves can be deadly, and I'm afraid this is an example."

Jim looked at Father O'Reilly then at his partner and asked, "What can I do?"

Father O'Reilly answered, "Didn't she just ask your help to prosecute the culprit that impregnated her?"

"Yes!"

"Then do what you can," the priest stated.

Bob Ortega spoke up, "Jim, it has to be a dying declaration to stand up in court. She has to be told she's dying, know it's the truth, and be asked to tell the truth."

"I remember," he said.

"Then do it. I'll be at your elbow, writing as you speak."

Jim went back to the table, took Flora's hand and his voice trembled slightly as he spoke. "It's not good, Flora. Do you understand that?"

115

She answered in a tired voice, "Yes, Jim, I think I know what you're saying. Oh, Lordy. Lord help me. I wish my Momma and Daddy were here."

"Do you still want me to prosecute Sweetpea Jackson?"

"Yes, yes, Jim. Please!"

"Do you understand, Flora, you are dying?"

She whimpered, choked back tears and replied, "Yes, I know I'm dying. It hurts so much. I just want it to stop hurting."

"Then you know you are going to die?"

"Yes, and I'm ready to meet Jesus. I just want to be forgiven."

Jim choked up, tears flowed down his cheeks and Father O'Reilly softly began to pray as he started the Last Rites.

Hospital staff motioned them back as they positioned a Gurney next to the examining table and moved the plasma, fluids and red blood cells for the I.V. to an attached tree. They pulled on the sheet upon which Flora rested and tugged her onto the Gurney.

The Mother Superior told them to go along as they moved Flora up to the operating room. As attendants moved the Gurney out the door, Jim resumed his position next to Flora's head.

"Do you swear that what you say here will be the truth, the whole truth and nothing but the truth; so help you God?"

"Yes I do!"

Then Jim went on, "Can you tell me how this happened?"

Her voice growing weaker, Flora spoke. "Sweetpea Jackson waited for me after school every day for a month. He sweet talked me, said he loved me, followed me, and swore in God's name he loved me and would do me no wrong. I let him make love to me, then he wanted me every day after school. We went to his house on Gundry every day and he showed me how to make love and suck him off. I loved him."

They arrived at the elevator and attendants pushed the up button.

"Flora, how old were you when this started?"

"I was thirteen."

"When was your birthday?"

"March 4th."

"Then yesterday you turned fourteen?"

"Yeah."

The doors opened and attendants pushed Flora into the elevator. It began to move upward.

"Can you remember what month this all started and you first had sex with him?"

"Yes, it was in October. I wrote in my diary. It was after school on October 13th. I was in love so I wrote the memory down. It was Tuesday, October 13th. Oh Lord, forgive me! We was off school the day before for some holiday, I don't remember what. Then on Tuesday, after school, Sweetpea walked with me. I was alone that day and he started to kiss me and I got all excited. He asked me to come with him and we got in his big car and went to his house on Gundry. I loved him, oh Lord, I did."

The doors opened, Jim and Bob stepped out of the way, and they moved down the hall toward the operating room.

"What happened then?" asked Jim.

Flora's voice continued to fade as she replied. "He showed me how to make love. I loved him.

"Flora, I have to ask this. Did you have intercourse?

"Yes."

"By that, did he put his penis in your vagina?"

"Yes. He showed me how to fuck and suck. Then he did me wrong."

"How's that?"

"I started getting sick in December and told him I thought I was pregnant. All my friends said that's why I was

117

sick in the morning. He laughed, said it's time I went to work. I said doing what. He say turning tricks like his other girls. I wouldn't do that. We been arguing ever since. I wouldn't let him fuck me no more. Then tonight I just had to get rid of his baby. He's a no good. Jesus help me and I loved him."

Jim followed Flora through the doors and into the operating room. And while the plasma, fluids and red blood cells were attached to the O.R. table, he continued to speak. "Did Sweetpea ever threaten you?"

"Yes, when he wanted me to turn tricks and we argued. Then he say he'd kill me if I ever went to the police."

They moved Flora onto the table. The gynecologist hurried into the room pulling on rubber gloves. An anesthesiologist, already in the room, stepped forward.

"Is there anything else you'd like to say?"

Flora groaned, visibly exhausted, spoke slowly, "Only to tell my Momma and Daddy I'm sorry. I love them so much. Please tell them I went to see Jesus."

The anesthesiologist placed a needle in the I.V. line.

"I'll tell them, Flora. Is there anything else?"

She stirred, and after a moment, looked at Jim and answered weakly, "It don't hurt no more, Jim. Thank you for helping me."

The weak pressure from her hand relaxed.

The officers walked out as the doctors went to work.

They went to the tiny coffee shop and began preparing reports. Hardly twenty minutes passed when Father O'Reilly walked in and sat with them.

Jim looked up from his work into the sad face of the Priest.

Father O'Reilly spoke quietly, "Flora has gone to the Lord. I'm sorry to report she died on the operating table. Her injuries were just too serious and too much blood lost."

Jim wept. Right in front of Bob Ortega, he wept while Father O'Reilly held his hand.

Bob called the station and advised them of the death.

Both officers remained in the tiny coffee room in St. Mary's Hospital, writing, until Homicide Sergeant Bill Millard and his partner Detective Carl Peele arrived. Bob Ortega briefed them on the death, statements of Flora Lewis implicating Sweetpea Jackson, and the already completed fact gathering.

The small brightly lit coffee room gave Jim his first real close-up view of Bill Millard. At 5' 11" and 220 pounds, he looked like a bear. His worn cheap double-breasted brown suit needed pressing and his wide floral patterned tie hung down from the unbuttoned frayed collar of a white shirt that was turning gray with age. He needed a shave and a haircut and smelled of bourbon. Jim wondered if he had just left the Apple Valley Steak House.

Carl Peele looked just a little bit better. Skinny at about 6' 3" and 185 pounds with longer brown hair and brown eyes, he had on a shabby navy blue double-breasted suit. He had his tie in the right place and appeared cleaner.

Their nicknames, in patrol, were Laurel and Hardy. Millard was big Oliver Hardy and Peele was skinny Stan Laurel.

"Okay," Sergeant Millard said. "Just another idiot using a coat hanger to get rid of a kid. You'd think the fools would get the message and go to a hospital in Tijuana. It's self inflicted, nothing for us here. You go ahead and file it all."

"Sure," Bob replied. "We'll finish it."

"Probably ain't much they'll do with that nigger pimp. Though you might just as well hammer him. Thirteen years old makes it crime against child, instead of statutory rape. Even so, a good attorney will make it hard to stick. Fucker will probably get it reduced to a misdemeanor."

"Why will it be so hard to get a conviction?" Jim asked.

Millard answered, "Cause juries are likely to believe that kid has been fucking since she was twelve."

119

"I don't believe that," Jim argued.

Homicide Sergeant Bill Millard examined Jim carefully. His brown eyes almost became slits as his face contorted in visible anger. He clasped his huge hands and replied, "I don't give a shit what you believe, kid. That's the way niggers live."

Jim, about to lose his temper, put his head down and fought to regain control of himself, looked up and straight into Millard's eyes and replied, "This little girl wasn't a nigger, and I'll do my best to stick it to that bastard."

Millard laughed and commented, "So you're going to save the world, eh'? Then go get his ass, rookie. You handle it, we're out of here."

They left. Both officers sat quietly for a moment.

Bob Ortega broke the silence. "You were right, Jim, but be careful. Somehow you hit his hot button. As a rookie you can't poke at Bill Millard. He's a heavy duty ass-hole."

Jim looked at Bob and angrily said, "Yeah, you're right. He's an ass-hole."

* * *

At the station, case notes in hand, with Bob Ortega at his elbow, Jim dictated to Isabel Packman as tears ran down all of their faces. The training paid off. The reports generated were complete, accurate, and the finest he ever filed.

At 6:30 AM, when it ended, he thanked Isabel and stood to leave.

"Just a minute Jim," Isabel said. "I want to tell you this is good work. You know I never give compliments. This time I want to say thanks for that little girl."

"Isabel, this is the hardest thing I have ever done in my life. That bastard nailed Flora the day after I started on this police department. She was just a little girl. I'll never forget

120

that. That's why these are the best reports I've ever done. Next, we'll roll his ass up."

"Okay, Jim. Go get that pimp bastard," Isabel said.

"Tomorrow," replied Bob. "We'll plan this at squad meeting and take down the Lay Back Hotel just before dawn. They'll all be asleep and unprepared. Then his home changes from the Lay Back Hotel to the Gray Bar Hotel."

Still on duty, they went to breakfast, nibbled with no appetite, ended the shift and went home.

* * *

Jim seldom said prayers. As he crawled into bed he took a moment and thought. Then he sent a silent prayer to God.

>*Lord,*
>
>*I don't often say hello or ask for anything. This is important.*
>
>*Please take little Flora Lewis and forgive her sins. She didn't know. She is really a sweet child.*
>*Oh, and Lord please, do the same for Peggy Evans. We have all made mistakes.*
>*And Lord, the Mother Superior and Father O'Reilly were wonderful. Please accept thanks from a Baptist that needed to be reminded that all of us on earth of all faiths worship One God.*
>*Amen.*

CHAPTER THIRTEEN

Sunday, March 6, 1960.

Jim wanted to be at work early. Still depressed about the death of Flora Lewis, he left the apartment at 9:45 PM and went to the station knowing that some of his fellow officers would be planning the arrest of Sweetpea.

Walking into the squad room, he brushed off his grief and joined planning activities. Bob Ortega, Lester Peabody and Red Price were in the rear, gathered around the pool table. Others joined the group and listened. Ortega had a copy of Sweetpea's rap sheet. Lester Peabody had been to the Record Bureau and made notes concerning Sweetpea's local arrests for violent crimes. Red Price, always the Marine, had gone to the City Building Department, examined a copy of the floor plans of the Lay Back Hotel, and drew a copy. He unfolded it on the pool table. Pool balls and cues rested on the corners to keep them from rolling up.

"Listen up, you guys," Ortega said. "For those of you that don't know him, Sweetpea's real name is Floyd (no middle name) Jackson. He's male Negro, 34 years old, 5' 4", 130 pounds, with black hair and brown eyes. His DOB is April 28, 1925. This asshole has a three-page FBI rap sheet that started in Biloxi, Mississippi in 1943. The first arrest was for petty theft and the next for draft dodging. After that he got bagged for pimping, procuring for the purpose of prostitution, transporting women across state lines for the purpose of prostitution, running gambling games, battery, assault with force, assault with a deadly weapon and attempt murder." Bob gestured toward Lester Peabody and said, "He'll tell you about this prick's Long Beach cases."

Lester began, "Seven of the assault cases involved his stable of girls. He beats the shit out of them to keep them in line. In the attempt murder case he shot another pimp who tried to take his girls and squeeze the Lay Back Hotel. He might be a little fart, but he's made a reputation as someone you don't want to fuck with. According to a snitch, he carries a little .25 Colt automatic in an ankle holster. Watch out!"

"My turn," growled Red Price. "Lean over, look and learn. This drawing is of the inside floor plan of the Lay Back. It has two stories, a long center hallway on each floor and stairs straight up at the front and the rear. The old place has baths in the center of the hallways on each side. Johns and girls come and go all the time. Sweetpea has a half dozen girls in rooms on both floors and he changes his own room every night. Guys on the Vice Squad tell us he's foxy and you'll never know where he'll be."

Red announced they would hit the Lay Back at 4:30 AM. A good hour because the radio would be quiet and few units would be out on calls. He assigned units to the front, sides and rear and urged caution. Red explained they didn't need a warrant because they had reasonable cause to believe a felony had been committed, that Sweetpea was the perpetrator, and they would kick doors until they had him.

"Remember," Red said, "this is not statutory rape. This is a felony. It's Crime Against Child; little Flora Lewis was only 13 years old when he started banging her."

"The radio code name would be 'Taking Richmond.'" Then he pointed to Jim Grant, laughed and said, "Jim did his best for that little girl. Now, taking Sweetpea will be just like Grant taking Richmond."

The guys roared.

There were no questions.

"Another thing!" Lester said. "You might want to know how he got his nickname. He tells folks a virgin's vagina looks like a sweetpea and he just loves to lick em', taste the sweet things and stick em'. That's why they call him Sweetpea."

"We send that fucker to the joint," Ortega remarked, "and somebody will be making use of his Sweetpea."

All the men he-hawed.

Sergeant Frank Gonzales came through the door and hollered, "Stop the jawing and let's get to work."

He walked to the tall oak watch-meeting table in the front of the room, threw down a thick binder, sat on a tall bar stool, began to sort loose papers, hammered on the wooden table with his mallet and started the meeting. The binder contained the watch report, a summary of all events that occurred in the city on each shift. He quickly read appropriate announcements, concluded the meeting and the men left for their cars.

As graveyard units went into service they were directed to a command post at Willow Street and Pacific Avenue. A wounded felon had escaped from officers. Afternoon units were conducting a search.

Jim and Bob arrived, saw a sergeant's car on the Department of Motor Vehicles lot, parked, joined other arriving officers and walked to the vehicle to receive directions.

They were told a marijuana dealer being pursued by narcotics officers crashed his car at Willow and Chestnut and ran. Since he was a fleeing felon (any quantity of marijuana constituted a felony), they shot him as he climbed over a fence and escaped. Being wounded didn't slow him down. Narcotics officers called for help and patrol took charge. The sergeant gave each officer a specific location to work and the search started.

Following directions to secure a north line on Twenty-seventh Street, Bob dropped Jim at Twenty-seventh and Cedar and then drove to Twenty-seventh and Pacific.

Jim stepped away from a streetlight and stood behind a tree in the shadows on the north side of the street.

Fuck, he thought, he didn't bring the shotgun. He just had the loaner revolver wobbling around in his holster. Too late to take corrective action, he hunkered down.

The radios were in the police cars. He had no means to communicate. He couldn't see a black and white or an officer in either direction. At about 12:15 A.M., the waiting began.

Cedar Avenue to the left front and an alley to his right front, he watched. A neat neighborhood of working class stucco homes, everything appeared tidy and nothing moved. A full moon loomed in clear eastern skies. An occasional dog's bark could be heard in the distance. A half hour went by.

Jim saw movement on his right front at the edge of the alley. First, a head peeked around the alley side fence then a figure limped into the area illuminated by the street light. Jim made him as male, about 25 years old, 5′ 10″, 165 pounds, with dark hair, and wearing dark pants and a sweatshirt.

He pulled the borrowed revolver slowly and silently from his holster, waited until the suspect reached the middle of the street, then yelled, "Freeze ass hole! Put your hands as high as you can reach and hold that position."

Lights came on in the adjacent homes.

The suspect stumbled, then complied, groaned and spoke, "You got me. Shit, I'm shot. Help me, will ya?"

Jim ordered the suspect to face away from him, approached from his rear, held the gun to his head, rapidly patted him down for weapons and placed him on his knees. He then handcuffed the suspect's left hand behind his back and then the right hand.

The front door of the closest house opened and a man yelled, "Who's out there?"

"Police," Jim replied. "I've got a wounded escapee in custody. Would you call the station and have them send a car?"

"Yes sir, right away."

"How bad are you hit?" Jim asked as he lifted the suspect back to his feet and looked him over with a flashlight.

"I think they got me in the ass," he answered, "and I don't feel so good. It's starting to hurt."

He remained bent over slightly, appeared under the influence of something, and looked like he had been eating weed. His lips were caked with shreds of marijuana. Jim saw a small hole in his pants at the fold of his right buttock and the area, while not dripping, appeared saturated with blood.

"What's your name?" Jim inquired.

"Jerry. Jerry Bailey," he replied.

A plain car followed by a black and white skidded around the corner and stopped with their headlights illuminating Jim and the suspect. The officers hurried out and took charge. Narcotics officers from the plain car recognized Bailey as their suspect, put him in their car and left for Seaside Hospital at 14th and Magnolia. All units working the area were released from the search for regular duties.

Bob Ortega came for Jim, picked him up and they checked back into service.

Several minutes passed and new directions came by radio.

"Unit One. Contact narcotic officers at Seaside Hospital and standby with the prisoner."

Jim grabbed the microphone and answered, "Unit One 10-4, from Willow and Magnolia."

"Shit," muttered Bob. "When a wounded or injured felon is in custody someone has to guard them until they're sent to the County Hospital Jail Ward. You were the blue suit that made the capture so narcotics just unloaded him on us."

Ortega drove to Seaside Hospital. They parked, went inside and went to the emergency room.

Jim Grant recognized Narcotics Officer Emilio Zapata. A huge man and former heavy weight boxer, he stood by the head of a gurney patiently chipping marijuana debris from the lips of the prisoner into a small evidence envelope.

Bailey moaned as an older doctor leaned over his disrobed torso and probed at a lump on his belly with stiff fingers. Jim recognized him as Police Surgeon Phillip Carstairs, a tough crusty competent physician that regularly handled in custody injuries and rape cases.

"Hell, this ain't bad," Carstairs reported to the suspect. "The bullet entered through the fold of your butt as you crawled over the fence. The fatty tissue closed over the wound, restricted hemorrhaging, and the projectile passed through. It's this lump on the front of your belly."

Bailey grunted, "Doctor, it hurts. Can I have something for the pain?"

"Shit, kid," replied Carstairs. "You're already loaded. I don't want complications. We'll just ship you straight to the Sheriff's Jail Ward and let them pay the bills."

Carstairs wrote instructions to County authorities, passed the slip to Jim, and stated, "Take his ass to County and it'll also save the City of Long Beach the ambulance bill."

Emilio Zapata stood up, waved the envelope and said, "I'm done. Take him!"

It took two hours to transport and await admission of the doper. County Hospital staffers and Deputy Sheriff's were pissed at having him dumped on them. Bob shrugged, looked innocent, and said they were only transportation officers.

Finally back in town at 3:30 AM, they hustled back to the parking lot opposite the Navy Base and Jim found another stolen Austin Healey.

"One each night," chortled Bob as they waited again for the tow truck. "I work with you and every night we're swimming in shit. You're making me a fucking hero."

The radio squawked.

"Attention all units. Richmond WILL NOT be taken tonight. Repeat, Richmond WILL NOT be taken. Robert E. Lee is away. Unit One did you read?"

"Unit One, 10-4."

"Oh, fuck," exclaimed Jim. "I really wanted to take him tonight."

"That's the breaks, partner," Bob said.

They went to breakfast, completed leftover paperwork and checked out at 7:30 AM.

* * *

At 8:25 A.M., Jim stood at the door of the Long Beach Uniform Company on the south side of Broadway west of Long Beach Boulevard. He hoped someone would come in early.

The company supplied police uniforms, guns, holsters, handcuffs and almost everything else. Recruits and veteran officers bought it all here. The city only supplied a badge, metal hat emblem and call box key.

One of the business partners walked up at 8:30 A.M., recognized Jim, opened the door, turned off the alarm system, unlocked gun display cabinets and provided immediate service. Jim told him about the burglary and the loss of his gun. The owner sympathized with his loss, reminded Jim that Long Beach Uniform Company represented Smith & Wesson in the area and then mentioned that a very special gun had recently arrived from the factory.

He showed Jim a brand new blue steel .357 Model 19 Smith & Wesson Combat Magnum with a four inch barrel and a special factory target hammer and trigger. Jim immediately chose that gun and then selected a new cross draw holster. His fast draw Jordan Holster had not been easy to access in the car. The total, with tax, came to $98.21 and Jim wrote a check.

Back in his Golden Hawk, he drove straight to the pistol range to zero in the new revolver. At the range he began at the twenty-five yard line with sand bags and a bench rest. In fifteen minutes he correctly adjusted the sights and fired three patterns of three rounds; each of which could be covered with a twenty-five cent piece. Then he fired standing with right hand, left hand, and two-hand hold positions. The special target trigger and hammer combination responded beautifully.

Finally, he used a silhouette target and fired a score of 99.6%. Smiling, confidence restored, he turned in the target frame and sandbags and headed for home.

A ringing telephone greeted him as he unlocked his apartment door.

Jim snatched it and answered, "Hello."

"Captain Green here."

"Yes sir."

"I've been calling since 8:00 A.M. I wanted to catch you before you went to sleep."

"I'm sorry, Captain. I stopped at Long Beach Uniform, bought a new gun and then went to the range."

"That's part of what I'm calling about. The report is right here in front of me. Somebody broke in and took your gun."

"Yeah, a bad break."

"I'm not sure it was just a bad break," said the Captain. "I'm afraid my secretary screwed up, opened your note, and left it on her desk. Now others know about that letter from Peggy Evans to Roy Jensen."

"Oh."

"Well, I'm worried about that. I wonder if the burglary is a result of that mistake."

"Is that possible?"

"I've seen stranger things. It's all the more important to keep the rest of this secret. Do you still have the letter?"

"Yes sir, it's in a safe deposit box at F & M Bank."

"Outstanding."

"Thank you, sir."

"It's time to meet and discuss the letter, evidence and some strategy. A task force is working on this and it remains top secret."

"Yes sir."

"I want you to meet with the Task Force this afternoon at 5:15 P.M. I'll be there."

"Yes sir."

"Good. Then come to the Towne Theater in Bixby Knolls. Wear a suit and tie as if it's a business interview. Tell the doorman you have an appointment with Mr. Winterton in the executive offices. When you enter go to your right front, knock on that door and you'll be admitted. Bring Peggy's letter. Tell no one. Not even your mother."

"Yes sir."

"Oh. And, Jim, take care that you are not followed to or from the F & M Bank. Stay armed. These precautions are important."

"Yes sir."

Jim set his alarm for 4:00 P.M. and hit the sack.

CHAPTER FOURTEEN

Monday, March 7, 1960. 5:00 PM

Jim drove northbound on Long Beach's only freeway and turned east on Del Amo. The 4:00 P.M. alarm had come too soon. He'd slept lightly and remained tired. Dressed in a suit and tie, he'd been to the bank and had the letter from Peggy in his pocket. He watched warily to see if others were following. It looked all clear as he turned south on Atlantic to the Towne Theater just north of San Antonio Drive.

He parked in front, looked around, picked up the newspaper article that named Dr. August French, then left the car and went to the theater entrance. The doorman readily accepted his explanation and pointed out the office door to the right rear of the lobby.

Following instructions, he knocked. The door promptly opened and he looked his grinning former partner Leo Jefferson in the face. Surprised, he instantly understood why Leo had been so cagey about his new assignment.

"Damn, I'm glad you're here," Jim exclaimed.

"I'm covering your ass, Jim," chortled Leo as he grabbed him by the hand and pulled him into the room. "I have some people I want you to meet."

Jim rapidly met the other three members of the four man Long Beach Police and Los Angeles County Sheriff's Department task force. He shook hands with Sergeant Joel Patterson, the second member from Long Beach. Then he met Sergeant Clay Landsberg and Deputy Eric Hanson of the Los Angeles County Sheriff's Department.

Captain J. C. Green, on the phone, waved from behind a desk in the rear of the room.

"Shit, Jim," Leo Jefferson said. "You never even told me about this. It's good. We started Tuesday of last week. I ain't seen anything move so fucking fast."

131

The Captain hung up and gestured for them to gather around him. They walked over and took chairs about the desk. Jim passed the letter and newspaper article, circled in ink, to the Captain.

J.C. put on a pair of reading glasses and read the letter. Not a man moved. Then he read the newspaper article.

Looking up, J.C. spoke, "You've all heard me speak of Jim Grant. Now you've met him. He's a rookie and has done this job as well as could be expected from any veteran. I've told you before that his digging around developed the information that led to the creation of this task force. Now I'll tell you that this is an incredible, powerful and damning letter."

The Captain paused. "At first I couldn't imagine the letter would have much importance. Now I understand. It makes a hell of a lot of sense. She couldn't send it to her folks, so she sent it to her former boyfriend. She expected his loyalty and got it. I think I should read this to all of you before we continue the meeting."

The Captain solemnly read the letter, then the newspaper article. No one spoke. He took off his glasses and cleaned them, then quickly wiped a single tear off of his cheek.

"We're going to have to defend this in court, and it may not be admissible," Captain Green said, "but it sure as hell is solid information. It'll be sufficient to enable us to get warrants and then make searches. It names Ivan Slade, Johnny Redden, Doctor August French and identifies Ben Clarey's apartment as the site. That arrogant fucking Lawyer Johnny Redden met her in person and named Doctor French. What a dumb shit. It just shows he thinks he's too smart for the law."

"Sergeant Patterson," the Captain directed. "Summarize for Grant all that's been done. He'll have to keep working patrol, but he's too valuable out there to be kept uninformed."

132

"Yes sir," Patterson responded, looking toward Jim. "We've worked hard. Copies have been quietly made of all Long Beach Police information filed on Peggy Evans' death. Sergeant Landsberg and Deputy Hanson obtained all of the Coroner's reports concerning the scene and the autopsy. Information has also been retrieved, for background purposes, on Ivan Slade, Johhny Redden and Ben Clarey. We know that Sergeant Bill Millard and Detective Carl Peele of Homicide have a close friendship with Attorney Johnny Redden. We're asking around quietly to learn just how close they might be."

Patterson thought for a moment and continued. "We work out of this office after 5:00 P.M. when staff has gone home. Everything we gather goes into a separate safe before we leave."

Captain Green waved the letter. "This widens the net. Now we have our sights on the doctor that did the work." He waved the paper. "This newspaper article probably confirms his I.D., but we still need more information."

Green again thought for a few seconds. "I think we should carefully and quietly obtain a search warrant for Clarey's apartment. The blood loss was tremendous.

If we can find blood from Peggy Evans in that room we can squeeze Clarey. I also want the doctor interviewed when the search warrant is served. We'll have them both at the same time and sweat them before the word gets out."

All nodded.

"Is there anything I should or should not do?" Jim asked.

"Yeah," Captain Green answered. "Find Tokay and see what the word is on the street. Then call me. Use a pay phone."

"Yes sir."

"You're tired, Jim," Green said. "Get out of here. You'll soon have to go back to work. Keep a personal

133

record of your overtime on this case. We'll file for that after this goes public."

"Yes sir."

* * *

Jim Grant arrived early, eager to participate in the final plans to arrest Sweetpea. He walked through the squad room door at 10:45 P.M. The moment he stepped inside he heard Bob Ortega yell his name.

"Hey, Jim. Come here."

Bob leaned over the pool table, cue in hand, intent upon a shot in a game of rotation. Red Price stood on the opposite side chalking a cue stick.

Jim walked to a nearby chair, put down his gear, straightened his tie, and approached the pool table.

"Aw shit," exclaimed Bob as he miscued and sunk the eight ball. "You win, Red. All I can think about is putting that fucking Sweetpea in the jug." He dug in his pocket and handed Red a quarter.

"I hope you shoot your revolver better than you shoot pool," Red replied.

"Don't worry about my shooting. Worry about Jim using a borrowed gun."

"No sweat," Jim interjected. "I bought a new Combat Magnum this morning. Have a look."

Jim removed his new S & W four inch, opened the cylinder, emptied the six cartridges and passed it to Bob.

Bob whistled, "Not too bad. It's all about money. When you're single you get all the new toys you want. Shoot it yet?"

"I hit the range this morning right after I got it. That target trigger and hammer combination works well. It shoots beautifully."

"Mind if I look? Red asked.

"No, go right ahead."

134

Keeping the cylinder open, Red pressed forward the cylinder release, cocked the piece, sighted on an imaginary spot on the ceiling and pressed the trigger. It snapped smoothly.

"Very nice, it feels polished."

"Red, get your ass up here," hollered Sergeant Frank Gonzales. "It's squad meeting time. I want you to announce assignments. We're taking Richmond tonight. The Vice cops say Robert E. Lee is back in town."

Red passed back Jim's gun, grinned and said, "Maybe you can break it in tonight."

Again, the strike was scheduled for 4:30 A.M., and assignments were made. Red asked that Units Two and Seven under Lester Peabody hit the front. Unit Six would guard the west side of the building and Unit Four cover the east side. Unit Three and Unit One (Jim and Bob) were to go in the rear under direction of the Red Price, with his rookie Zeke Walker.

Routine information dispensed, the squad meeting broke up. The night began for the graveyard watch as midnight approached.

A typical Monday night / Tuesday morning, the shift started slowly. Bob recommended an early breakfast and Jim, always hungry, agreed. They discussed locations and decided on Curries, near Sante Fe and Anaheim, and checked out of service at 2:30 A.M.

Curries made a reputation in the 1940s for terrific ice cream. They specialized in banana splits, ice cream sundaes, root beer floats and malts. They also offered an array of typical American food including hamburgers and pies. Countertops and booth tables were red Formica trimmed with chrome strips and wooden counter stools sat on cast iron bases. Chrome decorated most everything. It was on mixers, dispensers lining the back bar, salt and peppershakers, the tops of sugar containers and paper napkin holders. Coca-Cola posters adorned the white walls.

A Wurlitzer Juke Box stood in the corner and Frank Sinatra's "New York, New York," filled the room. The aroma of cooking hamburger stimulated their hunger.

Seated at the counter, they ordered coffee, cheeseburgers, and pieces of apple pie (always a safe and nutritious menu for cops). A tired waitress turned and placed their orders on clips facing the cooks.

Looking around Jim saw the usual crowd. The bars closed at 2:00 A.M. and those that didn't need to hurry home and were still hungry came here.

"Hey, Bob," someone yelled. Jim thought, shit, now we have a conversation with some late night drunk.

Bob Ortega waved and called back, "Hi, Michael."

The man, looking like a waiter, walked to the counter. He wore black pants, a white shirt, black vest and black bow tie. Michael turned out to be Michael O'Donnell and Jim learned that he worked at the Apple Valley Steak House.

Sure enough, he'd had a few and wanted to talk. He took a seat next to Bob at the counter, ordered and began yakking. The burgers arrived and Jim listened with half an ear.

"Too bad you guys aren't living off the fat of the land like Homicide," Michael remarked.

"What do you mean?" Bob asked.

"Shit, I mean Bill Millard and Carl Peele from Homicide," Michael said. "They must be in the Apple Valley four nights a week. If the boss doesn't let them eat and drink free, somebody else is picking up the tab. Talk about living high off the hog, these guys have taken mooching to a world record level."

"No shit," Bob interjected.

Jim, now interested in the conversation, unseen by Bob and Michael, took notes on a napkin.

"Yeah. Friday night Millard and Peele were alone. They had prime rib and seven Jack Daniels and water each. I

136

waited on them and counted. The boss ate their bill. Do you think they'd leave a tip for my help? Fuck no!"

"Shit," Bob replied. "That is a freebie."

"That ain't all. Saturday night, they're back in with Johnny Redden, the Attorney, and Ivan Slade, the engine rebuilder on the West Side. Twenty minutes later Dr. French, the social wheel, joined them. They bullshitted, sucked up the booze again and choked down lobsters. This time French picked up the bill. It was over a hundred bucks. At least Slade tipped. I scored a twenty. That's better than a poke in the ass with a sharp stick."

"That's high living," Bob said.

"Fuck. Tonight, it's Millard, Peele and Redden. The drinks don't change, but they're onto New York steaks. They got their heads down like they're thick as thieves. Redden got the tab and I got ten bucks. In two years I've worked there I've never seen Millard and Peele cough up a nickel. You can't believe the number of times the boss picked up their check. I bitched. You know what he said? He said, 'Michael, don't sweat it if you like your job, it's my money.' I've never seen anything like that in my life. Do you guys get to take people out and eat for free?"

Bob answered, "No, Michael. Maybe half price like this place, when we're on duty, but we don't get taken care of like that."

The meal finished and the bill paid, Bob and Jim said goodbye and returned to service. They patrolled aimlessly and waited for 4:30 A.M. and Taking Richmond.

* * *

The radio had been quiet for an hour and all units were available. Then, at 4:18 A.M., the silence ended.

"Taking Richmond is authorized. Proceed as directed. Say again. Taking Richmond is authorized. Assigned units, take your places. Synchronize your watches. At the radio

137

beep the time will be 4:20 A.M." A silence of about thirty seconds followed.

"Beeeep."

"Kick-off is 4:30 A.M."

Jim remembered from his academy training that when code named strike teams are directed to an arrest or make warrant searches, units do not to reply to the radio. Persons listening on the frequency must not understand the numbers of units deployed or their destination.

Bob Ortega, as passenger officer, had set his wristwatch.

Jim drove east on Anaheim, turned north a block from the Lay Back Hotel, and approached the rear through the alley with headlights turned off. He parked behind Red Price's black and white four buildings west of the hotel. Bob took the shotgun and they joined Red and partner, Zeke.

Whispering and looking at their watches, they walked to the alley door of the Lay Back Hotel. At precisely 4:30 A.M., they entered.

The rear door led to a long hallway that ran the length of the old stucco building. Jim saw other officers silently coming through the front door at the other end of the hall. Kind of touchy, he thought, we don't want to start shooting at a suspect between us.

A stairway on the right side, parallel to the hallway, led up to the second story. Jim started up the stairs.

Nothing moved. Not a sound could be heard.

Faded peeling yellow paint decorated the walls. Crummy plywood slab doors painted a blotchy yellowed white were on each side of the hallway. The old hotel smelled of a mixture of dirty laundry and stale beer and wine combined with bad body odor and old cigarette smoke.

Shabby worn and faded green carpet covered the old wooden floors. No matter how carefully and slowly Jim walked, every step caused the floor to creak. New gun in hand, slowly approached the top of the stairs.

Peeking over the top of the stairs he looked down the hallway. No officers had entered from the other end. He paused and looked back.

Bob Ortega, Zeke Walker and Red Price were looking down the first floor hallway toward the front of the building. Red looked up and motioned to the others to continue down the first floor hallway. Red, with shotgun at port arms started toward the stairs.

Jim, at the top of the stairs, moved down the hallway and sneaked past the first closed door on his left. As he looked forward, he heard a faint creak behind him. He glanced back over his left shoulder and saw a small man with his right hand extended coming from the door he'd just passed. Jim lunged down and to his right, hat falling away as he heard the crack of small caliber handgun.

He rolled to his right, leaped up from the floor and raised his revolver.

Part way up the stairs, Red heard the shot and swung the shotgun up and ready he looked toward the top of the stairs and Sweetpea appeared running right toward him. From six feet away, Red fired. The double-ought buckshot struck Sweetpea in the face at an upward angle and blew the rear of his head off.

Jim looked toward the already collapsed suspect, a mille-second too late to shoot, and was splattered across the chest and face with Sweetpea's gore. At that same moment Sweetpea collapsed like a broken water balloon.

Shouting cops came running.

Jim's shirt and tie were covered with blood, brains and mucus. It dripped from his face. Turning toward the wall, he dropped to his knees and vomited. Then he slowly stood, holstered his gun, and started to pull off his breakaway tie.

Red yelled, "Jim, did he get you?"

"Naw, just close, that's all," Jim replied. Tie in hand, he stooped over and retrieved his hat.

Bob Ortega ran up the stairs after hearing the shots and croaked, "Jesus Christ, Sweetpea's shit is all over you."

Looking up, every doorway in the hall seemed filled with faces. Sailors pulled on uniforms and girls were tying their robes as the hotel came to life.

"Come on, Jim," Red urged, grabbing his elbow, "let's get you to the john." He steered him down the hallway, past gawking whores and their johns, to a bathroom.

Jim flushed his face under a faucet, took off his uniform shirt, and tried to scrape the gore off with a pocketknife. The work merely smeared the mess.

Red exclaimed, "Jesus, did you see the hole right through your left sleeve just below the armpit? A few more inches and you would've bought the farm."

"Damn straight," Jim replied as if disgusted with the matter. Trying to conceal his shaking, he threw his shirt and tie to the floor. "That was too close."

Red picked up the clothing, rolled it up, and stuffed it in a wrinkled paper Cole's Market grocery bag, remarking, "It might be ruined, but it's still evidence. Maybe we ought to keep it."

"You keep it," Jim said as he put his hat back on his head and walked bare-chested back down the hallway. "No matter what it costs, I'll buy another one."

Homicide had already arrived. A quiet night, the Coroner's Office reportedly even announced they were on their way. The place now crawled with cops.

Jim, no longer smoking, turned and said, "Hey Red, can I bum one of your Camels? I've got to have a smoke."

"Sure", Red replied, bending over and retrieving his cigarette pack from his right sock. He shook one out, handed it to Jim, and remarked, "You did a good job, but you should've waited for me before you started down the hallway. Remember, this is combat. We can't be perfect,

140

and it's great to be lucky. You're the luckiest bastard I ever saw."

Smoke lit, Jim inhaled deeply and walked over to look at what had been Sweetpea crumpled on the floor. His skull crown nearly all gone, one remaining eye glassily peered sightlessly upward.

Yeah, Jim thought, that's the last little girl you'll destroy. Your rotten low life is over, wasted. I hope little Flora Lewis is looking down.

Christ, Jim thought, it's going to take forever to file paperwork on this fucking escapade. It's nearly dawn now. It's Tuesday morning, March 8th. Some probation this is.

Thirty-three days and it will be over.

CHAPTER FIFTEEN

Tuesday, March 8, 1960

Jim had already been home, showered, put on a suit, returned to the station, parked and headed for court. No matter how hard he tried, he couldn't stop thinking about the close call with Sweetpea. Only a few more inches and he would have bought the farm. Thinking about the close call increased his heartbeat and brought on a cold sweat. He started looking at everything around him to break away from the memories.

He cut through Lincoln Park on his way to the Jergins Trust Building. Crossing Broadway he looked to the right at the shuffleboard courts; playing had already started. He passed the old turn-of-the-century Carnegie Library in the middle of the park. Retired men wearing suits sat on oak slat park benches under the stately trees reading newspapers. An older woman pitched birdseed to milling pigeons. A drunken panhandler, seeing him coming, scurried away. He passed by the statue of Abraham Lincoln, a reminder of the influence of the Grand Army of the Republic in the early settlement of Long Beach, and then by a Civil War cannon with stacked balls at the corner of Pacific and Ocean.

There were few places in America on March 8th with weather at about sixty degrees at 9:00 AM, and Jim understood why this climate attracted retired people from the mid-west to Long Beach. They sure wouldn't have any more snow to shovel. The breeze off the ocean, the smell of salt air, and the bright sunshine combined to make a glorious morning.

He joined the half-dozen people waiting for the signal to cross Ocean Boulevard.

A small three-wheeled open electric cart driven by a bent over old man whizzed by on the sidewalk, nearly hit him and several others. It turned into the street in defiance of the red signal. Right in front of an approaching '36 Ford, the old man panicked and stopped. The sedan slammed on the brakes and skidded sideways. The old mechanical brakes were not so efficient. Angered, the driver screamed, "You old fool, you almost got killed!"

The signal now changed to green for the crosswalk. The old man continued on his way, holding his right arm high, waving his middle finger at the driver of the Ford.

Those that waited muttered about the stupidity of the old man and proceeded across Ocean Boulevard. Jim followed.

The subpoena compelled the appearance of Jim Grant and Leo Jefferson at a preliminary hearing for Ronald Albert Cole. They had arrested him for Grand Theft Auto of a '58 Volkswagen on February 26th. The hearing was required in Municipal Court to determine if sufficient cause existed to make the arrest and hold over the prisoner for trial in Superior Court.

The court appearance had been rushed, only ten calendar days after the arrest, because the new County Courthouse at 415 West Ocean had been completed. Frantic activities were underway. Schedules were accelerated and juggled, court records moved, and new courtrooms and offices organized.

Leo waited outside the courtroom door. Jim decided this presented an opportunity to funnel information to the task force and pulled Leo away from others and down the hall. He gave his notes of the conversation of Michael O'Donnel that described activities of Homicide Sergeant Bill Millard and Detective Carl Peele at the Apple Valley Steak House, and their many meetings with Johnny Redden, Ivan Slade and Dr. French.

Leo read them carefully, whistled and said, "The foxes are in the chicken house. It looks like these guys are all in cahoots."

"If Dr. French performed the abortion that killed Peggy," said Jim, "that puts Millard and Peele in a hell of a position to mess with evidence or kiss off the case."

"Yeah," Leo replied. "And good old Johnny Redden, the Attorney for the oppressed, is right there with his arm around Slade the rapist. He sure takes care of his clients."

"Do you suppose that Millard and Peele just get free drinks and free meals? Or more?"

"Shit. You've got something there," Leo answered. "The owner at the Apple Valley does that for them anyway."

Deputy District Attorney Vince Isaacson came from the courtroom, glanced at Jim and Leo, and with face flushed, put his head down and came over to where they stood. He radiated anger and sputtered, "That fucking Redden has done it again."

"Done what," Leo asked?

"That prick brought in the former owner of the VW," a steamed Isaacson ranted. "He put him on the stand and the guy swore Cole had a part ownership in the Volkswagen and had a right to drive the damn thing. He even had a written agreement from them. All fucking lies. I'm sure it's bought and paid for. He claimed he'd had an argument with Cole over the car, hid it from him and he was looking for it. He said he didn't tell Cole he was trading it in, so when he happened by and saw the car, he mistakenly took it."

"No shit," Leo responded.

"That fucking Redden even had the gall to bitch about today being Cole's birthday," Isaacson complained. "The gullible fucking judge bought it and our GTA suspect walked. He dismissed it all."

"How the hell does this happen?" Leo asked.

"I'm sure they paid off the car owner. That's how," Isaacson replied. "It's all perjury, and one fucking day I'll prove it."

144

Deputy District Attorney Isaacson, his day ruined by Attorney Johnny Redden, marched off, following people carrying boxes of files, on the way to offices in the new building.

Jim and Leo, their court day over, just looked at one another.

* * *

Sleep did not come to Jim. He rolled and tossed as he relived the shooting over and over again. For a while he lay awake, then he dozed off and woke covered with sweat. Dreaming, he again felt the gore of Sweetpea hanging from his face. For hours he tossed and in his dreams scraped blood, brains and mucus off of his shirt and tie. He awoke exhausted, rushed into the bathroom and scrubbed his face and hands. Then, slowly he shaved and showered.

As he dressed, he thought, after tonight I'll have two days off. That's good. Maybe something will provide a lift.

He just had to escape from his apartment. Just for a break in routine, he left his car behind and began to walk. Only about a mile to work, it would take twenty minutes. He didn't want to be seen in uniform and then asked to answer some fool's question. Cool and windy, he put on his loose fitting Army field jacket to conceal his police Melton jacket, uniform, leather gear and gun. He carried his hat in a paper bag in one hand and his brief case in the other. His head throbbed.

He figured he'd stop at the Olympia Café, about the half way to work, and grab a sandwich. Still only 7:15 PM, he had plenty of time. Depressed, he didn't feel like hurrying. In fact, he just wanted the world to slow down.

The Olympia, across Ocean Boulevard from the Civic Auditorium on the northeast corner of Long Beach Boulevard, did a brisk business twenty-four hours a day. Locals came in before and after movies at the Ocean

145

Boulevard theaters. Tourists came and went from the nearby Pike and Rainbow Pier, and sailors loved the place.

Jim sat at the far end of the counter on the east wall with his briefcase and paper bag near his feet. From the corner, he could see everyone in the place. Booths lined the windows facing the streets. The owners were Greek and all of their salads were superb.

He ordered a Greek salad with coffee and glanced restlessly at a discarded newspaper as he waited for his order.

Alone, Tokay Rainwater walked into the restaurant. Jim waved at her and she came over to the counter and took a stool beside him.

"You look like shit," Tokay stated. "What's the matter, you tired?"

"It's been a long week. Sometimes it's a bitch to work nights, go to court and sleep days. After tonight I'm off and I'll get some rest. How are you doing?"

"I'm going back to Anchorage," Tokay said.

The waitress arrived, and Tokay ordered a burger and Coke.

"Is something wrong?" Jim asked.

"Yeah. Clarey came to my room in the Stillman Hotel about an hour ago. He gave me the evil eye and told me I was easy to find. He said he heard I got drunk the other night and started blabbing about Peggy. The fat fuck said I'd better shut up and leave town. He got nasty, said he's speaking for others and he means it."

"He scare you?" Jim asked.

"Yeah. Damn straight. I just called my sister to wire me money. She'll send it to Western Union on Friday night after she gets paid. I'll take the Greyhound to Seattle Saturday and then catch the ferry to Anchorage. I'm going back to my village. I sure don't want to go, but I'll be safe. They come looking for me and I'll use a rifle and blow their balls off."

146

Jim studied her thoughtfully, and replied, "Maybe it's better if you do get away for a while. But, I'd still like you to call me Saturday morning before you buy a ticket. If you go, I'd like a number where I can reach you."

"Jim, I'm not coming back. Those fuckers will get me."

The waitress returned to the counter and placed their orders in front of them.

"How about if they're in the slammer?" Jim asked. "Would you come back then?"

"Sure," Tokay answered. "But, I'm not going to testify. I'm no fool."

"If they're in jail," Jim continued, "the District Attorney's Office would pay to bring you back and give you a hotel room while you testify. That's a free trip. When it's over it won't do them any good to try to get you. And they'll be looking at a long vacation with the State of California. It'll be all over for them."

Tokay thoughtfully munched on her burger and replied, "Maybe, Jim, just maybe."

"Give me the phone number. You can make the decision when I call."

Tokay wrote a number on a paper napkin and pushed it over to him.

"You keep this, Jim. I don't want it anybody else's hands."

Small talk continued until 9:15 PM and Jim went on to work.

* * *

Exhausted after the events of the last twenty-four hours, Jim left the squad meeting and loaded his gear in the assigned police car while Bob checked them into service.

The wind picked up, rain came, palm frowns blew and weather pushed aside everything. Finally, near dawn, the

147

storm passed, a few billowy white clouds remained and it became clear, cold and calm.

Jim took the wheel at 6:00 AM and drove slowly down Long Beach Boulevard from Willow Street. Traffic picked up, pedestrians appeared and buses stopped for those on their way to work.

At Anaheim Street, Bob asked Jim to check out a guy on a bus bench. A big white dude with a cowboy hat, long sleeved denim shirt and Levi's with a big silver rodeo belt buckle sat on the bench. 6′ 2″ and 240 pounds, and buffed out like a weightlifter. He also looked like he just got out of the joint. Men lifted weights in prison and this guy looked like he had muscles in his shit.

When released these ex-cons look like they belong on the cover of a muscle magazine. When they have been out a while, the equipment isn't as available, they don't keep in shape and they lose tone fast.

Jim parked fifteen feet from the bench and both officers got out of the car and approached together. Jim, with arms crossed over his jacket front, came warily from the driver's side and Bob, hands at his side, from the passenger's side. The big cowboy stood up and faced the officers as they walked up.

Jim saw his right hand move back slightly. Then he saw a .45 automatic in his right rear pocket.

With his left hand, like a rattlesnake striking, Jim grabbed the cowboy's right lower forearm. At the same instant, as quick as a flash, Jim swung his .357 from under his jacket into the cowboy's face.

"Move a muscle and you die, asshole," Jim yelled as he pushed the barrel of the gun into the cowboy's left nostril.

Bob suddenly saw the cowboy's right hand at his hip pocket, held vice-like by Jim, resting on the butt of a .45 automatic. Bob frantically clawed at his own revolver to cover the suspect.

Jim spoke again quietly and slowly, "You're big and you're strong and if you move a muscle I'm going to blow your fucking head off. Let go of the gun now." Jim cocked the Magnum. The end of the barrel still rested in the cowboy's left nostril.

The big guy quivered, whimpered, released his hold on the .45 automatic, lost his bowels and peed his pants. The stench enveloped the officers.

"Don't shoot, don't shoot," whined the big cowboy as he was pushed to the ground, his gun taken and handcuffs applied.

Jim inspected the Colt Government .45 automatic. Fully loaded, a round rested in the chamber, it had been cocked with the safety off. He released the magazine and put it in his pocket, ejected the chambered round and put it in his pocket and then shoved the now empty automatic into his gun-belt.

It only took another minute to load him into the car, with Bob riding behind Jim next to the prisoner, and head for the station. They went to the station fast with the police car windows venting the foul smell. In five minutes they had their prisoner seated on the bench at the booking desk while they filled out paperwork.

Old Sergeant Chuck White climbed their case.

"God damn it," White roared, "you guys are making a habit of bringing shitters into my booking desk. This crap has to stop. Next time one of you idiots is going to keep the prisoner outside until the paperwork is finished. Then you can hurry him through and up to jail."

They quickly completed the work, delivered him to jail and went in to finish the reports.

The cowboy had copped out. He had just been released after doing ten years in prison in Arizona for attempted murder of a police officer.

Reports completed, Bob said, "Thanks. I didn't see that fucker go for his gun. I've never seen anybody react faster. You saved my ass."

Jim nodded, looked at the clock and noticed it was 8:00 AM and March 9th. He replied, "I just saw it coming and I already had my gun out of the cross draw holster in my hand under my jacket. He didn't know I was ready."

"You sure were ready," Bob exclaimed.

"Let's go home," Jim said. "Thank God I'm off for two days. I've got to get some sleep."

* * *

Jim slept restlessly, awakened, drank coffee, read the paper and cleaned up and dressed to meet the McKenzies as promised.

The Pacific Coast Club, just east of the Villa Riviera, catered to the wealthy families of Long Beach. In 1920's Spanish-Moorish style, it towered six stories over Ocean Boulevard. The dining facilities and halls were at the Ocean Boulevard level, guest rooms in the tower, and the beachfront rested three stories below. Part beach club, dinner house, spa, and athletic center, it partnered with the Los Angeles Athletic Club providing membership privileges for the elite.

In sport coat and tie, Jim came through the front door early at five minutes before 7:00 PM. This first visit to the Pacific Coast Club made him feel special. He looked about in admiration.

"May I help you, sir?" asked a tuxedoed Negro waiter.

"Yes, please," replied Jim. "I'm meeting Attorney and Mrs. McKenzie for dinner."

"Yes sir, right this way," directed the waiter. He led him through a Spanish-Moorish style portico, across the dining room, and to a table overlooking the beach. He pulled out a chair for Jim and he sat down.

"The McKenzie's called and said they will be just a few minutes late, Mr. Grant. May I have a waiter bring some refreshments?"

"Thank you, I'll wait," Jim replied. He thought, wow, the maitre d' knew I was expected. He even knew my name.

Looking out at the view, lights from boats loomed in the distance. The florescence of the surf sparkled as the waves fell in rhythm with the curvature of the beach. The mountains of Catalina Island loomed under a full moon.

When they'd built the Club, Long Beach claimed to be the center of world motion picture production. Major studios came, and then fled to Hollywood in the mid-1920s. Silent screen star Fatty Arbuckle and others lived in stately homes with facilities stepped down the bluff. Homes at the top, pools on the mid-level and stables at the beach. They swam and rode their horses in the surf. They'd all dined and danced here.

Interior floors were of polished oak, Persian carpets had been carefully placed and the huge wooden beams artfully painted in the Moorish style. Jim could just visualize Rudolph Valentino, with his cape, walking into the room to the music of the lone pianist in the corner.

Jim stood as the maitre d' ushered Craig and Debra McKenzie, still wearing her pearls, to the table. She gave Jim a hug, introduced Craig and they shook hands. Jim was pleased at the genuine cordiality of the greeting.

Craig "The Gray Wolfe" McKenzie looked impressive. White, mid-40s, he stood 5' 10" and weighed about 165 pounds. Average sized, with eyes of light blue, and a full head of gray hair combed back, he looked distinguished. And tough.

The gracious maitre d' fussed over them until they were seated. Debra ordered a Daiquiri, Craig ordered a Haig & Haig Scotch on the rocks, and insisted Jim have the same.

"Thanks again for helping Debra," Craig stated.

"Yes, you're my hero," Debra said, smiling at him.

151

"I was just in the right place at the right moment. The rest was training and duty," Jim replied, embarrassed by the praise.

"I thought you were a businessman when I saw you," laughed Debra. "You stepped out of the way and I thought, is he scared of that jerk? Then you tripped him and he landed right on his face. Smack. I heard him hit. You were all over him. It was beautiful."

"I didn't want to wrestle him and ruin my suit," Jim admitted, grinning.

"And that *suited* the bum," punned Craig.

They all laughed.

Drinks arrived. Craig insisted that they celebrate with lobster.

They talked about their different backgrounds, schools, the Army (Craig served in the 1st Infantry Division in Korea and came home a Captain), their interests and the future. Craig and Debra proudly showed pictures of their high school age children. Jim expressed his anxiety about police work and probation, which would end April 12$^{th.}$

Debra ordered the desert, selecting crème' brule' for all. There could be none better; they devoured it.

Jim had finally relaxed. Contented, filled with fine food and three scotches, his evening came to a happy close. These were good friends. He liked that.

Craig and Debra lived on Treasure Island in Naples. They insisted that he come to dinner. He couldn't refuse. They set a date at their home for 6:00 PM, Wednesday, April 13th. It would be the day after the end of probation.

Craig laughed and said, "We'll party. I have the Haig & Haig. You'll be off probation and your attorney will be with you. That's me. From now on, I'm your attorney. Remember that!"

CHAPTER SIXTEEN

Thursday, March 10, 1960

Jim went to bed at 2:00 AM and slept through the night. He didn't even dream. Awake and refreshed he thought about the dinner with Craig and Debra McKenzie, the great time and the medicinal value of Haig & Haig. Up early, at 2:00 PM on Thursday, March 10th, after sleeping twelve hours, he felt wonderful and looked forward to another evening off.

He had just finished making a liverwurst sandwich with Dijon mustard and a slice of onion and was pouring a large glass of milk when the phone rang.

"Jim, this is Captain Green. How are you?"

"Just fine, sir!"

"Good. You had a hell of a week. First Sweetpea and then you and Leo captured that Arizona cowboy. All of it was good work."

"Thank you, sir."

"Leo Jefferson reported the information about the Apple Valley meetings. That was important; it can't be a coincidence and it makes Millard and Peele look dirty."

"Yes sir."

"We're searching Clarey's apartment Friday night at midnight. When that goes down everybody in town will know, so you might as well be there. I'll have the Patrol Watch Commander special assign you and your partner to help. We also plan to pick up Dr. August French at about the same time. He's supposed to be at a party at the Petroleum Club and the Sheriff's crew will wait for him to leave, hopefully after Clary's already named him. The doctor will probably be tired and have a few drinks in him. Joel Patterson and Clay Landsberg will pick him up and take him to Lakewood Sheriff's Station and sweat him."

"That's good."

153

"Jim, are you ready for Clarey?"

"Yes sir, I can't wait."

"Is there anything new?" Captain Green asked.

"Yes sir. I saw Tokay last night. Clarey hunted her down at the Stillman Hotel, threatened her and told her to get out of town. She's really scared. She's going back to Anchorage."

"We might need her to testify," said Captain Green.

"I asked her to call me Saturday morning before she buys a ticket."

"That's good thinking."

"Is there anything else I should do?"

"No. I'll be at Clarey's Friday night," Captain Green said. "Then we'll know where this is going and who we'll roll up."

"Yes sir."

Off the telephone, Jim leaned back and took a big bite of his liverwurst sandwich then washed it down with milk. What a feast.

* * *

Jim spent the afternoon running errands. He went to the bank, the cleaners, stopped at the market and then drove home. He unloaded the car, put the cleaning and groceries away, cleaned and vacuumed.

Thursday evenings were suitable for casual dress. He put on Levis, navy socks, cordovan penny loafers, a tan long sleeve shirt with a button down collar, a cordovan belt and his 2" off duty Smith & Wesson in a shoulder holster. He covered the gun with a lightweight navy waist length jacket.

Hungry again, Jim drove to the Mexico City Restaurant near Orange Avenue and South Street in North Long Beach. A local place, with the finest shredded roast beef enchiladas in the world. Jim ordered, feasted on guacamole and taco

154

chips and, while eating, washed it all down with a Lucky Lager beer. Then he smothered the enchiladas in salsa and devoured the mess along with the beans and rice. He paid the $1.80 bill and left a thirty-five cent tip.

Curious about the Apple Valley Steak House, he decided a visit would be in order. He drove to Broadway and Alamitos, parked around the corner to save the valet parking tip and walked back to the south facing entrance.

Several groups were arriving at 7:00 PM and when Jim came through the door he noticed that most were older people, from their late 30's through 60's. An affluent crowd, he recognized several judges, a number of attorneys, a bail bondsman, a local doctor and a Long Beach Police captain.

The end of the horseshoe bar faced the door. An older portly gentleman wearing a gray business suit, with combed back gray hair and tired blue eyes seemed to greet everyone by name. Jim slipped past to the west side of the bar, sat down and tried to be inconspicuous. There were only a few open stools. He ordered another Lucky Lager, sipped the beer slowly and watched.

The piano player sitting west of the bar took requests. He played well and everyone seemed to know him. All of the restaurant tables were covered with white linen tablecloths. The waiters wore black trousers, white shirts, black vests and bow ties.

Booths lined the walls behind the piano and an exit led to the adjacent alley. There were tables in a dining room east of the bar and a doorway opened to a private room on the south front of the building. When the door opened Jim saw men playing cards.

Jim asked for a menu and looked it over. His mouth watered when he saw ½ pound Shrimp Cocktails Supreme for $1.75, abalone for $4.00, prime rib (the cattleman's cut) for $3.75 and lobster for $4.75. He noted that bar whiskey was seventy-five cents. Prices are a bit high, he thought, but it's a good place to bring a date.

He sipped his beer and looked around at the other patrons seated at the bar. Directly across the horseshoe bar, fifteen feet away, sat Ronald Albert Cole, the GTA suspect they captured in the Volkswagen. Since he'd never seen Jim out of police uniform, Cole looked past, not even recognizing him.

Jim did his best to remain composed and not look directly at the car thief. He glanced over from time to time and got the impression Cole had a companion seated to his left. Jim asked the bartender about the location of the men's room, left his beer on the bartop and walked in that direction, which took him around the bar and right past Cole and his friend. After a few minutes he returned from the men's room getting a second good look. He thought his little walk went unnoticed.

Cole's male friend on the barstool looked young, maybe twenty-five, appeared short and portly and had a brown crew cut. Jim felt sure he'd remember him.

He waited another half hour and thought it smart to get out and left.

* * *

Jim drove east on Ocean Boulevard to the spot where single gals gathered on Thursday nights, the Anchorage Bar on 62nd Place half way down the Peninsula. Had he gone farther on, the Peninsula becomes a dead end. This spit of land between Alamitos Bay and the beach has very short streets leading north to the Bay and south to the beach. Almost resort-like, homes and apartments fronted on the water. In summer, many dwellings converted to beach rentals and the residents traveled abroad. During winter young schoolteachers, college students and naval officers in groups of two, three and four rented the apartments.

At the Anchorage, Thursday nights were legendary as girls gathered to look for dates. That attracted the guys, including naval officers, attorneys, cops, firefighters, lifeguards, college professors, college students, and everybody else.

Arriving before 8:00 PM guaranteed a parking place and a seat. Later meant a four or five block walk and standing, drink in hand, in the crowded bar. Standing wasn't bad though, because it provided a greater chance to mingle.

Jim parked a half block away, crossed to the west side of 62nd Place, entered and sat at an open table in the front of the room. Across from him a hood hovered above a fire ring where natural gas burned continuously. The walls and ceiling were pickled pine and old nautical pieces and pictures hung everywhere. A red stained and waxed concrete floor completed the picture. Not fancy, just functional and nobody cared. They were at the beach. Tap beer and mixed drinks were the fare. Customers didn't even read the menu in the Anchorage.

Jim ordered a Budweiser on tap. A generous mug promptly appeared on the table. He handed a dollar to the grinning young waitress and received fifty cents in change; he gave her a big tip – twenty-five cents.

"Hey kid," yelled an older big guy, waving a hand that held an unlit cigar.

"Hi!" Jim automatically replied, without recognizing him. Then he remembered it was Jeff Lewis, the day officer that helped him when he caught the guy that snatched Debra McKenzie's purse.

"Grant, what are you doing here?" Jeff asked as he came to the table.

"Just checking out the pretty ladies."

"You've come to the right place. I've been coming here for fifteen years. I'm still checking them out".

"Sit down, join me." People now were rapidly filling the room.

157

"Nah. A gal I know will be here in a minute. Just wanted to say hello," Jeff remarked.

"Hey, Jeff. Jim," somebody yelled.

They both looked toward the door as Bill Burns, the Deputy City Prosecutor, came toward them. In his early thirties, he stood 5' 10", carried a little too much weight, wore his sandy hair in a short crew cut and always displayed a huge grin. Burns always wore suits, but tonight he looked like a beach bum, wearing a raggedy old Hawaiian shirt, sun bleached and paint stained jeans, with a few holes here and there, and old paint splattered deck shoes. Everything looked clean, but funky.

"Bill, you been working on your boat?" Jeff asked.

"Nope," laughed Bill. "But I want the girls here to ask me if I've been working on my boat. That's my scheme. I'm an eccentric rich guy with a boat."

"Sit down," said Jim, gesturing toward the empty seat.

"You bet, you've got a table. That's a good deal," replied Bill.

Jeff Lewis saw his friend come in, excused himself, and joined her. Jim and Bill chatted amiably as they watched people enter.

My God, thought Jim, how does a guy pick a babe from among so many beautiful chicks? There were blondes, redheads and brunettes. At that moment a slender gal with glossy black hair walked by, glanced his way, and tossed her hair slightly with a turn of the head. A beauty among beauties; was her glance an invitation? Too late, another guy with beer glass in hand suddenly appeared next to her and started a conversation.

The ladies were short and tall, dark and fair, beautiful and cute, twenties and thirties, with short and long hair and they were almost all available. What a bazaar. Jim couldn't stop looking. They were all about the place, talking to each other, talking to guys, sipping drinks and enjoying Thursday night out.

Jim stayed near Bill Burns and watched him work the cuties with his boat stories. He talked to several girls and nursed his beer to make it stretch. While he spotted several that spurred his interest, he hadn't hooked up. Nonetheless, he watched the action and enjoyed himself.

Midnight came and passed. Cops on the graveyard shift were just awakening at midnight. Jim felt fresh and alert and noticed most other people were fading and leaving. The crowd thinned.

Bill Burns had a little petite brunette in tow, a nurse. Jim overheard that she loved kids and worked in pediatrics at St. Mary's Hospital. They left hand-in-hand.

Only a dozen people remained at 1:30 AM. Jeff Lewis, still there, talked with three guys on the other side of the room and it appeared to be a heated argument. Jim watched, then decided Jeff could handle anything that came his way. In his late forties, he had a lot of experience that combined with his 6'2" in height and 220 pounds of muscle. His hands looked like hams. Still, he looked a little tipsy.

Then the tone escalated and the hackles stood up on the back of Jim's neck. He knew it would be a fight. The confrontation continued, challenges thrown and accepted and they all started for the door. Three of them would be against Jeff.

Jim followed them. Outside, they walked toward the nearly empty parking lot south of the bar. The three who wanted to kick Jeff's ass paid no attention to Jim. By walking behind and being screened from Jeff by the others, he appeared to be a spectator. No one else followed.

The tallest, a lean slender fellow, stood closest to Jeff and loudly challenged him, "Three of us against one, you big fucking cop. We're going to stomp your ass!"

"It's three against two," Jim said.

All three turned to face him. When the tall lean guy looked away, Jeff threw a powerful huge right hand. It hit home – on the tip of the jaw with a crack. He flew eight feet across the lot and went down in a heap.

His friends ran.

"You made that a short fight," Jeff said. "I don't think I could've handled them without your help."

"Hell," Jim replied, "I didn't do anything but watch."

"Bullshit, you made the difference. I owe you."

"Don't you think we ought to get out of here?" asked Jim. "Somebody is going to call the cops. This could get embarrassing."

They watched as the would-be assailant stumbled up from the ground, looked toward them fearfully, held his jaw and staggered toward Ocean Boulevard.

"Yeah! Let's split," Jeff said. "I'm on vacation. How about meeting for breakfast at Hof's Hut in the Shore?"

"Sure," Jim replied and started toward his car.

* * *

Second Street in Belmont Shore seemed empty at five minutes before 2:00AM. The only cars remaining were in front of Hof's Hut. California law compelled bars to close at 2:00 AM and many of the late crowd from Belmont Shore's gin mills migrated in for an after hours meal and coffee.

Jim arrived first, saw a few booths open on the left side of the room opposite the counter and took one. Jeff came through the door a minute later and joined him.

In just a moment the waitress had brought carafes of coffee, poured them each a cup. They both ordered patty sausage, with eggs over easy and "those potatoes" (a combination of fried potatoes, onions and bell peppers) with English muffins.

"Word has it that you're doing good, kid. I can see why. You've got some street smarts," Jeff said.

160

"Thanks. I just try to look, see what's there and act without offering them time to think. It's a paratrooper thing"

"That worked tonight. You noticed, I caught that prick looking away and knocked him on his ass. The rule is to win."

"He dropped like a turd from a horse's ass."

"Enough of the horse-shitting," laughed Jeff. "I like you and owe you, so I want to drop some information that might be personally beneficial."

"What's that?"

"You've got enemies, kid."

"Who?" Jim asked, curious and unaware anyone would be out to get him.

"Those pompous pricks in Homicide, Millard and Peele."

"How so?" Jim inquired with new concern.

"I don't know what they're up to," Jeff replied. "But I overheard them the other night at the Apple Valley. They had their heads down and were grumbling about you sticking your nose into one of their cases. They were pissed and they were serious."

Jim recalled the note Captain Green's secretary left out. They knew! This was not an idle warning; it was cause for serious concern. Jim had an empty feeling in the pit of his stomach.

The waitress returned and shoved the steaming food, smelling heavenly, in front of them. They attacked it ravenously.

"Thanks for the warning."

"Watch you ass, Jim. I ain't shittin'. Watch your ass."

CHAPTER SEVENTEEN

Friday, March 11, 1960

Jim looked forward to helping serve the search warrant. He hoped convincing evidence would be found that tied Ben Clarey's apartment to Peggy's abortion death. Early for squad meeting, at 10:00 PM, Jim walked into the police bungalow.

Big Sergeant Frank Gonzales already sat at the tall briefing room table, books and papers spread out, as he prepared for the coming meeting. Jim liked him, considered him friendly, hard working, demanding and honest. Popular with the troops, Gonzales supported those that worked hard and made life miserable for those that were lazy.

The sergeant glanced up, reached among his papers, retrieved a memorandum and pushed it across the table.

"Glad you came in early, Grant. This is for you and Ortega. There'll be no Unit One tonight. You're excused from the squad meeting. You're special detailed to dicks on a confidential deal. Have a black and white ready and grab Bob when he comes in and then report to Captain Green's office. Don't say anything to anybody and don't check in on the radio; just slip out."

"Yes, Sergeant."

Jim grabbed a set of car keys, carried his gear out, checked the vehicle and moved it alongside the station. He caught Ortega on his way in and advised him of the assignment. Ortega threw his gear in the car and they went to Captain Green's office.

Jim knocked and Leo Jefferson opened the door and motioned them inside. Captain Green and Sergeant Joel Patterson were looking at a construction blueprint on the desk.

Two other men Jim knew from the police academy were waiting. Criminalist Simon Goldstein handled the classes on

162

crime laboratory procedures, and Identification Technician Henry Holcolm taught crime scene searches and fingerprint recovery. They only worked together on major crimes and used a specially equipped van.

Captain Green, waving the search warrant, said, "Men, we're going to search an apartment. It belongs to a guy named Ben Clarey. We hope to find bloodstains to help establish that a young girl died there. At the same time we'll look for fingerprints that'll show who has been there. The reason I'm not saying more is that we strongly believe people inside this department may be interfering with this case. I've got to order you to discuss nothing you see or hear tonight. This is so serious that an information leak could cost your job. The secrecy must be absolute. For that reason we'll stay off the police radio. Army surplus walkie-talkies will be in each car; we'll only talk with each other. Does everybody understand?"

The Captain looked slowly around as each person nodded affirmatively.

"Okay, Patterson, they're yours. Tell them how we'll proceed."

Sergeant Patterson called them over to the desk and showed them blueprints of the floor plan of the apartment building. He explained that Clarey lived in a fashionable third floor walkup with an ocean view on Alamitos Avenue. A half block north of Ocean Boulevard, the building rested on the northwest corner of Medio and Alamitos. There were two apartments at each level. The apartments had two bedrooms and two baths with stairs accessing the third floor units from the front and rear. A top unit belonged to Clarey.

The sergeant then produced a detailed map of the city block bisected by east/west and north/south alleys which crossed one another in the middle. A Department of Motor Vehicle records search revealed Clarey had a Volkswagen. Patterson pointed on the map to the location of his garage on the east side of the alley. He told them Clarey kept his car garaged with the door down so it would be impossible to tell if he were home.

Sergeant Patterson told Ortega and Grant to park their police car just west around the corner in the intersecting alley. Next, he asked that Goldstein and Holcolm put the crime scene van a block west, next to a pay phone. He said Captain Green would be waiting there with his plain car. The Korean War surplus olive drab walkie-talkie radios were passed out for each vehicle. Patterson and Jefferson would be out front in a plain car. All would monitor their walkie-talkies.

At midnight sharp, Patterson and Jefferson, hoping Clarey would be home, would go to the front and knock. Ortega and Grant would already have slipped up the rear stairs to the back door. Captain Green would call the apartment simultaneously, from a pay phone. If no one answered, they would return to their cars and watch the alley until Clarey returned. Patterson expected him to come into the alley from the south to approach his garage. On a signal, by walkie-talkie, from the front of the building, the black and white would pull forward and block the north end of the alley. Patterson and Jefferson would come from the south and block his rear.

Patterson then asked if there were questions. No one spoke.

"I want to caution you all one more time," Captain Green stated. "No matter what occurs tonight, it'll not be discussed outside this group. You won't tell other police officers and you will not tell your wives. Am I understood?"

They all nodded.

"Good," said Green. "Let's get rolling."

They all synchronized their watches, left the office and drove to their appointed locations.

Grant and Ortega were in their assigned alley position at 11:30, lights off and walkie-talkie turned on.

"Jim, you know all about this caper, don't you?" Bob asked.

"Yeah, I do," Jim admitted, "but I swear it's real secret and I can't tell you about it."

"I understand; Green's a straight shooter. If he says to keep it under wraps, I will. But, when it's all over I want to hear about it from A to Z."

"That's fair."

At midnight, the front and rear entrances covered, Patterson and Jefferson knocked and the telephone rang inside. No one answered the door or the phone and they retreated to their vehicles. The wait began

Finally, at 2:30 AM, the walkie-talkie whispered, "A candy apple red Volkswagen just came around the corner. It's turning into the alley. Get ready. Block him."

Jim already had the car started; he accelerated, slid into the alley, skidded to a stop and turned on his reds. Patterson and Jefferson, headlights on the VW, blocked the rear. Jim and Bob, guns in hand, scrambled from their car.

"Police," yelled Patterson. "Come out of the car with your hands up."

"Don't shoot, don't shoot," exclaimed the little 5'3 pear shaped guy with a brown crew cut, as he stepped from the car into the lit up alley. "I didn't do anything."

Jim recognized Clarey. He had seen him in the Apple Valley seated next to Ronald Albert Cole. Bells went off and he thought, this no coincidence. He's with a VW thief, he drives a VW, and Slade's shop paints VWs. Shit, mused Jim, how long does it take a guy to get a clue. The VW thing had been sitting under his nose all the time.

An apartment across the alley faced the garages. The commotion drew people outside. Curious, they asked questions. A good police strategy is to leave an area when bystanders have gathered unless it is absolutely necessary to stay. Simply put, why prolong a situation that could result

165

in confrontations with curiosity seekers. The officers moved quickly

Leo Jefferson patted Clarey down, found no weapons, and put him in handcuffs. Sergeant Patterson asked Jim to search Clarey's car and put it in the garage. He searched the car, found nothing, drove it into the garage and returned to the police car.

Leo Jefferson placed Clarey in the plain car and they drove away to let things return to normal. Jim and Bob followed.

Sergeant Patterson, via walkie-talkie, arranged to meet with Captain Green. They all gathered on a darkened lot where Green and the crime scene van had parked. Clarey looked like he'd been drinking and appeared scared. Patterson turned on the dome light in the detective car, showed Clarey the search warrant and read it entirely. Clarey whimpered, but said nothing.

Jim still had the key-ring to the VW. The apartment keys were on the same ring. They convoyed back to the apartment, parked quietly, brought Clarey along, and walked up the stairs.

The telephone inside the apartment rang while Sergeant Patterson tried the key; the door opened and they entered. The phone stopped ringing. The drapes were closed, lights were turned on and they pushed Clarey, still whimpering, into a living room chair. Captain Green took the phone off the hook and left it lying on the end table.

Grant and Ortega were told to watch Clarey and the search began.

Henry Holcolm went first, meticulously searching for fingerprints. He dusted, used a flashlight to examine results, and lifted prints as he moved from the living room straight back through a hallway, to a bath on the right, a bedroom on the left, and a second bedroom and bath in the rear.

The Criminalist, Simon Goldstein, followed on his hands and knees and carefully combed back carpet fiber in

166

his search for bloodstains. He used masking tape in the hallway at several locations to mark possible discoveries. Then, in the front side bedroom he marked an area of about four square feet with masking tape.

Captain J. C. Green patiently listened as Sgt. Patterson interrogated Clarey.

Leo Jefferson stood with Grant and Ortega while the search went on. Jim motioned to Ortega to watch Clarey and pulled Leo aside. He told him of the association of Clarey and their VW thief, Ronald Albert Cole. Then he described Clarey's VW and the painting of Volkswagens at Slade's place. Leo whistled and said he'd work on the auto theft angle.

By 3:45 AM the search had been completed, the area diagramed, and samples of carpet cut and removed from several probable locations. Criminalist Goldstein unpacked gear in the kitchen and began to work on the counter with his microscope.

At 4:30 AM, Goldstein poked his head out of the door, motioned for Captain Green and Sergeant Patterson and they went into the kitchen. In a few minutes they returned.

Patterson sat down opposite a quivering Clarey. He calmly described the investigation, told about the letter naming Redden as the coordinator, Clarey's apartment as the abortion site and Doctor August French as the physician. The letter had brought them to Clarey's apartment.

He explained that the search warrant had been lawfully obtained and that bloodstains just found had been identified as probably belonging to Peggy Evans.

Clarey burst into tears and talked and talked and talked. He accused Ivan Slade of raping Peggy and making her pregnant, Johnny Redden of organizing the abortion and Doctor French of bungling the job and killing her.

He said French sedated Peggy at about 2:00 PM and did the work in the front bedroom. He left after telling Clarey it would take about four hours for her to recover and then she could go home. It was over by 2:45 PM and she looked okay. At about 7:00 PM, he went in to see her, shook her arm and realized she was dead.

Clarey described his panic, several telephone calls to Slade and Redden, and that Redden finally arrived with a sleeping bag. They cleaned Peggy, put her in the bag and waited until the Pike closed.

At 1:30 AM Redden parked his car in front with the deck lid unlocked. They carried her downstairs, put her in the trunk and then took her to the roller coaster, removed the bag and left her.

Henry Holcolm had brought a manual typewriter. He took notes of Clarey's disclosures and typed a complete statement. Then Clarey made corrections on all of the copies, initialed each correction and signed all three copies.

Captain Grant directed Bob Ortega to watch Clarey and he took Jim Grant, Leo Jefferson and Sergeant Joel Patterson to the back bedroom.

Captain Green closed the door, turned, held both thumbs up, and spoke. "You did good work tonight. We have hard evidence and Clarey's admissions will be a big help.

"This still won't be a walk in the park. While Clarey named Ivan Slade and Johnny Redden and Dr. French, no evidence or statements implicate Millard and Peele. We need to get warrants for Slade, Redden and French. When we do that Millard and Peele will know they're in harms way and take cover. That makes continued secrecy important.

"Another thing, we're going to have a tough time keeping Clarey, an accessory to the death, in custody. If he gets out I'd bet that he'll tell them he blabbed."

The meeting over, they went back to the living room and prepared to leave. Goldstein and Holcolm were finished, their gear loaded in the van, and they went home.

The kitchen clock read 6:00 AM and Captain Green told Grant and Ortega to book Clarey for investigation of a felony. They were only to make a one page cursory report providing no information and cite the Captain as having directed the arrest. Captain Green took two copies of Clarey's statement and Sergeant Patterson took the remaining copy and they went to the station.

Jim and Bob walked into booking with Clarey in tow at 6:15 AM.

Sergeant Patterson and Leo Jefferson hurried into booking and called Jim outside. Bob Ortega stayed with the prisoner.

"The Sheriff's thing turned to shit," exclaimed Sergeant Patterson shaking his head. "French was cut loose."

"What happened? Jim asked.

"French left the Petroleum Club early, so they arrested him at about 11:15 PM and went to Lakewood Station and tried to sweat him. They gave him details about the abortion and he still wouldn't talk. He yelled for his attorney and they let him call Redden. Then Redden called a Deputy Chief of the Sheriff's Department that he's known for years. A drinking buddy, the guy called Lakewood and they let French go."

"Why didn't they call us?"

"They did," responded Patterson, "and we were off the radio."

"What now?"

"They have a bondsman waiting, writ in hand, to take out Clarey. He'll be released as soon as his fingerprints clear our record bureau."

Like Sergeant Patterson said, Clarey beat them out the door.

CHAPTER EIGHTEEN

Saturday, March 12, 1960

Jim awoke well rested but frustrated. He reflected on the accomplishments of the night before. They had successfully searched Clarey's place, discovered bloodstains, obtained his damning admission, and then booked him. Redden got Clary out of jail fast, but how could they refute the evidence and get themselves out of trouble? They had nothing implicating Millard and Peele, but Jim felt confident and believed it a job well done.

Still, when Tokay Rainwater called, he couldn't convince her to stay in town. She was scared, warned him that Clarey was out of jail, and believed Slade would kill to cover his tracks. She left for Seattle.

Restless, Jim decided to grab a bite to eat and kill some time on his way to work. He put his field jacket on over his uniform, stowed his gear in the car, and at 6:00 PM he drove up Orange Avenue through a forest of wooden oil derricks onto Signal Hill.

When the oil boom erupted in the early 1920s, the producers incorporated the tiny town as a separate city to avoid Long Beach regulations and taxes. Surrounded by Long Beach, the oil kept coming and Signal Hill somehow kept the small town atmosphere.

He turned right on Willow Street and then into an oiled dirt lot on the northwest corner of Cherry Avenue. Curley's parking lot was nearly full, an operating wooden derrick in the center. He drove slowly past old pickups and an occasional new Cadillac until a space appeared.

An oil-field bar and eatery with a wild reputation, Curley's made the best chili in town. If oil field roughnecks and drinkers didn't bother you, the deal made the drive worthwhile. During happy hour, fifty cents bought you all the chili you could eat.

The people were fun. There were oil millionaires and down-and-out drunks and everything in between. They all knew one another and believed in hard work and the reliability of a personal promise. This was the way of the oil patch people.

Jim threaded his way through the crowd to the bar and ordered a Coke and chili. The bartender took his dollar bill, popped the cap off the familiar hourglass shaped bottle, grabbed an empty chili bowl, dropped thirty-five cents in change on the bar (fifteen cents for the Coke and fifty cents for the chili) and pushed it all toward him. Jim tipped him a quarter and headed for the chili pot on the north wall.

He dipped a ladle into the steaming brew, filled his bowl, heaped fresh chopped onions over the top, shoved a handful of packaged Saltine crackers into his jacket pocket, grabbed a soup spoon and a large paper napkin, juggled the Coke in the crook of his elbow and headed for an empty stool in the corner. Habit now, he always wanted his back to the wall. Corners were even better.

As he ate, he talked sports with a friendly tall, thin, bald old guy, probably in his early seventies, named Curley. With that name, Jim thought he might own the place. He didn't, yet knew everybody. They shared ideas about the Dodgers' possibilities for the coming year. They discussed Ron Fairly, who came from Long Beach and played first base, and then talked pitching.

Across the room, a familiar face headed for the chili pot. An automobile dealer named Greg Henderson, he'd seen him around with a few of the motorcycle officers. He had a car lot on Anaheim Street. Greg spotted him and came over carrying a beer and his chili.

"You work Watch One and your name's Grant, isn't it?" he asked.

"Yeah," he replied, surprised to have been recognized. "Aren't you Greg Henderson?"

"Yup, that's me."

"I've seen you around. You belong to the Motor Patrol Association (a support group for the motorcycle officers) and hang out with some of the guys."

"Yeah, it's a great bunch."

Old Curley stepped away and drifted into a conversation with a new arrival.

Jim talked awhile with Greg. They both refilled their chili bowls; Jim bought another Coke and Greg had another beer. They discussed construction progress on the new Memorial Hospital, acquisition of the right-of-way for the planned San Diego Freeway, development of the new El Dorado Park and rumors that the Chief of Police might retire. Time passed and Jim checked his watch, 10:00 PM and time to go to work

"I've got to run," Jim said.

"Would you do me a favor?" Greg asked.

"What's that?"

"I owe $50.00 to Lester Peabody," said Greg digging for a bill in his wallet. "It's been over a month. I haven't been able to catch him and I hate to owe somebody. I'd appreciate it if you'd drop it off."

He passed a fifty-dollar bill to Jim.

"Sure," replied Jim, "that's no bother. Count on me."

"Thanks. You'd better run. I'll see you later."

Jim left, drove toward the station, stopped for gas and arrived thirty minutes later. He parked, pulled off his field jacket, dropped it in the trunk, put on his police Melton jacket and hat, grabbed his brief case and started toward the squad room.

The new desk sergeant, Fred Carson, stood outside the squad room doorway, and called Jim.

"Hey, Grant!"

"Yes, Sergeant," Jim replied.

"Lieutenant Dickerson is inside, wants you to report to him in his office."

172

"Sure," Jim said, turning to go up the steps to the station, through the door, and into the Watch Commander's Office.

Jim hadn't had any problems with Lieutenant Dickerson, but knew the man had a rotten reputation with the troops. He came to work in 1935, attained an Associate of Arts Degree from Long Beach City College and considered himself a very important and intelligent command officer. Most men in the department had served in World War II, while Dickerson, according to stories, dodged the draft. Generally, the guys described him as a nitpicking short tempered, impulsive, inconsiderate micromanager. Jim thought that might be over-exaggerated. Rumor had it that he would soon be retired and a number of the guys couldn't wait to see him go. His nickname, "Dick the Prick," by itself, encouraged wariness.

Lieutenant Dickerson, at age 49, claimed he stood 5' 9" and weighed 135 pounds. The Civil Service Board had set the minimum height for the Long Beach Police Department at 5' 9". Many believed Dickerson had been stretched the morning he came in for his physical and to be measured. He was the smallest guy on the job. Red hair and green eyes topped it off.

When Jim entered, Dickerson stood up behind his desk, red faced and yelled, "We've got you now, you rotten son-of-a-bitch. We won't have any crooked cops here. You're fucking suspended."

Startled and speechless, Jim sensed a slight movement on his right and turned to see Detective Sergeant Bill Millard from Homicide. Big Bill Millard wore a rumpled double-breasted suit, and had his hair combed across his head to conceal a receding hairline. His face carried a sly smirk and his eyes had the look of a mean dog.

A host of warning signals erupted in Jim's mind. Sergeant Millard, a suspect, stood as his apparent accuser. What had he done?

173

"What the hell are you talking about? What did I do?" Jim blurted.

Millard, in his regular manner of speech, spoke deliberately in a low deep voice, "Hand me your wallet, Grant."

Without a thought, he pulled his wallet from his right hip pocket and passed it to Millard.

"Watch," said Millard opening the wallet. "Here is the $50.00 bill, Lieutenant. You take it. Look at that light lipstick smudge."

Millard passed the wallet back to Jim.

Jim knew. He had been set up. Greg Henderson had nailed him for Millard.

Lieutenant Dickerson took the bill from Millard's outstretched hand, curled his lips and scowled. He examined the $50.00. "Yeah, the smudge is there. Grant, you're a fucking shake down artist."

"What have I supposedly done?" Jim asked.

"You were at Curley's in Signal Hill," Dickerson replied, "and you followed a drunk out to his car, let him get behind the wheel, arrested him, shook him down for $50.00 and then kicked him loose. You're a low down no good puke."

"That didn't happen."

The phone rang and Dickerson snapped it up, answered curtly, listened and put down the receiver. He looked across at Millard, nodded toward the door, and stated, "They're here. Keep this fucker in the office while I talk to them."

"Talk to whom?" asked Jim.

"The citizen you shook down, who do you think?"

"And who might that be?"

"Mr. Greg Henderson."

"I just saw him at Curley's," said Jim. "Is he the guy I'm supposed to have shaken down?

"Yeah," replied Dickerson.

174

"He's not drunk," said Jim. "He probably had two beers."

"Just keep him here," ordered Dickerson, looking at Millard, and walked out of the office.

Jim stood quietly while time passed, and Millard stared at him from across the room. His head throbbed. He had never been so angry or so helpless in his life. He breathed deeply and counted to a hundred to maintain self-control. Time went by slowly and finally Dickerson returned.

"Thanks for standing by, Bill," Dickerson said to Millard. "I'm glad you called and let me know about this. Peele brought Greg in and Fred Carson gave him the Intoximeter. Drunk on his ass, he had a hell of a time blowing up the balloon. The first test showed .19% and the second .23% blood alcohol."

Jim looked at his wristwatch. It was 11:45 PM. Only an hour and forty-five minutes had passed since he left Greg Henderson at Curley's. How, he questioned, did Henderson get so drunk so fast? Why would Henderson set him up? There were just too many questions.

"You're dog meat, Grant," Dickerson snarled. "Give me your fucking badge and I.D. card. You're summarily suspended pending dismissal."

Without a word, Jim unpinned his gold badge from his left breast, took his I.D. card from his wallet and gently placed them on the desk.

"Report to the Chief's Office, 9:00 AM Monday morning," Dickerson directed. "Now get your ass out of my sight."

Jim, devastated, walked to his car and drove home.

* * *

Jim rolled and tossed all night, plagued by unanswered questions. He got up on early Sunday morning, March 13th.

To keep busy, he cleaned the apartment and then polished his Studebaker.

While he worked he tried to dope things out. He remembered being pleasantly surprised Greg Henderson recognized him and called him by name. Now he knew, Henderson had come for him like a snake for a rabbit.

Lester Peabody warned him, Jeff Lewis warned him and even Tokay told him how dangerous they were. He hadn't listened and just hadn't been cautious.

No doubt they followed him from home on Saturday evening. Just being at Curley's created the opportunity for the set up.

Then it came to him; he really needed help. He could call Craig McKenzie.

Jim put down the polish cloth and walked back inside to use the telephone.

CHAPTER NINETEEN

Sunday, March 13, 1960

At 10:00 AM, he called Craig McKenzie to ask his help. Debra answered and he received a warm and friendly greeting. Craig came on the line. Jim told him that he really had a serious problem. Craig responded with an invitation to come to the McKenzie home immediately. Jim hurried over.

Debra McKenzie opened the door as he came up the walkway and hugged him. Craig stood right behind her grinning and then shook his hand.

"It's great to see you, Jim. Come in," Craig urged.

"Thanks," Jim replied. "You don't know what this means to me."

"Let me show you our home," Debra said, "then you guys can go to work."

Debra quickly showed him the house; a small pretty place on Treasure Island, it had a terrific view of the bay. In a few minutes she had him calmed down, then ushered him to Craig's den and office, poured coffee, and left the pot.

Craig became very serious, assured Jim all conversations were between attorney and client and therefore confidential, and he needed to know everything to do the job right.

Jim had thought about what he would say to Craig. It seemed wrong to tell an attorney about confidential information concerning the Long Beach Police Department, but he could see no other option.

A yellow legal pad at hand, Craig took up a pen and wrote as Jim talked.

Jim unloaded everything. He started with the death of Peggy Evans, told of the expanding investigation, the involvements of Slade, Clarey, Redden, Dr. French and Homicide Investigators Millard and Peele. He described the organization of the task force and the search of Clarey's apartment, the finding of the bloodstains, admissions by Clarey and his booking and release.

Finally he told Craig about his encounter with Gregory Henderson and the fifty-dollar bill given him for delivery to Lester Peabody. The accusation and involvement of Millard and Peele having been described, Jim explained the results of the tests that he had not witnessed and his summary suspension by Lieutenant Dickerson.

Craig grilled him extensively about the departure time from his apartment, the route driven to Curley's in Signal Hill, those persons he saw or conversed with in Curley's and his departure time, route to work and arrival time.

Then Craig asked about what occurred in the Lieutenant's office, the time he thought Greg Henderson arrived with Peele, the estimated time of the tests and finally what time Dickerson took his badge and sent him home.

Having heard the explanation, Craig reached for the pot and refilled the coffee cups. Then as Jim started to speak, Craig waved with a hand in the air to signal that his attention remained with his notes. He finished reading, made several other notes, and then looked up.

"Sorry," said Craig, "I was in the middle of some thoughts. I apologize for the interruption."

"No problem. I was just going to say I appreciate your help. Just telling about all this came as a relief."

"I don't want to give you any false hope, but I think I can help."

"What can be done?"

"Let me ask a few more questions before I answer," Craig replied. "Have you contacted Captain Green?"

"No, sir."

"Relax, its Craig."

"Okay. Craig."

"That's better."

"Should I have called the Captain?"

"It couldn't have hurt, he's a good man, but I don't want you to call him now. Let me do some work first."

"Yes, Craig."

"I'm glad you called promptly. This might be Sunday, but things can be done. I have an old friend in Signal Hill that knows everybody and where all the dirt's buried. I'll call him and see if he knows Curley. We'll need to talk to him."

"That's a good start."

"He can testify that he saw you in an ordinary conversation with Henderson. He might even have seen him pass you the fifty-dollar bill. He'll be able to describe Henderson's state of sobriety. It's even possible that he knows Henderson. Signal Hill is a small place; everybody there knows the history of everybody else. It's one spot in Southern California where you can't hide from your reputation."

"What do you mean by hide from your reputation?" Jim asked.

"What Henderson did to you is so crooked it stinks. Good people don't do bad things without tremendous cause. Bad people do them without hesitation. Henderson proved he's a low life. We'll just have to dig into his past and I think his reputation will prove me right."

"Okay."

"Speaking of reputations," Craig said, "I'm not at all surprised that Johnny Redden, Bill Millard and Carl Peele are in this shit. Redden and Millard think the laws are made for other people. Ask them, and they'll tell you how smart they are. Since I do criminal work, I've seen them in the courtroom many times. I pity poor Peele; he's just along for the ride and he'll take gas with the rest of them."

"Is there anything I can do?"

"Lay low. Go home. Just hide out. I don't even want you to answer the phone. If I need to call, I'll let it ring twice, hang up and then ring again. In any case I'll call you,

179

using that code, at 8:30 Monday morning. I'll need to let you know if you should appear in the Chief's Office at 9:00AM. Right now my intuition tells me I don't want you to appear. Delay will enable more preparation."

"I understand."

"Good. Get home and get some rest."

* * *

Seeing Craig McKenzie had been immensely helpful. Craig believed in him and knew that his reputation as a defense attorney was excellent.

Jim returned to his apartment and a ringing telephone. He let it ring. He looked about for a book to read, pulled *Andersonville*, by MacKinlay Kantor, from his shelf. He bought books when they captured his interest and set them aside. He loved Civil War history and enjoyed reading. Now he had the time and he soon lost himself in the story.

The callers were persistent. Jim cocked an ear for the code and no calls came from Craig. The phone rang about every forty minutes all day and into the night. At 2:00 AM, he put down the book and turned out the light.

* * *

Jim sat waiting for the call at 8:30 AM. He had set the alarm for 7:00 AM, but the phone started at 6:30AM. It rang incessantly. He showered, shaved and dressed in his court clothes. A suit, white shirt and tie made him ready and presentable. Still, he didn't really want to go see the Chief of Police. Not yet.

At 8:30 AM on the nose, the telephone rang twice, then about thirty seconds passed and it rang again. For the first time in hours, Jim answered it.

"Jim, this is Craig. Has anyone tried to come by and contact you?"

"No one has come to the door, but I'll bet my phone has rung a hundred times."

"Good. I'm glad you've followed instructions. A lot of people are looking for you."

"Who?"

"Leo Jefferson, Captain Green, and the Chief. Jefferson heard the rumor about your suspension at a City Employees Baseball League meeting on Sunday after church. He called Captain Green at home and the Captain called the Chief. The Chief had been kept informed about the Task Force's case, doped out the connection with Millard and Peele and he blew his cork. He went to Dickerson's home, chewed his ass, and said he should've gone through proper channels, didn't have the authority to make dismissal decisions and threatened him with a suspension. He never told Dickerson about the case though. He just scared the shit out of him."

"My God! You mean they're on my side."

"Well some. No, partly. Don't get overly confident. I can't be sure. For one, I'll bet there are more than Millard and Peele that would do anything to see you found guilty.

"That means we have work to do and the investigation is still secret. I called Captain Green Sunday afternoon. He knows I'm your attorney. I can't say he likes it, but he seemed to grudgingly accept it. It'll still take some strong evidence to clear you, but we have a chance. He wants you to continue to behave just as if you think you're dog meat."

"Hell, that's not hard."

"Then I called Chief McNaughton at his home. When I said you were my client, he didn't seem pleased. Then I told him I didn't want to go though the station switchboard and that calmed him down."

Instantly, Jim recalled a story told by Red Price about the switchboard operators. He said they could recognize every voice on the department and were famous for tattling on everybody about everything. Red said they listened in on conversations. He warned that they knew who screwed whom, the names of those that would be promoted and who would be fired. Jim had thought nobody scared Red; they did.

"I leaned on McNaughton to arrange the conference," Craig continued, "and it took some doing. I had to push him hard and he seemed displeased that I knew as much as I did. Knowing about Millard and Peele helped force the meeting. Saying I would take it to the paper cinched it."

"Oh," Jim replied. That worried him.

"Your meeting with the Chief is rescheduled for 9:00 AM, Friday, March 18th. Put that on the calendar."

"It's on."

"We'll meet in my office in the Ocean Center Building."

"Why there?"

"I told the Chief it would prevent gossip and keep it secret; he liked that."

"Oh."

"I left a message for my old timer friend in Signal Hill. Like I told you, Signal Hill is a tiny place. I hope we can identify Curley."

"Me too."

"Even so, Jim. We don't know what he'll be able to remember."

"Is there anything I can do? I'm just sitting around."

"Yeah," Craig replied. "Don't answer the phone."

"I know. I know."

"Well, maybe there is something else." "I'll call you at 5:00 PM."

"I'll be waiting."

"Oh. Another thing, Jim."

"What's that, Craig?"

"Stay out of your white Studebaker Golden Hawk. Everybody knows your car. It's the only one in town. If you go anywhere, everybody will know."

"Yeah. I guess that car stands out."

182

* * *

Jim changed out of his suit to work clothes and looked around for something to do. Unable to do anything in his own defense, he just had to use up energy.

The telephone made it worse. It rang and rang.

It seemed that he had never had so much time on his hands. He cleaned the apartment like a recruit preparing the barracks for inspection in parachute jump school. He worked in the bathroom, proceeded to the kitchen, did his bedroom, then the dining area and living room. He even cleaned out and rearranged his kitchen cabinets. The place sparkled.

The phone rang twice at 5:00 PM, then thirty seconds later it rang again.

Craig reported his friend positively identified Curley. Fearful of being accused of corrupting a witness, he gave the information directly to the Chief of Police. He told Jim the interview had to be kept secret from Millard and Peele and conducted so as to be beyond reproach.

"I'm glad he's been found," Jim said. "But, I'm not so sure he'll be much help. We don't even know if he'll remember me, much else recall anything important."

"You'll never know until you ask," Craig replied. "My old buddy from Signal Hill knew him right off. When I described Curley and asked about him, he laughed, said he knew damn sure who it was. He said the guy's name is Curley Johnson, a tough old oilman who has more money than God, balls as big as footballs, and integrity a mile long."

"Well, that's a little encouraging."

"I have a message for you," Craig said. "Captain Green wants to talk to you, but don't call through the station switchboard. You're to call his home after 5:30 PM. Write down his number. Do you have a pen?"

183

"Go ahead."

"It's Hemlock 50114. Call him. Oh yeah, another thing, call Leo Jefferson. He'd like to talk with you."

* * *

The Task Force didn't go to work until 5:30 PM so Leo couldn't be reached. Jim also didn't want to interrupt the Captain's dinner hour, so to kill time he sat down to read. The Civil War prisoner of war story had captured his interest.

At 6:40 PM, he called Captain Green. The supportive response made him feel good and broke the ice.

"Am I glad you called," Captain Green said. "I've tried to phone and it just rang."

"I'm sorry, I haven't answered the phone at all. I've just been thinking."

"I understand, though I wish you'd called me first. From my point of view, without any other information, it appears that Millard set you up."

"Thank you. That's just what happened."

"McKenzie said it's fine to talk to you about this. He's your attorney, but is that all right with you?"

"Sure."

"You must have felt trapped."

"Trapped, scared and confused."

"That makes me understand why you grabbed McKenzie. At first I didn't like that."

"I'm sorry, sir," Jim replied. "It happened at about midnight Saturday, I just didn't know what to do. I didn't think it was my place to call you."

"I think it's a good thing to have McKenzie in your corner. He's the best. Understand though, some people in the department think since you got an attorney you're guilty."

"I never thought of that."

"Don't worry about what they think. Just work on the problem."

"I'll try."

"Tell me, from your memory, what happened."

"Yes, sir."

Jim described the Greg Henderson incident in great detail just as he remembered, reported that Craig McKenzie had identified a witness and that the event happened in Signal Hill Sheriff's jurisdiction. He explained that the Chief had been asked to arrange a meeting."

Captain Green remained supportive and expressed confidence that everything would work out. Then, he laughed, changed the subject to that of the Task Force's investigation, and told Jim that Sheriff Peter Pitchess exploded when he discovered that one of his Deputy Chiefs had interfered in the arrest of Dr. French and caused his premature release.

As if ice had broken and the weather changed, Jim began to regain confidence. He believed he had Captain J. C. Green's support.

He described the two-ring telephone code and politely asked the Captain to make use of it. Green thanked him, told him to continue to keep in touch, to call him at home and then hung up.

A great deal relieved, he felt as if some of the weight he carried had disappeared. He admired J. C. and coveted his respect.

A few minutes later, Jim called the Task Force Office. Sgt. Joel Patterson answered.

"Garfield 64441, Patterson here."

"Sergeant Patterson, this is Jim Grant returning Leo Jefferson's call."

"Jim, it's good to hear from you. I hope you're bearing up okay. Millard and Peele sure whacked you. What a trap. Understand, we know what's going on and we're with you. You got that?"

"That's good to hear. I felt like I got run over by a Mack Truck. I'm not out of the woods yet."

"Keep the faith, Jim. Hey, Leo knows you're on the phone and can't wait to tell you something. Here he is."

"Hey, Jim. How come you don't answer your phone. I ought to kick your honkey ass. Don't you know you got friends here and we're with you?"

"I'm sorry Leo. I just wanted to hide."

"Hide shit, just hang in there baby. Things are going to work out."

"I'll answer next time. But, call, ring twice, hang up, and call again."

"Good. Things are cracking."

"What's happened?"

"Your idea about VWs hit big time pay dirt. I called the California Highway Patrol and all hell broke loose. They already have a unit working with some special guys from the Department of Motor Vehicles on this VW theft problem."

"They're already on it?"

"Yeah. But they didn't have jack shit. I told them about the Slade possibility and they went nuts. They've done a records search on dozens of VWs stolen around Long Beach and never recovered. They're doing more record searches to identify VWs insurance companies sold as total wrecks. They think they were bought for their factory identification, then the tags removed and put on stolen cars. Then they're repainted and sold as if repaired."

"Great, this is moving."

"You bet. The CHP has a search warrant to check the numbers on Clarey's candy apple red VW. It'd been sold as a total wreck. I got to go right now," Leo said. "I'll keep in touch. Bye."

CHAPTER TWENTY

Tuesday, March 15, 1960

After lunch, Jim's phone rang twice, went dead for thirty seconds and rang again. He picked it up.

"Jim, this is Leo."

"How did the search go?"

"You won't believe this. The California Highway Patrol doesn't do searches like we do. Last night we went to Clarey's apartment, he's not home, so we leave. We're back there this morning and he's still not home. I had to hassle these CHP guys before they'd cut the padlock and open his garage."

"Where's Clarey?"

"God knows, we don't. Nobody's seen him."

"What happened then?"

"The garage door is opened and there's his sweet looking candy apple red VW. The CHP rolls it into the alley and their expert checked all three Vehicle Identification Numbers. They're on the dashboard in the lower left corner below the windshield, under the hood and on the frame tunnel. The guy says the plates were pinned with slightly different rivets. It looks legal. Only an expert would know. They say it's a work of art, close, but not a true match. The VINs have all been switched. The car is hotter than a Jalapeno pepper. You did it, Jim. You hit those fuckers where it'll hurt. And wait till you hear the rest."

"That's great. You mean there's more?"

"Hell yes," Leo exuberantly replied. "The VIN numbers were from an auctioned total wreck. According to the DMV records, Ivan Slade bought it and then transferred title to a dealer and the dealer transferred it to Clarey. And Jim old boy, Gregory Henderson was that dealer."

"He's part of this club. That's why they could pull him in and set me up."

"10-4, baby," Leo exclaimed.

"No shit," Jim responded in surprise. "That's great information. Wait till Craig McKenzie hears this. It'll turn the tables on those bastards."

"I gotta run," Leo said. "We have to hand search all the resale records on wrecked VWs . The tough part is yet to come. The experts know the identification plates have been switched, but they can't come up with the number that's been removed. What stolen car is it? When we get to court, somebody has to testify that car 'A' got stolen, ID plates were removed, replaced and it became car 'B'. I don't know how we'll match them. I'd hate to see us only having a low-grade felony for tampering with identification numbers."

Fifteen minutes passed and the phone rang again. The code being right, Jim answered.

It was Craig. Jim told him about the call from Leo.

Craig laughed, and said that's what he was calling about. Captain Green had already called him and that's why the CHP Chief Records Clerk would be at the Friday meeting to testify. "The Task Force is convinced that Millard and Peele are crooked as a dog's hind leg."

Craig urged him to stay in hiding, "You're not out of the woods. I want you to wear your best suit and be forthright. We need to clear you and make the roof cave in on those bastards."

"When will this accusation against me end?" Jim questioned.

"In law, we say it'll only be over when it's over."

* * *

Officer Grant had been put in the library of Craig McKenzie's law offices on the fourth floor of the Ocean

Center Building at 110 W. Ocean Boulevard on Friday morning

March 18th. The wall clock read 9:25 AM. He'd arrived, wearing his suit, at a quarter to nine. A receptionist led him there, left him, and had no idea what had occurred since.

The southeasterly view from the office looked across Rainbow Pier at the Pacific Ocean. The Flag of the United States, high on the pole in front of the Municipal Auditorium, danced smartly in the wind. The morning sun came straight into the room; it shone brightly and then would be concealed for a moment by a few moving clouds from a distant Mexican storm. The shadows and the reflections bounced off the water and made the room shimmer. A beautiful morning, Jim thought. Maybe it means good fortune has come.

Craig came and shook his hand warmly explaining he would be first up. He said that Chief of Police McNaughton, Personnel Captain O'Reilly and Chief of Detectives Captain Green would be on one side of the conference table and he would sit with Jim just opposite.

A state-of-the-art Grundig reel-to-reel recorder with a three-hour tape would record the proceedings. After Jim's interview finished, they would remain in the room as Curley Johnson and then Inez Malone of DMV Records were interviewed. Then Craig said, "Just relax and be yourself and you'll do fine."

Yeah, Jim thought, sure just relax. I've been stripped of my badge, I can't carry my gun and it's a dismissal hearing.

Craig opened the door to the conference room and led Jim to the table. Chief McNaughton on the left had a troubled look on his face. Captain O'Reilly sat in the middle and Captain Green on the right; they both had pleasant smiles.

Jim worried about the troubled look and then those pleasant smiles. Were they undertaker smiles, just professional smiles or were they smiles indicating support?

Jim had only seen Chief of Police Tom McNaughton from a distance. A white male, he wore glasses and looked about sixty years old. A big heavy man, he had a round face, dimpled chin, gray hair turning bald and blue eyes. He wore a black sharkskin double-breasted suit, worn but neat. He'd joined the Long Beach Police Department in 1927, ten years before Jim had been born.

The conference room had two doors, one at each end of the table. Large framed pictures of Presidents Washington, Lincoln, Grant, and Theodore Roosevelt decorated the walls, two on each side. The black walnut conference table and matching armchairs completed the law office decor. A microphone sat in the middle of the table. Captain O'Reilly formally opened the hearing, "All parties are now in the room. I am Captain O'Reilly and this proceeding is being recorded. Let the record show that Officer Grant is present with counsel, Attorney McKenzie, and that Chief of Police McNaughton is present as well as Captain Green."

"This is a very unusual hearing," Captain O'Reilly said, "as it will involve testimony concerning an investigation of possible illegal activities of several police officers. It is therefore essential that all matters discussed here be kept secret. All persons present are asked to maintain that secrecy."

"First," Captain O'Reilly said, "Captain Green will present a synopsis of a related ongoing investigation. After that, Officer Grant will be given an opportunity to speak and be questioned. Then each of two civilians will be interviewed, then excused. A discussion will follow." Captain O'Reilly took his seat, motioning for Captain Green to stand and proceed.

Captain Green, a tall man, seemed to tower over the table. He opened a large manila envelope and removed and passed around 8 ½" x 11" black and white glossy photographs of Peggy Evans. The coroner had taken them under the Cyclone Racer at the Pike. They were startling as

190

they captured the death of a nude beautiful young girl. Chief McNaughton and Captain O'Reilly looked closely at the pictures and seemed moved.

Captain Green held one of the pictures in his hand, looked, cleared his throat, and began, "This isn't about Officer Grant taking a bribe. This is about the investigation of the death of this young girl, Peggy Evans. So, I'm starting with that case. Peggy Evans body was found at 3:10 AM on Sunday, December 28th, and Officers Price and Grant were called to the scene. Homicide Sgt. Millard and Detective Peele were called and handled the investigation. Later, the Coroner's report described the death as an abortion gone wrong. An investigative unit, separate from homicide, has worked on the case and has developed evidence identifying those involved as including Ivan Slade, Attorney Johnny Redden, Ben Clarey and Dr. August French. They also believe that Homicide Sgt. Bill Millard and Homicide Detective Carl Peele have helped those involved."

"It doesn't stop there," Captain Green continued. "It's also linked to an auto theft ring involving all of these people plus Ronald Albert Cole and Gregory Henderson. And to be fair, none of the evidence on hand would probably have been discovered were it not for the work of Officer Jim Grant. Those in on the investigation think Grant was framed to get rid him."

Both captains smiled. The Chief frowned.

Captain Green produced a Bible, walked down to Jim, placed it on the table to his front, asked him to stand and put his left hand on the Bible and raise his right hand. He admonished him "to promise tell the truth, the whole truth, so help you God."

Jim answered, "I do."

Captain Green then asked him to describe, as best he could recollect, including times of occurrence, the events of Saturday evening, March 12th.

191

"I left home at about 6:00 PM and drove up to Curley's on Signal Hill, parked and went in to eat. I got chili and a Coke. I met this friendly old timer named Curley, talked sports, and Greg Henderson came in. I knew he hung around with Motor Patrol guys. I didn't think he knew me. He came over and called me by name. We talked, refilled chili bowls and talked some more. When I got up to leave, Greg asked me to deliver $50.00 he owed Officer Lester Peabody. I said sure, put the bill in my wallet, left Curley's, stopped for gas and drove to work. Then Sgt. Carson met me at the squad room door and sent me to the Lieutenant's Office. That's when I learned about the accusation. Lt. Dickerson left me in his office with Sgt. Millard while Henderson took Intoximeter tests. I never saw Henderson at the station. Lt. Dickerson said Detective Peele brought him in and that the two Intoximeter tests had readings of .19% and .23% blood alcohol."

Jim's statement concluded, Attorney Craig McKenzie asked to hold his questions until after testimony of the two civilian witnesses.

Captain Green first looked at the other Command Officers. They nodded and he agreed.

Then Chief McNaughton spoke up, "Before we continue, I'd like to make a few points and ask a few questions."

A moment passed. No one responded.

The Chief took off his glasses and used them to gesture, stating, "To be honest, I've gotta say this. I've been in this town my whole life. I get around at community events; that's part of my job. I know Slade, Redden and French. That doesn't make me a crook. Millard and Peele know em' too, and I don't think that makes them crooks. Cops have been mooching free meals since the beginning of time and that doesn't make all cops crooks. Everybody I know goes to the Apple Valley.

I've known Bill Millard since he hired on in '40 and Carl Peele since '41. I've been kept aware of this case. I've damn sure watched its progress. When things look dirty, it's my job to make sure we dig deep. Okay, we're digging.

"Now, this meeting is to dig into something else. It's about Grant. His conduct is the reason we're here. Some things about him bother me and I want to yank them into the open. Part of me is bothered cause I'm an old cop. In my time when a police officer got in trouble with the department he went to his commanding officer. When he got an attorney, I started thinking he was guilty. Okay, these are new times and I'll accept that, but I've got questions."

"Ask them," Attorney Craig McKenzie replied.

"All right," the Chief said looking right at Jim. "You're accused of jacking up a drunk driver in a bar parking lot. To me a cop would have to be money hungry to do that for $50.00. I'm told you drive an expensive Studebaker, have a nice apartment with your own furniture and that when your gun got ripped off you replaced it with one more expensive and didn't even blink. Can you explain all that?"

The Chief's statements steamed Jim. It made him think he was being called a thief. He turned red and came near losing his temper. Then he took a moment to pause, and replied. "Sir," Jim said bluntly, "I'm cautious about how I spend my money. In my life I haven't had much. In the paratroops we were paid on the first of each month. And, I learned you had to make it last. That is, if you blew it on gambling, booze and women you wouldn't have any more until the next payday. I also learned to buy right. I bought my Studebaker ten months ago from Jamestown Motors; it was one year old.

"I bought used furniture so I could pay less for an unfurnished apartment and I didn't need much. When they took my gun, I wrote a check to Long Beach Uniform. I had to have it and I bought it. The money was in my account. I sure didn't like to buy another gun. I had to have another gun, and I want the best I can get – not fancy, the best for performance. It'll be simple to check my bank account and talk to Jamestown Motors."

The Chief smiled ever so slightly, and spoke, "Let's hear the witnesses."

Green left and returned with Curley Johnson. He saw Jim when he walked in and grinned. He had an older, but neat, gray herringbone suit on and looked good. Not bad for a guy that age, thought Jim.

Captain Green properly swore him in as a witness and he took a seat on the right side of the table. Green took a chair just opposite in order to look at him directly when asking questions. The interview now became quite formal.

Green asked, "Please state your full name and address for the record."

"My name is Curley Johnson. I live at 3622 Country Club Drive in Long Beach."

"Is Curly a nick-name?"

"Nope, that's what my mama named me."

"Mr. Johnson, what's your occupation?"

"I'm an oil man. Been one for fifty-five years."

"Do you still work?"

"Yep. Manage my leases. It keeps me busy."

"Do you know anyone in this room?"

"Yep. Seen the Chief a few times at the Petroleum Club and I met Jim Grant, there at the end of the table, last Saturday evening at Curley's."

"That's Curley's at Willow and Cherry in Signal Hill?"

"Yep."

"Have you seen him since?"

"Nope."

"About what time did you see him and what happened?"

"I guess about 6:00 PM or a few minutes after. Me and the boy here was having us a bowl of chili and talking sports and up comes that Greg Henderson. I just kinda

194

backed away. No offense to you, Jim. Henderson's a weasel. I don't truck with him. Then they talked and had more chili."

"Anything else happened?"

"Yeah, I heard Henderson say he owed another cop, don't remember his name, fifty bucks, and asked Jim to give it to him. He took it and left. Heard him say he was going to work."

"You said you don't truck with Henderson. What did you mean?"

"Mean I don't truck with him – I don't do no business with him. Son-of-a-bitch is a liar, a cheat and a car dealer. Being a car dealer gives him lots of chances to mess over people. I don't like folks like that."

"I get the picture. How do you know about him?"

"I've seen him from time to time. I know a widow woman that bought a car from him. He cheated her from hell to breakfast. I talked to him about it. He wouldn't own up. I was disgusted, got pissed and wrote her a check myself. That took care of it. Wouldn't buy a car from him if he was the last dealer in town."

Captain Green looked around at the other Command Officers. "Any other questions?"

"Yes, please." Craig said.

"Did Henderson look drunk when he talked with Officer Grant?"

"No."

"Did you see Greg Henderson again that evening?"

"Yeah, I did."

"When and where was that?"

"He left right after Jim went out the door. Seemed to be in a hurry. I walked out headed for my Cadillac. There he was next to a green '56 Chevy four-door sedan talking to some big guy, built like a bear. I never saw the likes of it; the bear handed him a ½ pint and he chug-a-lugged it."

"You saw Henderson chug-a-lug it?"

"Yeah."

"By a half-pint, do you mean whiskey?"

"It looked like a half-pint whiskey bottle to me."

"Anything else happen?"

"I got in my car. When I was backing out and leaving, I saw a skinny guy get out of the Chevy. He stayed with Henderson and the bear drove away right in front of me."

"Anything else?"

"No, I went home."

"I have no further questions," McKenzie said, poker faced, to Captain Green.

"We appreciate your help, Mr. Johnson. You're free to go," said Captain Green motioning for Curley to follow and leading him from the room.

A few seconds later, he returned with a small slender woman. About 60 years old, she looked professional in a brown suit and wore her gray streaked dark brown hair in a bun. Granny glasses partially obscured her brown eyes. She clutched a folder of notes and documents nervously. Captain Green swore her in and the questioning began.

"Please state your full name."

"Inez Elizabeth Malone."

"What is your occupation and where do you work?"

"I'm Chief Clerk of Records, Southern California Division, of the State of California Department of Motor Vehicles. That's in the Los Angeles DMV office."

"Have you been involved in an investigation of thefts of Volkswagens in the Long Beach area?"

"Yes, sir."

"These questions, as I have explained to you before, pertain to confidential Long Beach Police business. Your answers will not be disclosed to others. Have any probable suspects been identified in this investigation?"

"Yes, sir."

"Would you please explain?"

"We've been working with the California Highway Patrol on this case for months," Inez reported, fumbling with her folder and then glancing at her notes and some documents. "The problem came to our attention because too many Volkswagens were being stolen and few recovered. We believed it to be a large theft ring. Finally on Monday, as the result of information from LBPD, a search warrant uncovered a Volkswagen that appeared stolen. It looked like the Vehicle Identification Number plates had been replaced with plates from another car. The CHP officers believed the rivets were not those used by the manufacturer. They impounded the vehicle for tests. Then our experts positively determined that the VIN plates had been removed and replaced by those of another vehicle. We traced the car and found out it had been bought at auction for salvage. That means it had been declared a total wreck and sold for the value of useable parts."

"Did you determine who bought the car as salvage?"

"Yes, sir."

"And, who was that?"

Mrs. Malone looked through her papers and replied, "Mr. Ivan Slade with a business address of 1713 Sante Fe Avenue in Long Beach."

"How did this car reappear as registered?"

Again she looked at her records and answered, "Mr. Slade signed the title over to a dealer, Mr. Gregory Henderson of Henderson's Motors on East Anaheim Street in Long Beach, and he sold the car to a Mr. Ben Clarey that lives on Alamitos Avenue in Long Beach."

"Thank you. Mr. McKenzie, would you like to examine the witness?"

"No further questions. Thank you,"

Captain Green looked toward the Chief of Police. He gestured that no further questions were necessary. The witness was excused and left the room.

197

Craig McKenzie rearranged his notes and requested to make some observations. Captain Green urged him to proceed.

"The need for secrecy has made this a very unusual procedure. The accusing party, Mr. Gregory Henderson, is not present. The testimony received links him to the auto theft investigation and some of those involved are also suspects in the Peggy Evans death. Clearly Mr. Henderson is involved with parties who may wish to derail this investigation."

Craig McKenzie stood up and continued.

"Other testimony, from Mr. Curley Johnson, reveals that Henderson chug-a-lugged a half pint of liquor right after Officer Grant left for work. His description of the two men with Henderson clearly describes Millard and Peele. I'm certain that Millard gave Henderson the half pint to chug-a-lug. Then, it seems that Millard went ahead, told his story to Lt. Dickerson, who then confronted Officer Grant. Peele later brought Henderson to the station. A half pint is a lot of liquor. I'd like to refer this board to the Intoximeter tests. The first showed a blood alcohol reading of .19% and the second a reading of .23 %. That evidence is in accord with the testimony of Curley Johnson. The digestive system needs time to enable alcohol to enter the blood stream. As time passed Henderson became more intoxicated and the second higher test is proof that occurred. I think the testimony and evidence exonerate Officer Grant. I have nothing further to say."

"I don't much know Curley," the Chief said. "But I do know nobody could buy his testimony. His reputation for honesty is as solid as they come. He's convinced me they set it up. Those DMV records showed the connection. This is a damned frame-up. They must really want to get rid of Grant. On probationary stuff, it's my call, and I don't see he's guilty." The Chief turned to Jim. "This is over. Captain

O'Reilly, make arrangements to give him back his badge and get him back to work."

"Just a moment," Captain Green interrupted. "We're in a spot. If we put him back in uniform, they'll wonder why and ask questions. If we answer those questions, we're going to screw up the Peggy Evans case and the auto thefts."

"Damn it," responded the Chief. "You're right."

"Let's keep the reinstatement confidential and put Grant undercover on the Task Force. I can use him there," Captain Green suggested.

"Do it," said the Chief.

"I'll handle the Personnel records, quietly," Captain O'Reilly replied.

"You did well, Grant," the Chief said. "I knew you were clean when you got testy answering my question." He stuck a hand out toward Jim to shake. "I like your style."

Grinning, Jim pumped the Chief's hand.

Captain O'Reilly, smiling, winked at Jim. The Chief looked at his watch, excused himself and left.

Now Jim grinned.

"I've been working on the purchase of a used undercover car," Captain Green said. "I'm going to deliver the purchase order to your apartment along with your badge and I.D. card. The car's a '56 De Soto. It's at Glenn E. Thomas Dodge on Anaheim. Pick it up, park it a block from your apartment and leave your Golden Hawk where it is. You use the De Soto. Report to the Task Force office at 5:50 PM on Monday, March 21st. Remember, keep this reinstatement secret."

"Yes, sir."

Jim turned to Wolfe McKenzie, the big grin still wrapped around his face and said, "Thanks, Craig. You turned it around. I owe you."

"No you don't," Craig replied. "It's between friends. I'll see you at the party at my place on April 13th."

199

CHAPTER TWENTY-ONE

Monday, March 21, 1960

Although his troubles seemed to be over, and Jim answered the phone normally, he did as directed and said nothing about the reinstatement. When asked about the problem he always replied, "My attorney said to let him answer any questions." That usually stopped the questions.

On Monday, Jim left his Studebaker parked in front of the apartment and didn't want another soul to know he intended to pick up another car. He walked to Cherry Avenue and then took the Ocean Boulevard bus downtown. At Long Beach Boulevard he transferred to another bus, rode north to Anaheim Street and got off. Then he walked a block west to the car dealership.

Jim had waited until Monday morning to call for an appointment so he could take delivery on the same day he started work undercover. He fidgeted and looked at new cars while waiting for the Used Car Manager at Glenn E. Thomas Dodge to return from lunch. The telephone receptionist had assured him that Mr. Rooney would be available at 1:00 PM. In a hurry for no particular reason, he wanted to pick up the '56 De Soto sedan and go. He had the City of Long Beach purchase order in his hand.

Mr. Rooney walked in at 1:40 PM. A nice guy, he apologized saying he had a special Downtown Lions Club board meeting and had been delayed. He examined the purchase order, commented that everything appeared proper, handed Jim a double set of car keys and took him to an adjacent storage lot. The four-door dark green DeSoto sat near the front of the lot; a visor-shade about 12" in depth hung above the windshield the width of the car. He unlocked the door and sat behind the wheel. A Deluxe model, it had plastic seat covers over mohair upholstery that had never been sat upon, a radio, a heater and a Fluid Drive automatic transmission. It looked perfect for a trip to the Social Security office.

Jim thought about it for a moment and decided there couldn't be a less conspicuous vehicle in town. He started the engine and the big V8 purred. The odometer of the four-year old vehicle showed 12,762 miles. If the car were waxed it would look new. It should always be kept waxed, he thought, because that makes it the perfect undercover vehicle. No one would ever suspect a cop would use this car.

Jim thanked Mr. Rooney and drove away. He accelerated west on Anaheim from the dealership, felt the slow slushy shift of the Fluid Drive transmission and turned north on Sante Fe past Ivan Slade's engine rebuilding shop. He laughed. No one would ever know if he nosed around.

* * *

At 5:30 PM, Jim came through the door of the Towne Theater and turned to the executive offices doorway. He knocked, Leo let him in and the small crew clapped. It felt good. He'd become one of them.

Task force meetings began with a discussion of related news and information. Sergeant Joel Patterson opened the meeting with a startling announcement, "Men, somebody got into the Chief's safe over the weekend. Peggy's letter was taken and Ben Clarey's signed statements are gone. The Chief went right through the roof and personally picked detectives to work the case. They got nothing. There aren't any prints."

"What about Millard and Peele?" Leo asked.

"They're away at a state homicide investigator's conference in San Francisco," replied Patterson.

"A nice arrangement," Leo responded.

"Yeah," Patterson said.

"Our witnesses are gone too," Leo added. "Tokay's in Alaska. Roy Jensen and Al Kaufman went to sea on the Segundo, and Geri Kaufman's on her way to Connecticut to be near Al's next assignment at the Submarine School. And I don't have any idea where Clarey is. I can't find the bastard."

Sergeant Patterson spoke up. "Millard and Peele must think they've demolished the investigation. The evidence has been taken, the witnesses are gone or run out of town and they think Jim's been fired. They must be celebrating."

"They didn't get everything," Leo said.

"You're right," Patterson replied. "We've still got the third signed copy of Clarey's admission in our safe here. If we have to, we can bring back all the witnesses. Clarey's around somewhere, we'll just have to find him."

"I worried about whether the loss of Peggy's letter will create a stumbling block," said Patterson. "She'd named Slade, Redden, Clarey, and Dr. French and we used that information to get a judge to sign the warrant to search Clarey's apartment. That gave us the carpet stained with Peggy's blood and then Clarey's admission. With the letter gone, they might invalidate the warrant, wipe out our search and kill Clarey's admission."

No one responded.

Sgt. Patterson said he already called Captain Green and discussed the problem. In turn, Captain Green called the District Attorney's Office and asked that a Deputy D. A. be assigned for assistance. The request had been approved by mid-day. They assigned Deputy D. A. Vince Isaacson and he was expected at any moment.

Leo explained that DMV and the California Highway Patrol were examining each of the cars transferred from Slade to Henderson and then to private owners. So far, eleven had been examined and all were found to have replaced VIN plates. They still couldn't identify a specific stolen car as one of these eleven.

A knock at the door announced Isaacson's arrival. Enthusiastic about the case, he plunged right into the work. They all participated in an in-depth case discussion and then he asked to review all of the accumulated paperwork. In a few minutes he had a mountain of paper piled on a desk at the rear of the room. He sat alone, in concentration, absorbing every possible detail.

Jim remembered the court incident when Isaacson became angered because Attorney Johnny Redden had sold a bill of goods to a judge and succeeded in getting Ronald Albert Cole released on the VW theft. The old veteran that piloted seventy-six World War II bomber missions over Germany had a reputation for tenacity. Jim figured the Task Force had the best Deputy District Attorney in town.

Vince Isaacson could provide expert guidance in the prosecution of Slade, Clarey, Redden, Millard, Peele, Henderson and Cole.

The work continued.

* * *

At 9:00 AM, Tuesday, March 22nd, the phone rang and Jim grabbed it.

"Jim," an excited voice said. "This is Captain Green."

"Yes, sir."

"Clarey's dead."

"What?" Jim replied, startled. "Did you say Clarey's dead?"

"His body's been found. A fishing boat trolling near Catalina snagged it and called the Coast Guard. He'd been wrapped in fishing net. They responded, brought the body back to their base on Terminal Island and turned it over to the Coroner's Office."

"When did this happen?"

"They picked up the body at about ten last night. Karl Schultz from the Coroner's Office just called me. No one else here in the station knows."

"They're sure it's him?"

"They found his wallet and driver's license. I'm sending them a set of his fingerprints for a positive identification."

"What do you want to do?"

"I sure don't want Homicide in this," Captain Green replied. "It's a Sheriff's case. They found him beyond the Avalon City limits. That's still Los Angeles County, even if it's underwater. Their homicide has the autopsy, but I want you there. The Corner and I go way back. I'll arrange it and you can also give them an eyeball confirmation. They'll open him up right after 9:00 AM tomorrow morning. Can you make it?"

"Yes, sir."

"I'll call so you'll be expected. You go ahead and work your Task Force shift this evening," Captain Green instructed. "Then handle the autopsy in the morning."

"Yes, sir," Jim replied. "But I have to tell you, I've never been to an autopsy. I don't know what to do."

"Hell, don't worry about that. Sheriff's Homicide will do a lot of the writing and handle the evidence. Karl Schultz can tell you what you what to do. He's been in the Coroner's Office for thirty years. Don't let his cigars run you off. Pay attention, and learn."

"Yes, sir."

"Oh," Captain Green continued. "This messes up your schedule. You're working Monday through Friday now, and the Task Force hours are 5:30 PM to 2:00 AM. Work an 8:00 AM to 5:00 PM shift Wednesday for the autopsy and don't go in that evening. That'll give you Wednesday evening off and you'll return on Thursday at 5:30 PM for the Task Force. Does that work?"

"Yes, sir."

"Good, Jim," the Captain concluded. "I need to know everything possible about his death as promptly as the information can be obtained. Call me at home at 5:30 PM. You can handle that. Make that call overtime."

The telephone had only been down for second, and it rang again.

"Hello, Jim," purred Donna.

"Hi. Are you in town?"

"Yes. Only for a few days though, it's a rush trip. I have a client that simply must have some select Asian antiques to redecorate her place. I'm gathering them in Beverly Hills and West L.A."

"That's great," Jim replied.

"Can you make dinner on Wednesday evening?" Donna asked.

"Absolutely. What time and where?"

"Meet me at 7:00 PM at the Sky Room in the Breakers International Hotel," Donna paused. "And bring an overnight bag."

She hung up.

My, Jim thought, what a change of luck. A few days ago I had no job and no female prospects. Now I've got a great assignment chasing criminals that I want to catch, I'm horney and I'm going to get laid.

* * *

Jim parked the big De Soto in the Coroner's Office lot next to L. A. County General Hospital at twenty minutes before nine on Wednesday morning, March 23rd. He walked into the business office, identified himself, stated his purpose and waited. In a few minutes, Karl Schultz, wearing green surgical scrubs, hurried out, gave him a friendly greeting, took him to their small coffee room, pulled him over to the urn and poured them each a huge mug of steaming java.

"Karl," he said, "I know diddily squat about autopsies."

Karl laughed, and replied, "You've wrecked my day. Every once in a while I get a smart ass that pretends they know what's going on. Then I say nothing and it fucks with their mind. Since you're honest, I'll teach you the ropes. You'll learn. Besides, Sheriff's Homicide Detective Logan will be here. He'll do most of the work."

"Will you be able to determine the date and time of death?"

"He's been in the water awhile, that makes it harder. I've been at this for thirty years and I've looked at thousands and thousands of deaths. I'll be able to make an estimate accurate to within about twenty-four hours of the actual time of death."

"Does an autopsy take long?" Jim asked.

"It depends upon age, the state of decomposition and a multitude of other factors. In this case we'll spend about two hours. He was young, healthy, bound and wrapped in fishnet, and I expect the cause of death to be drowning. We'll still do the whole drill, expectations don't do in this work; we don't want to make any mistakes. I'll talk you through it. You take the notes."

"How are you doing, Dr. Schultz?" Los Angeles County Sheriff's Department Detective Rick Logan asked.

Dr. Schultz introduced the two men.

"I didn't know you were a doctor," Jim said.

"Well, I don't go around tooting my horn," answered Dr. Schultz, "probably because I did it the hard way."

"What do you mean, the hard way?"

"Well, I came to work here at the Coroner's Office in 1929 while I worked my way through UCLA. Then the Depression hit. The job paid well, and I just kept slugging my way through school. They wouldn't let you go to medical school part time, so I got a master's degree in pathology. Then World War II broke out and I enlisted. The Army looked at my education and background, put me in the Medical Corps and sent me to Medical School at the University of Chicago. A special course, seventeen of us went to school full time for three years. I interned on the front."

"That's a great story," Jim replied.

"Then I came back. They made me a Medical Examiner, and I did the same work. I get a little uncomfortable sometimes with this doctor, doctor shit. The old guys knew me as Karl or Schultz, so that's the way I like it. Sometimes though, when I don't like somebody or something that's going on, I put on the doctor role."

Detective Rick Logan broke in with a discussion of the interest LBPD had in Clarey. An agreeable guy, Rick immediately offered to help Jim as the work ensued.

"Everything okay?" Karl asked.

Jim and Rick were ready.

"Put these on," he instructed. He threw them each a set of green scrubs, gloves, a mask and then asked their shoe sizes. Then he brought them each a pair of rubber boots. A jar of Vick's was pushed in front of them and Karl showed them how to put a dab in each nostril. Jim's eyes watered.

"Follow me," Karl said pulling on his own mask.

They walked down a hallway, the sickening odor of death growing stronger as they drew closer and turned through a door into the autopsy room. The Vick's still didn't squelch the smell. The strong odor of disinfectant mixed with the pungent smell of rotten human meat. It brought a little bile up in Jim's throat. He forced it back down.

The walls and floor were of pale green tile, all the better to clean with a high pressure hose. The white ceiling had hanging lamps with green steel shades and 250 watt light bulbs that brightened the area. Six stationary stainless steel tables in two rows of three were neatly arranged in the austere setting. The tabletops were pans that had drain lines running to floor sumps. Scales rested on small tables with rollers.

He barely recognized Clarey's body, blackened and bloated, on the nearest table. The odor was now so bad that Jim had to swallow to keep from gagging. Coming closer, Jim saw that his arms were bound behind his back, fishing net had been wound around his torso and he wore the same clothes he had on when booked. Jim immediately confirmed his identity and told Karl Schultz and Detective Logan about the clothing. Schultz signaled his partner, Terry Hawks, and photographs were taken.

Detective Logan directed the rope bindings be cut as far from the knots as possible, to preserve them, and the fishing net carefully unwound and the clothing set aside. They pulled butcher paper from a huge roll, tore it off in sections, then placed it in layers between rope pieces, net remains and clothing in boxes to be taken to Sheriff's Homicide for evidence.

Karl pointed out bruises on the arms, neck, mouth and face. More photographs were taken as they explained bruising confirming that Clarey had been bound, beaten and gagged before death.

Karl announced each autopsy step in a loud voice, while they systematically sawed and cut their way into key body parts. The running fluids, the stench, and the sounds from the saw nearly caused Jim to vomit. He struggled not to show his misery.

They worked with surprising speed, removed and weighed organs, recovered tissue samples, and probed and examined critical areas.

Karl waved for Jim to come close when he cut into the lungs. He told him they expected to find them filled with salt water and said that signified drowning. He also explained that if death occurred before entering the water, most of the air stayed in the lungs. They cut in and the salt water flowed. Working fast, several samples were collected for laboratory analysis.

Their work concluded, all walked out of the room. They pulled off the masks, yanked off their scrubs and boots and tossed them in a huge bin, and went down the hall. Now out of the autopsy room, he took a deep gulp of fresh air, shook off the nausea and felt an odd sense of accomplishment. Clarey was a victim and entitled to justice and this had been a necessary step in that direction.

Karl led him back into the coffee room where they sat down, poured more coffee and talked. Rick and Jim took notes as Karl explained that the victim had been securely bound, beaten, gagged, wrapped in fishing net and tossed overboard. He assured them that Clarey had still been alive when he hit the water.

"He drowned after he hit the water," Karl said. "Bound and gagged as he was, he sure as hell didn't jump off the boat. And, they didn't bind him up and gag him after he drowned."

"When did he die?" asked Jim.

Karl pulled out a pocket calendar, thumbed it open, studied it for a few minutes and replied, "I'd estimate his death, give or take twenty-four hours as Sunday, March 13th. That's ten days ago."

Jim also had his calendar in hand and looked at the dates. He replied, "We arrested Clarey very early on Saturday morning, March 12th and booked him at about 6:15 AM. The bail bondsman took him out with a writ at about 6:40 AM. He still wore the same clothes when he died."

"That's close," Karl said.

Satisfied that the work had been completed, Jim changed the subject to the death of Peggy Evans. He asked Karl Schultz if any fibers had been found on the body? And, if so, could they have come from a sleeping bag?

Karl went to get the file. Jim briefly described their unsolved Peggy Evans case to Detective Logan. Karl returned several minutes later with a huge manila folder. It contained all of Peggy Evans' case information. He thumbed his way through miscellaneous documents and photographs, then fished out his laboratory report. He read the document and confirmed that tiny pieces of goose down had been found on her body.

Jim asked, "Could they have come from a sleeping bag?"

Karl answered, "If it's a good quality goose down bag, not a cheap bag filled with duck feathers."

* * *

At 5:30 PM Jim called Captain Green. He reported the results of the autopsy, explained the condition of Clarey's remains, and the Coroner's estimate that put his death within twenty-four hours of his release.

Jim also reported that the rope that bound him, his clothes, and the fish net wrapped around him were taken by Sheriff's Homicide Investigator Rick Logan.

Captain Green thanked him and said he'd be in the Task Force office when Jim reported for work Thursday afternoon.

* * *

Jim parked the De Soto northbound on Pine Avenue just south of Ocean Boulevard at 6:30 PM. Only a block west of the Breakers International, the diagonal spot easily accommodated the big car. He ignored the nickel an hour parking meter; parking was free from 6:00 PM until 8:00 AM.

He thought he looked good, wearing a white sport coat, charcoal flannel trousers, a white shirt, with a maroon knit tie and black wingtip shoes. He left his overnight kit in the car, walked the few steps to Ocean Boulevard and turned east past the State Theater on the front of the Jergins Trust Building.

He took a deep breath and enjoyed the view. Looking east down the palm lined boulevard, the United Artists and Fox West Coast Theaters were on the left and the Wilma Hasting's School of Modeling on the right. Other buildings, some nice and some just plain brick, filled in space. The Villa Riviera apartment building stood imposingly at the end of the street where Ocean Boulevard jogged slightly to the left.

He passed Locust Avenue and turned into the Breakers International Hotel. The sidewalk curved alongside the valet driveway leading to the front entry. Ballyhooed as "The only European Hotel at the edge of the sea," it opened during the boom in 1926. The likes of Colonel Charles A. Lindbergh had stayed there, the finest hotel in Long Beach.

He walked through the entry and glanced to the right at the elegant formal lobby with pillars faced with mirrors, Persian carpets, deep upholstered chairs, couches and tables. Then Jim turned left to the elevators, one of the three opened and he ascended to the top floor.

The Sky Room had fine dining and dancing. The black and chrome bar stood above a glistening waxed hardwood dance floor in a room surrounded by windows overlooking the city and the ocean. In Jim's opinion, no better 1920's art deco example existed. The combined textures of glass, tile, metal and mahogany were accented in sharp colors and made the "Roaring Twenties" come back to life. A six-piece combo in the corner on the city side of the bar played soft jazz.

Fifteen minutes early, Jim explained the reservation for Donna Stephano at 7:00 PM and asked for the small lone table in the southwest corner. Sergeant Patterson had told him this table had the best view in the city. The maitre d' smiled and directed a waiter to take him there.

211

Seated and waiting for Donna, Jim looked out; Patterson had steered him right. A spectacular view unfolded as the setting sun slipped beyond Palos Verdes Peninsula. Catalina Island loomed on the horizon, waves crashed across the beach and around the roller coaster as the skies darkened. In fifteen minutes everything changed, night fell, and lights came on illuminating the florescent surf. Rainbow Pier had blue lights, the Ferris wheel had red lights and neon glittered throughout the Pike below.

Jim turned from looking out the window and saw Donna stepping from the elevator door. She wore a low cut blue cocktail dress with a pale blue chiffon scarf that accented her cleavage. He waved, and she smiled. She look's great and those spectacular boobs are about to burst from that outfit, thought Jim. The maitre d' directed a waiter to accompany her to the table. Jim stood, gave her a hug, then she kissed him lightly on the cheek, and settled in the waiting chair.

She smiled broadly and squeezed his thigh under the table. Her soft touch stimulated him; instantly he had a boner. Jim reached over and took her other hand and pointed to the view. She smiled, squeezed his hand, and spoke, "This is going to be good. I hope you're ready."

"I can't wait."

"Let's eat. I have this view on the eighth floor. We can look between the acts."

They ordered drinks first, Donna a Manhattan and Jim a scotch and water. She talked about her trip, antique shops visited and treasures found. Next, they both ordered New York steaks, medium rare. They haggled a moment over salads and again chose the same dish, a dinner salad with Roquefort.

Their food served, they chatted, dined slowly and enjoyed the view. A vocalist joined the band and music changed from the jazz of the Twenty's and Thirty's, into more contemporary music. They played "Mack the Knife" and then "Volare."

They declined dessert, the bill discreetly appeared and Jim reached for his wallet; Donna smiled, put her hand on his arm and slipped her American Express card onto the tray. A few minutes later her card and the credit voucher were returned; she picked up her card and signed the voucher.

"Hey, Jim," a voice called, as they started for the elevator.

Craig and Debra McKenzie waved from a table on their right front. Jim introduced Donna and they were invited for a drink. They sat down and enjoyed the drink with friendly conversation. The band played and the ladies slipped away to the powder room. Jim quickly brought Craig up to date regarding his work, the disappearing evidence and the death of Clarey. The ladies returned chatting like old friends. The vocalist sang "A White Sportcoat (And A Pink Carnation)" and the group took a break.

That signaled the departure of Jim and Donna. They said goodbyes, slipped to the elevator, stepped off on the 8th Floor and went into Donna's room.

* * *

A moment later Jim burst back out of door; quickly closed it and hurried down the hall. Like a dumb shit, he had left his overnight kit in the car. Not only that, he groaned inwardly, he had forgotten his most critical need - condoms.

Down the elevator he went, crossed Ocean Boulevard at a run, west across Pine Avenue to Long Beach Drugs at Pine and Ocean. They were still open. Inside and breathless, he purchased a large economy size tin of Trojan's. In a hurry, he didn't take the offered bag.

213

Outside again, he bolted back across Ocean Boulevard, returned to his car, retrieved his bag, and ran back to the hotel. Out of breath at the elevator, he waited.

The door opened. There stood Craig and Debra. He grinned sheepishly, overnight kit in one hand and tin of condoms in the other.

"Goodnight," they said in unison as they stepped past him.

He stepped inside, punched number eight, and waited. Good grief, he thought. What will they think? Back on the eighth floor again, he hurried back to the room and knocked.

Donna opened the door. This time she didn't have a towel on. She smiled and remarked, "That was fast. I hope you didn't tire yourself out."

CHAPTER TWENTY-TWO

Thursday, March 24, 1960

At 5:25PM, Jim walked through the Task Force office doorway with Captain J.C. Green. Sergeant Patterson, Leo Jefferson and Sheriff's members, Sergeant Clay Landsberg and Deputy Eric Hanson were waiting. Deputy District Attorney Vince Isaacson had also arrived. They gathered around a conference table and the Captain presided.

First, Captain Green asked Jim to report on the autopsy. He responded, explaining that Clarey had been bound, beaten, gagged, wrapped in fishing net, and pitched overboard alive near Catalina. Then he explained that Clarey still wore the clothing he had on when he was released on Saturday, March 12th. He also repeated Deputy Coroner Karl Schultz's opinion that the death occurred about ten days before, on or about Sunday, March 13th.

"What do you suppose happened to Clarey?" Captain Green asked the group.

After a moment, Sergeant Patterson spoke, "It looks to me like they tied him up, beat the shit out of him and found out what he told us."

"Yeah," interjected Leo, "and that means they learned about Peggy's letter and Clarey's signed admissions. So they arranged to get into the safe and swipe them."

"And then they eliminated Clarey," Sergeant Landsberg volunteered, "thinking if the admissions were gone and he disappeared, they'd be okay."

"It sounds to me like an attorney figured that out," Deputy Hanson said.

"When the Chief found out his safe had been cleaned out, he got madder than hell," Captain Green said, "and you can bet he'll do his best to find out who did it."

"What do we do next, Captain?" Sergeant Patterson asked.

215

"Recommendations?" Captain Green looked around at the group.

"This is war," Leo replied. "I'd like to work with the CHP, get a search warrant for Slade's business, and take it down. We finally got a positive identification on one of the VWs. It had a marked custom exhaust system. Those pukes probably don't know we're onto the auto theft angle. If we nail them on that, one of them might cop out on the others to get a deal."

"I don't want to do that yet," Deputy District Attorney Vince Isaacson said. "If it's all right with you, I'd rather take them all out at once than take them piecemeal. I'm laying out complaint packages to get warrants on every one of them. I know Johnny Redden will pull every trick in the book; so I want this work to have every 'I' dotted and every 'T' crossed. If you guys will help on some minor follow-up stuff, I'll take the complaints in to get the warrants. I've already started confidential discussions with Judge Farley. He's a tough old bastard and we're arguing, but I'll get them as soon as I can."

Captain Green looked around at them; there appeared to be no dissent. "That's good advice. Let's go to work."

* * *

With errands to do, Jim left his apartment for work at 4:00 PM on Thursday, March 31st. More cautious now, he noticed a black '41 Nash four door sedan parked on the west side of Hermosa, ½ block north of First Street facing south toward his building. A guy behind the wheel slumped down as Jim glanced that way.

His original intention had been to go get the De Soto parked a block away. Instead, he walked to the curb, unlocked the door of his Golden Hawk, got in, fussed for a moment, and looked carefully back through his rear view

216

mirror. The man in the Nash stayed down, his head partly concealed behind a portion of the steering wheel.

Jim stepped back out of the car, locked the door, and walked casually south to Ocean Boulevard and turned west. Out of sight he ducked behind an old huge Italian Cypress growing at the corner of the building.

He waited and watched the Nash turn the corner. The driver, with a baffled look on his face, craned his neck looking toward both sides of Ocean Boulevard. Only thirty feet away as he drove past, Jim recognized lanky Carl Peele.

Jim immediately circled through the alley, cut between apartment buildings and made his way to the De Soto. He started the car, pulled out and slowly drove away from the neighborhood.

* * *

Vince Isaacson sat behind his adopted desk waiting as they arrived at 5:30 PM on Thursday, March 31st. The work had been slower than expected. The Captain, fit to be tied, arrived a moment later. The warrants were neatly arranged in front of Isaacson and he wore a grin from ear to ear. "I finally got them all," he said proudly.

"That's good," replied Jim, "cause when I left the house at four, Peele had me staked out. I made like a rabbit and lost him."

Captain Green frowned. "Maybe those bastards know you're back at work. If somebody got the safe open for them, God knows what else has been leaked. Be real careful, going into that safe shows they'll use any means possible to stop this investigation."

"I'll watch myself," Jim replied.

"We'd better scoop them all up tonight," Captain Green said turning to look at Deputy D. A. Isaacson. "That'll wipe out any threat. What do you say, Vince?"

"We can't," Isaacson said, "I checked on Slade after I got the warrants. I made up a phony name and claimed I wanted to talk to him. His secretary said he's on vacation in Hawaii. He's supposed to be back Friday afternoon April 8th."

"That's a week from tomorrow," Captain Green replied.

"Yeah, I know. It'll wait."

"I guess we'll have to," Captain Green replied, looking disgusted.

"Let me brief you on the warrants," Isaacson directed. "Knowing how slippery Redden is, I tried to assemble ironclad cases. No matter how hard I tried or how much we did, Judge Farley wanted more. Even so, some of these cases are pretty weak. Here they are."

"First: a felony arrest warrant names Ivan Slade; the violations include rape and conspiracy to commit abortion and auto theft. An accompanying warrant authorizes the search of Slade's business on Sante Fe Avenue. The information substantiating the rape and abortion came from Peggy Evans' missing letter, Tokay Rainwater, Geri Kaufman, Al Kaufman, Roy Jensen and the signed admission of Ben Clarey. The information supporting the auto theft charge and search comes from the arrest of Ronald Albert Cole, DMV and CHP records information on Ben Clarey's VW, the search warrant to examine his car, the subsequent discovery of VIN changes on other cars and additional DMV record findings. I got a high bail of $20,000 on this one."

"Second: a felony arrest warrant for John Redden. The violations are conspiracy to commit abortion and accessory to the manslaughter of Peggy Evans. But, I also got a warrant to search his home on Sorrento Drive, the boat slip locker, his 32' Chris Craft motor launch and his car. That's based on the same information as that of Slade. The judge would only go a $5,000 bail here."

218

"Third: a felony warrant names August French. That's for conspiracy to commit an abortion and for committing an abortion and manslaughter. Again, this is the same information already stated. The judge levied $20,000 here too."

"Fourth: a felony warrant naming Ronald Albert Cole for auto theft. They had no jury impaneled when Johnny Redden convinced the judge to dismiss the case, so there's no double jeopardy. Leo Jefferson and Jim Grant made the arrest and now it's back to life with the DMV and CHP information. His bail is $10,000 and I had to show all the other thefts and beg until the judge pushed it that high."

"Fifth: a felony warrant for Gregory Henderson. The violation is auto theft and the information comes from the DMV records and CHP examinations of salvaged vehicles that he sold. We got a $10,000 bail because we were able to show all the cars sold with switched ID numbers."

"Sixth: we have misdemeanor warrants for Gregory Henderson, Bill Millard and Carl Peele. They allege the filing of false information against a peace officer. The bail is $500 each."

"Shit," bellowed Captain Green, who seldom swore. "Can't we do better than that? Peggy Evans is dead, Clarey is dead, God only knows how many Volkswagens have been stolen, testimony has been fabricated to frame a police officer and this is all we can do?"

"Don't get pissed off, Captain," Isaacson replied, shaking his head in frustration. "We've got to do this right. Johnny Redden is a crafty fucker. He'll pull every stunt in the book."

"So what?" Captain Green snarled. "We don't need the search warrants. We don't need warrants to make the arrests. All we need is probable cause that they committed a felony and we can book them with no bail. That'd keep them on ice for a while."

"A while, my ass," snapped Isaacson. "The ass holes would be out with desk drawer writs and bail bonds in no time at all. Then Redden would be at the newspaper and all over our ass, screaming that the evidence stinks, we prejudged them and it's bullshit police work. Then we're really fucked."

All of the officers watched and listened. They all looked uncomfortable, like they shouldn't be hearing the argument.

"Redden is tagged for conspiracy and being an accessory to manslaughter," Captain Green grumbled. "A sharp attorney will claim he had a responsibility to advise his client and then not disclose the results. Then they'll point out that Clarey is dead."

"Those are damn near the words of the judge, and he barely issued that warrant," Isaacson replied, "and he agreed that the information from Clarey made Redden look guilty as sin."

"Shit."

"Well, we got the search warrant and he's letting us look every place I asked."

"Yeah. You did that all right, especially for his Sorrento Avenue home and the dock and boat."

"Thanks."

"What about Redden helping dispose of Peggy's body?"

"I argued to beat hell that Redden helped dump her at the roller coaster. With the conspiracy, there's plenty of case law to make him a principal to the manslaughter. Yeah, the judge said, and who'd testify? Clarey won't. He said bring him corroborating evidence. Like I said, we need to squeeze these fuckers."

"That's not all," said Captain Green. "You just have misdemeanor warrants on Millard and Peele."

"Yeah, and I agree with you there, too. But, look at the meager evidence that they framed Jim. There's just one witness, Curley Johnson. That's going to be a tough case to prosecute. Two cops and one car dealer will try to make him look like a criminal. Taking a free meal isn't a crime. Spending hours at the Apple Valley with those pukes isn't a crime. The judge said that's what attorneys are supposed to do. We can't link Millard and Peele directly to Peggy Evans' death or Ben Clarey's death or to the auto thefts. Clarey didn't help us there. So far, we can't tie them to the burglary of Jim's apartment or of the Chief's safe. How many times do I have to tell you, our best chance is to squeeze these fuckers. One of them has to rat out on the others."

"You're right, Isaacson," Captain Green sighed. "I'm a hard head, but now I understand. This is the way it has to go. And, I guess the warrants make it iron clad."

"We're not alone," said Leo Jefferson. "CHP wants to help. They've found nineteen Volkswagens with bad VINs."

"Good," Captain Green answered. "Sergeant Patterson, let's plan the arrests and searches so they all happen at once. We can't have any leaks on this. Slade will be back Friday, April 8th. We have a week to put together the best damn coordinated take down in the history of the Long Beach Police Department. By God, it better be perfect. Let's do some surveillance on Slade's place and develop some good strategy."

CHAPTER TWENTY-THREE

Thursday, April 7, 1960

Jim handled the stake-out of the engine rebuilding shop alone. It made him feel important, as if he wasn't a rookie. He went to Goodwill and paid a dollar for a large double-breasted black suit and black fedora. He wore the outfit with a pillow inside his shirt to make him look fat. Dark glasses finished off the outfit.

He slipped up in the De Soto at varied times and watched operations all week. He saw Ronald Albert Cole coming and going frequently. He learned that the engine re-building operation closed at 5:00 PM daily, but the paint shop worked nights until 3:00 AM. They even worked on Saturday and Sunday nights. When regular workers were gone, the paint shop crew kept all three gates locked.

On Thursday, April 7th, the Task Force worked late into the night coordinating the final plans to make arrests on Saturday night simultaneous with the service of the search warrants. Five different locations were involved requiring separate operations, men and vehicles. That meant help from other agencies.

Because of Jim's stake-out report, they chose 11:30 PM for the strikes. All units would work on the Los Angeles Sheriff's north county radio frequency and stay in touch.

Captain Green assigned Leo as the LBPD supervisor on the Slade search. Jim would assist.

Leo made arrangements for help from the California Highway Patrol and the State Department of Motor Vehicles. The CHP generously promised three two-man cars, plus a sergeant and two auto theft investigators from their South Los Angeles Station. The DMV committed two identification specialists. Leo also asked for two animal control officers from the Long Beach City Animal Shelter in case they had to deal with the guard dogs. Based on Jim's surveillance, they expected Ivan Slade and Ronald Albert Cole to be in the shop at the time of the raid.

Sergeant Joel Patterson, assisted by Deputy D. A. Vince Isaacson, had the duty to arrest Johnny Redden and search his home and boat. They'd have three two-man teams from the Sheriff's Department, all surveillance experts, on Redden from the time he left his office on Friday afternoon until the 11:30 PM Saturday takedown.

Captain Green planned to have three of his own selected loyal detectives along for the arrest of Millard. He said he'd figure out some way to pick up Henderson later.

Captain Joseph O'Reilly wanted to be personally involved. He'd arrest Peele. He intended to have a patrol sergeant and a two-man patrol car with him.

Sheriff's Sergeant Clay Landsberg and Deputy Eric Hanson were assigned to pick up Dr. French. They arranged for help and planned to watch his medical office from 11:00 AM, Friday and continue surveillance until 11:30 PM, Saturday. This time, they vowed, they'd sweat him without interference.

At mid-day on Friday, April 8th, the teams began to deploy.

* * *

Leo and Jim, wearing army field jackets over their uniforms, parked the De Soto in the California Highway Patrol South Los Angeles Headquarters lot at 9:30 PM, Saturday night, April 9th. A young highway patrolman immediately challenged the presence of the two scruffy LBPD officers. Leo and Jim opened their jackets, displayed Long Beach Police uniforms and badges, were waved into the station and guided to the squad room.

True to their word, the sergeant, six officers for three cars, two CHP auto theft investigators and two DMV vehicle identification specialists awaited their direction.

Leo took charge, addressed the troops from the briefing desk and passed out information. He gave each car mug shots of Slade (from an old drunk driving arrest) and Cole. He taped a large drawing of Slade's business buildings across the front of the chalkboard and passed copies to each unit.

The CHP sergeant assigned a car to each side and the rear. They were to enter adjoining properties and secure the perimeter.

Leo and Jim would park the DeSoto across the street. The Animal Shelter truck would be concealed around the corner. The perimeter troops would proceed to their posts, arriving precisely at 11:30 PM. The sergeant, two highway patrolmen, two auto theft investigators and two DMV specialists would arrive in front at 11:30 PM.

The property and buildings were discussed in detail. Leo explained the entry and search and the responsibilities of those involved. A few minor questions were answered, watches were synchronized, and Leo and Jim departed.

* * *

At 11:15 PM, Leo and Jim were parked across from Slade's place. Each individual unit leader checked in on the Sheriff's frequency. Leo acknowledged for their group. At 11:29 PM Leo pointed as CHP units turned south on Sante Fe and approached.

They shrugged from their jackets, jumped from the De Soto, and ran across the street toward the locked gate. Animal control officers followed with their loop dog restraints on poles. Jim had the big bolt cutters on the lock and it snapped as support came up from behind. The officers all had guns out.

The dogs, in their kennel, started barking frantically.

Jim ran for the second gate, reached the lock, and snapped through it easily. Four men from the paint shop ran back toward the rear.

"Police!" yelled Jim. "Stop!"

They ran out of sight.

Leo, motioned to the animal control men and yelled, "Make sure the dogs don't get out."

The CHP sergeant, with two highway patrolman and one investigator stood guard outside, while Leo, Jim and the other investigator rushed into the lighted auto body and paint shop. The DMV experts followed.

Two freshly painted Volkswagens were inside. The workers had fled. Leo left the DMV specialists to go to work, and they went back outside.

Jim considered the next move as the most risky. Their surprise over, they had to cross another twenty feet of open area to reach the third gate, cut the lock, and get through. Anxious, scared, hearing the frantic barking of the dogs, he ran forward, stumbled, and fell on his face. He jumped back up, reached the padlock, cut through and they were at the machine shop, engine re-building and parts storage building's front door. No one had fired a shot.

He tried the steel door, but it wouldn't budge.

Leo asked the CHP sergeant to leave a man covering the door, waved them to follow, ran to the right and around the building toward the rear. They went past three demolished VWs. Rounding the corner of the large building, they saw an open door. Thirty feet to their front, Ronald Albert Cole and two other men were climbing up the eight-foot chain link fence. They were near the top, when two CHP officers, hiding beyond nearby trees, stepped out and pointed revolvers at them. They yelled, "Freeze."

One guy fell from the fence, screamed and clutched his ankle. Jim thought the ankle looked broken. Cole and the other man climbed slowly down. The CHP sergeant directed them to their knees with their hands behind their heads. All three suspects were handcuffed and searched. A loaded and cocked Colt Government Model .45 automatic was taken from under Cole's loose fitting jacket.

The injured suspect complained, tears flowing down his face, that he wanted a doctor. The CHP sergeant looked at the ankle, untied and removed the shoe and the swelling ballooned.

"Relax," the sergeant said. "It ain't going to kill you. We'll deal with this later."

Leaving the sergeant in control, Leo, Jim and a CHP investigator went through the rear open door into the darkened building. With guns drawn and flashlights in hand, in a slow systematic fashion they searched for more suspects. Finding no one, they reached and unlocked the front door. They told the CHP on guard there to go around back, along with the investigator, and help his sergeant.

Relieved about their progress thus far, Jim turned to Leo, gestured toward the lighted office and party room areas and asked, "Are they next?"

"Just a minute," Leo said, as he holstered his revolver and walked back into the building. He came out a few moments later carrying a large sledgehammer.

"What's that for?" Jim questioned.

"I worried about the gates and padlocks and dogs out front," Leo answered, "and forgot to bring one of these. In a second, I'll show you what it's for. Let's go finish up."

They hurried over to the office door. Leo stood on the jamb side and Jim on the other. This door was also made of steel and they found it locked. Leo grinned, gave the sledge a mighty side-swing and struck the jamb. It hit with a crash and the door popped open.

Leo said, "See. It's just a different kind of key." He dropped the sledge against the wall, drew his gun, motioned to Jim and they went inside.

226

They slowly checked the reception area, offices and the bathrooms. They found no one. Leo waved at Jim and whispered for him to stop and listen. He did. They heard someone walking in the room above. They went back outside and stood underneath the stairs leading up to the party suite.

Leo whispered his instructions, "Have your gun ready. We're going to be exposed on the stairs when we go up. I'll go first. You come about ten feet behind me. Come fast. Got it?"

Jim nodded, a sinking feeling in his stomach.

Leo, with his gun in his right hand, grabbed the sledge in his left and ran up the stairs. Jim hesitated to allow about ten feet and rushed up behind him.

They ran to the landing, about six feet long, in front of the door. Leo took cover against the wall between a window and the door. Jim hunkered down behind him under the window. They listened and heard nothing.

Leo turned the doorknob – it was locked. He hit the jamb with the sledge. It broke and the door slammed open. Leo peeked in and Jim moved up near his back. Warily, they looked around the room. Leo moved to the right and Jim ran left. Paratrooper style, Jim thought, as he swept around the couch while covered by his partner. Again, they found no one. They looked at each other and Leo motioned toward the hallway.

Twack, came a muffled sound from the back. Something thumped and rattled.

"What was that?" Jim asked.

"Small caliber handgun, maybe."

There looked to be three rooms off the hallway. At the end, an empty bathroom stood open. They worked their way down the corridor, opening the doors and clearing each room. The first bedroom checked okay, then they looked in the second and again heard thumping. This time they knew it came from the last room.

227

Jim stayed to the left of this door and Leo the right side. Jim tried the knob. It turned and he threw it open.

Slade lay in the middle of the floor, sprawled on his back, looking up. A slight amount of blood seeped from his nose. He clutched a little .25 caliber automatic pistol in his right hand. The hand wasn't moving, but his legs were. The heels of his worn wingtip shoes tapped against the hardwood floor. All appeared involuntary, like an epileptic seizure. One leg kicked again, then both legs thrashed a tattoo on the floor.

Leo stepped on Slade's wrist and pried the gun from his hand. He moaned, rolled a little to one side and opened his mouth. A little more blood dribbled from his nose. He groaned and made gargling sounds.

"What happened?" Jim asked. "Can we do something?"

"I think he shot himself through the roof of his mouth. An automatic pistol ejects the empty case each time it's fired and there's an empty cartridge case on the floor next to his head. I think that puny little slug went into his brain and bounced around. If he doesn't die, he'll be a vegetable."

"Ambulance?"

"Yeah, do that."

Jim ran down the hall, used a phone to call and returned.

Slade's heels beat another tattoo on the floor.

Leo took the discarded .25 automatic into the living room and put it on the table. He told Jim to stand by and went out to get on the Sheriff's frequency and inform Captain Green.

The body movements subsided. Jim, nauseated by the sight, stepped into the bathroom and spit bile from his mouth. Then he washed out his mouth and spit the water out. At least, he thought, Leo isn't here to see me act like a wimp. Still needing something to kill the bad taste, he went back down the hall to the party room kitchen. He opened the refrigerator, took out a Coke, used a bottle opener mounted

228

on the front of the sink and popped the cap off. He took a gulp, glanced toward the kitchen table and saw a note on lined paper.

The note read:

April 8, 1960
Dear Mary,
I'm sorry. I did wrong and let you down.
Please forgive me.

Ivan

Jim left it where it rested.

Leo came upstairs with the Long Beach Fire Department ambulance crew. Slade was still alive, so they took him to Seaside Hospital.

Jim showed his partner the note. Leo took out another Coke, opened it, took a sip, and finally spoke, "The Captain says we're detectives, we'll handle. Let's ask for the on-call identification technician and start writing."

Leo called the station for the technician. He went out to the car, brought back his briefcase, took out chalk and marked the location where Slade's body formerly rested. Then he dug out report forms and started filling in the blank spaces.

They diagrammed the apartment, took measurements of the body location, retrieved and marked the note, recovered the single spent cartridge and put it in a small marked paper bag and made a bag for the .25 automatic.

The identification technician arrived, took photographs of the apartment and bedroom where Slade had been found, dusted everything and lifted obvious prints.

They sat together and meticulously prepared a report of events leading up to the discovery of Slade's body. Finished about 2:30 AM, they went down to check on the progress of the CHP and DMV teams.

The CHP sergeant reported the two newly painted VWs had no identification numbers and that VIN plate sets, with new rivets lying alongside, were found on a bench. He said VIN numbers from two of the three wrecked VWs behind the paint shop had been removed; the third still had intact plates. Then he laughed and showed them a small bucket with plates from about twenty cars. Finally he said that Ronald Albert Cole wouldn't even give them his name, but the other two guys were talking.

Leo thanked him, asked if he would send over copies of the reports to LBPD, and they left.

They went to Seaside Hospital for information about Slade's condition. Leo told the hospital clerk Slade had not been arrested and therefore treatment costs would not be paid by the city. He explained it as a suicide attempt. They confirmed that Slade had shot himself in the roof of the mouth, the damage appeared extensive and that he probably wouldn't live. Leo wrote down the name of treating physician and they left.

At about 3:15 AM, Leo and Jim walked into the station to file reports.

Lt. Victor Dickerson standing near the door, saw Jim and toadied and stammered, "Officer Grant, I... I... I have to apologize for my actions when Bill Millard accused you of shaking down Greg Henderson. Captain Green told that you were framed. If, if there's any thing I can do to make amends, please, just tell me. I really am sorry."

Jim nodded. "You didn't know."

A smiling Isabel Packman helped them file.

Reports done, Jim and Leo walked out of the steno office and into the hallway at the booking desk.

Captain Green came through the door into booking wearing a grin. Behind him came Bill Millard, complaining with his hands uncomfortably clamped in handcuffs behind his bear body, "Damn it guys, don't do me this way. The cuffs hurt, can't you just put them in front of me?" Two detectives followed.

Millard saw Jim, sneared and said, "I thought you were in the middle of this fucking set-up. Let's see if you can make it stick."

Sergeant Frank Gonzales at booking, reached across the desk and slapped Millard in the head. The blow knocked him back to the wall. "Shut up, asshole," Gonzales snarled. "You don't talk to a real cop that way."

Jim watched while they took Millard's wallet and personal property. Millard kept his head down. His badge and police identification card were removed from his wallet and passed to Captain Green. The accompanying detectives took him into the elevator and to jail.

An elated Captain Green motioned them into his office and explained that Millard and Peele and Redden were arrested separately and hadn't seen one another. He said Millard came to his door, was greeted and arrested at gunpoint. He refused to say anything and demanded his attorney.

Peele, immediately after being arrested, told Captain O'Reilly he would meet with someone from the District Attorney's Office and discuss cooperating in return for immunity. His badge and I.D. card were taken and he said he could provide important evidence against Redden.

The Captain didn't want to let a day go by. The meeting had already been scheduled with Vince Isaacson for 1:00 PM, Sunday, April 11th in Captain Green's office. Leo and Jim were told they would now work the day shift and then were asked to come back in and attend Peele's interview.

The Sheriff's team arrested Dr. French, told him about how Clarey died, and he said he'd talk. He told them everything and also said Millard and Peele were collecting $300 a week from him for hush money. They'd discovered a year ago that French had been performing abortions and squeezed him. Dr. French was then taken to the Long Beach Police Department and booked.

231

Sgt. Joel Patterson arrested Johnny Redden at his front doorway. The warrants were presented and he exploded in anger. Refusing to talk about the case, he saw Vince Isaacson with the police officers and profanely proclaimed the arrest as a frame-up. He raved and ranted that it was unlawful, unjust and an outrage. They searched the boat-slip locker and boat and found nothing. He threatened lawsuits all the way to jail and was booked.

Captain Green had dispatched a patrol unit to Gregory Henderson's home. They awakened him at 3:00 AM, showed him the warrant, placed him under arrest, transported and booked him. He said nothing.

Captain Green thanked Leo and Jim again for the good work and sent them home at 5:30 AM.

CHAPTER TWENTY-FOUR

Sunday, April 10, 1960

Jim came back through the station door at 12:55 PM.

He still felt great about the arrests the night before and the warm welcome of those graveyard watch officers he'd seen. Red Price had given him a hearty hello. The word had spread like wildfire. His friends knew he had been set up and the ass-holes responsible were in the slammer. They knew Millard and Peele would be cops no more.

He went directly to Captain Green's office. The outer door stood open and Dep. D. A. Vince Isaacson, Leo Jefferson and Sergeant Joel Patterson were inside.

"Right on time, Jim," Green said. "Go with Leo and bring Peele down to my office. I want him interviewed here. It won't be like an interrogation room, cause I want to keep him in a mood to cooperate."

Leo and Jim went to the jail, brought Peele from his cell, signed him out, handcuffed his wrists without saying a word and took him out. Jim knew that felony prisoners were always kept separate from their accomplices so Peele wouldn't know anything about the scope of the other arrests. He looked haggard, needed a shave and reeked of overnight body odor. They walked him to the Captain's office.

Captain Green sat behind his desk. A chair stood to his right, back to the wall, for Peele. The Captain pointed and he took a seat.

Vince Isaacson sat across from Green with Peele on his left. Sergeant Patterson took the chair to the right of Isaacson, also opposite the Captain. Jim and Leo brought in chairs and sat about four feet behind Isaacson and Patterson.

Jim sat, and looked about at the setting and thought about the circumstances. He looked again at Captain Green's F.B.I. National Academy certificate, pictures of his family and his World War II military experiences and knew this would be handled professionally. He remembered riding in the back seat of the police car after arresting Tokay when she drunkenly made accusations about Peggy Evans' death. That coincidence and his curiosity had directly led to this interrogation. He was proud to be a part of this concluding investigation.

Captain Green had decided that an interview by Dep. D. A. Isaacson would be the best tactic. He told Peele that the District Attorney's Office would have to approve any negotiated agreement and Isaacson would handle the interview.

Peele nervously nodded. He wanted to make a deal for less prison time. He knew the drill, only now he sat on the receiving end.

Isaacson briefly described the matters to be discussed as cases involving Peggy Evans abortion death, Ben Clarey's murder, Volkswagen thefts, the theft of evidence from the Chief's safe, the framing of Officer Jim Grant and the extortion of Dr. French.

Former detective Carl Peele blanched and spoke in a choked voice, "The only things I had a hand in was squeezing Dr. French, getting Grant out of the way and taking the stuff from the Chief's safe. If you'll cut a deal, I can get the sleeping bag they carried the girl in when they dumped her and I can get the stuff from the safe."

"What do you want?" Isaacson asked.

"I know I can't skate. I want three months in L. A. County Jail," Peele begged. "You gotta help me."

"You're looking at ten years in the State Penitentiary. Minimum," replied Isaacson, "All I can offer is a year in the County. You'll serve about ten months. That's the best I can do."

"I'll take it."

No you won't," Isaacson directed. "You'll listen to the conditions."

"Tell me."

"You'll produce the sleeping bag and documents, name the person who helped you get the stuff from the safe, tell everything you know and testify against those involved. In return, you'll get the year. If you roll over on me," Isaacson ordered, "I'll make sure you get ten years and I'll pick the joint where you'll serve the time."

Peele didn't ponder his choices more than ten seconds, then stammered his reply, "I'll do it. Type it out and I'll sign it."

Jim, watching it all, understood. Peele, as a veteran detective, knew exactly his options. He knew he could have some life left or he could try to protect Millard and Redden. Peele made his choice for Peele. Jim thought Millard, given the choice, would squeal on Peele. He saw no honor among these thieves.

They waited. The agreement typed, Peele, nervous and sweating, studied it and then signed his name.

Then he talked. His dialogue came forth as a report in the language of an experienced investigator. He knew a tape recorded every word and played to the situation.

"Bill Millard," he said, "over the years, developed a close relationship with Johnny Redden and talked with him about everything. Millard pushed business toward Redden and they helped each other. Redden shared everything he knew with Millard. They were like brothers, and when I became Millard's partner, they both accepted me and spoke openly all the time.

"I thought we got into bad shit about two years before, with an abortion. The family of a deceased young girl hired Redden as their attorney. He prodded Millard to follow up on the case and they tracked down Dr. French. Redden played golf with French and didn't want him arrested. By then, the family had calmed down and decided they didn't want the publicity and backed away. Redden saw it as an opportunity to milk the doctor. Redden figured they could hit him for $300.00 a week; they did. Each of them took a hundred. French didn't even know his golf buddy got a share.

"Slade became our shit house buddy, too," said Peele. "We used to go over to his place once in a while and we'd party with the young girls and get head jobs. Then Slade got in trouble with the Evans girl, so Redden arranged the abortion by Dr. French at Clarey's apartment. It went bad, and she died. Then Clarey called for help. Redden called Millard, and Millard told him to put the body in a sleeping bag, take it under the roller roaster and dump it. Then we took the report and fiddle-de-fucked around with it. We didn't want it coming back on our friends.

"The next evening at the Apple Valley, Redden told how he'd followed instructions and dumped the girl. He told us he'd put the sleeping bag in his trash. I started thinking about it, didn't like the smell of things, went by his house and the bag was still in the can. I took it. Just for insurance.

"Then bad things happened. We heard about Grant's nosing around and the letter to the boyfriend. Millard and me busted into the kid's apartment and searched it. We didn't find shit.

"Later, the Sheriff's picked up French and went to Lakewood Sheriff's. Redden got his call, realized other people were working on the abortion death and got worried. He kept calling Clarey and no one answered. Redden and Millard figured Clarey got nailed at the same time as French'd been booked. Redden called a bondsman that had a blank writ and had him monitor the station. A cop buddy of the bondsman called him when Clarey came in. Then the bondsman called to learn what they booked him for, finished the writ, wrote the bond and sprung Clarey."

Peele's voice grew tired and faded as he progressed, thought Jim.

"They told me that Redden picked up Clarey and took him to his house," said Peele. "Clarey told what he snitched off and went to sleep on the couch. Redden called Slade and gave him the bad news. Slade got shook and came over at about 5:00 PM. He told Clarey he had a buddy in Avalon that could hide him. Clarey liked that and they left in Redden's boat after dark. Redden said later that Slade started asking Clarey questions and learned just how much he'd said. Then Slade got vicious, beat the shit out of him, tied him up, and made him tell everything. Clarey bawled and said when Tokay talked she mentioned Jim Grant and that he thought Grant was there when he got searched. He said Tokay told about the dead girl's letter. Then Clarey told about his signed admissions. Slade went berserk, wrapped him in an old piece of decorative fishnet from the cabin, tied on a spare anchor, and pitched him overboard. Redden couldn't believe it. Slade scared the shit out of him.

"Right after that, Redden told Millard about the girl's letter and Clarey's admissions. Millard knew the department had assigned somebody to work this on the sly. He decided to frame Jim Grant, figuring that at the least it would screw over his credibility. He thought they'd have the evidence in the Chief's safe. They always did on those secret deals.

"Millard leaned on me to get the stuff," continued a tired and broken Carl Peele. "Captain Green's secretary, Edna, knew the combination. So did about ten other people. She'd bragged to me about it. I squeezed her to come in on Sunday, open the safe, and bring me the papers. I kept them for insurance, too.

"I knew people were working on us," Peele concluded. "I just waited for the other shoe to drop."

"How long have you been screwing Edna?" Captain Green asked.

"About six years," Peele answered lamely.

"She's married," said the Captain.

"I know."

"She kept you informed about everything happening in my office?"

237

"Yeah."

"How'd you get Greg Henderson to burn Jim Grant?" Captain Green asked.

"Johnny Redden figured that out. He told Millard he'd look for somebody with credibility, like a businessman that didn't have an axe to grind with cops. Slade said to use Henderson and that he did business with him and he'd do as he was told. Henderson even belonged to the Honorary Motor Patrol Association. Millard said even the cops would believe him."

"What'd Millard give him to drink?"

"A half pint of vodka. He just chugged it down."

"When did you discover Slade ran a hot VW business?" Isaacson asked.

"Right after Clarey got busted," Peele answered. "We started asking Redden questions and he copped out on Slade. He said he bought total wrecks and developed a flawless method of switching VINs. He told us Slade did a terrific business and unloaded dozens of VWs."

"You took Grant's gun," Captain Green said. "Where is it?"

"It's with the other stuff."

No one spoke for a moment, and then Captain Green asked, "Any one have any other questions?"

No one answered.

"Okay," Green continued. "We're done for now. Peele, you go along with Leo and Jim. You show them where you put the documents, the sleeping bag and the gun."

Carl Peele, handcuffs on, stood. Leo Jefferson took him by the elbow. Jim Grant opened the door and they left.

* * *

Peele directed them to a storage facility on Anaheim Street. They went in and Peele opened his locker. They found Peggy's letter, Clarey's two signed statements, the

238

sleeping bag and Jim's missing gun. They returned Peele, tired and broken, to jail.

The documents were returned to the Chief's safe and they changed the combination. The sleeping bag and the gun went to the crime laboratory for analysis.

Jim called Sheriff's Homicide Detective Rick Logan, told him about Peele's statement, advised him to speak with Dep. D.A. Isaacson, and told him about the spare boat anchor tied to the netting wrapped around Clarey. Logan thanked him and he hung up.

Sgt. Patterson and Leo Jefferson later spoke with Dr. French. Afterward, they told Jim the doctor exploded when he learned Redden shared in the shakedown money. After that he cooperated completely with the District Attorney.

Captain Green called the Chief of Police and started the process to dismiss Edna. He called Isabel Packman to see if she would take the job; she did.

Jim filed necessary reports and went home at 5:30 PM. He saw Captain Green speaking with a police reporter from the *Press-Telegram* when he left.

* * *

The alarm went off at 6:00 AM, Monday, April 11th. Rested and alert, Jim rolled out. Twelve hours of sleep made him a new man. He showered, shaved and dressed for duty in the Detective Bureau.

Still driving the De Soto, he went to the Park Pantry at Broadway and Junipero for breakfast. An hour to kill before work, he started with coffee and then ordered Eggs Benedict. A *Press-Telegram* lay discarded at his elbow. He picked up the front section and saw headlines of the arrests.

Delighted, he feasted, read the article and then went to work.

* * *

On Monday, April 11th, Jim received a call from Debra McKenzie reminding him of the 7:00 PM, Wednesday party at their home. He expressed his appreciation and said he'd be there.

The Task Force disbanded and Sheriffs' personnel returned to their own duties.

On Tuesday, April 12th, Jim cleaned up what little paperwork remained and received some additional information.

The goose-down fibers from the sleeping bag were found to be a match to those found on Peggy's body. A torn place in the rotten fish net showed where the attached anchor broke away. More stolen Volkswagens were identified.

The evidence became overwhelming and now, it was rumored (and in the police department rumors swept through like the tide) that Redden wanted to testify against the others and negotiate a plea bargain. It was a fact – Redden begged the jail officers to call Captain Green so he could make a deal.

At 4:30 PM, Tuesday, April 12th, Captain Green called Jim into his office, confirmed the rumors about Redden, thanked him and complimented him for his work. Next, he collected the keys for the De Soto. Then he stood up, stuck out his hand, shook Jim's and congratulated him on completion of his probation. Now, he said, the City of Long Beach would start to deduct contributions for his pension and begin the City payments for their portion.

Then the Captain settled back in his chair and told Jim that his accumulated days off enabled him to be off until Monday evening April 18th, when he would report at 11:00 PM for the Tuesday, April 19th shift.

Jim went home at 5:00 PM. He thought about the past four and a half months – his field probation after the six-week academy. The time had seemed to pass so slowly, now it seemed like it went by in a blur. He remembered the euphoria of the best arrests and still felt the high of these last few days that closed the Peggy Evans case and the VW theft ring. Then there were fears: looking down the barrels of a shotgun held by a drunk, being shot at and nearly killed by Sweetpea Jackson, catching the Arizona cowboy before he could use his .45 automatic, being framed by Millard and Peele, and running about Slade's shops with bolt cutters and his revolver. He recalled the damning feeling of depression that came with the deaths of Peggy Evans and Flora Lewis and the autopsy of Ben Clarey. Finally he shook his head and thought, I've got to get off this Cyclone Racer. It's one hell of a roller coaster.

He pondered the use of his coming days off. It was Wednesday evening and he didn't have to be back to work until next Monday evening. He needed plans.

CHAPTER TWENTY-FIVE

Wednesday, April 13, 1060

Jim spent the day Wednesday with work and leisure. He polished the Golden Hawk and finished *Andersonville*.

Then got ready for the party. Debra said to wear casual clothes, so he wore a gray crew neck sweater over a white shirt, charcoal wool trousers, Argyle socks and black penny loafers. He also purchased and gift-wrapped a fifth of Grant's Scotch Whiskey for Craig and a pound of See's chocolates for Debra. He wanted to show his appreciation for their help and friendship.

Jim parked near the McKenzie home and walked to the door at 7:00 PM, sharp. Debra and Craig met him outside the front door. Debra gave him a hug and a peck on the cheek. Jim gave Debra the candy and handed Craig the scotch.

Debra pushed Jim inside.

"Surprise," roared about twenty people amid balloons and red, white and blue hanging crepe paper.

"Good God," Jim cried, his face as red as a school kid's.

Craig and Debra laughed until tears rolled. The crowd gave a cheer. The men Jim knew, the women he didn't.

Captain Green leaned against the door with a woman he recognized from the office pictures as his wife. At the Captain's elbow stood Leo Jefferson and his wife. Then he saw Lester Peabody, Red Price with a drink in his hand, Bob Ortega, Jeff Lewis, Dep. Coroner Dr. Karl Schultz, City Prosecutor Bill Burns, Dep. D.A. Vince Isaacson, Isabel Packman and even old Curley Johnson.

Almost all were with wives or girl friends.

A girl came running around the corner, shrieked, hugged him and planted a wet kiss on his cheek. Tokay Rainwater had come back; she loved to party.

242

Then somebody tapped him on the shoulder. He turned. Donna stood there. She hugged him close, gave him a huge kiss and her tongue tickled his. The crowd roared. She stepped back, looking gorgeous, with tight fitting black capri's, and a pink angora sweater that made her jugs look fabulous. What a body. He just had a glance and it made his body react.

Craig spoke up, "Donna has come all the way from New York for Jim's party. He's not due at work until Monday evening and they're going to Catalina tomorrow morning on the Grumman seaplane. She's decorating a New York penthouse for the Wrigley's and they have an invitation to stay at the Wrigley home on the hill."

The crowd went, "Oooooh."

Jim grinned and thought, I've died and gone to heaven. That'll be Thursday night, Friday night, Saturday night and Sunday night on a great roller coaster that matches the Cyclone Racer. It'll be another euphoric high ride. Damn, will I be able to make it?

Donna clutched his arm, knowing his thoughts, gave him her most lecherous smile and whispered, "You'll make it."

EPILOGUE

The academy training had, Jim learned, been a foundation for good police work. He'd not forgotten the lessons. He'd made probation.

There were times when he'd done well and sometimes he had made mistakes, but after the Cyclone Racer roller coaster of events, he still believed in the rule of law, justice and the American system. He knew that was corny. He understood the system wasn't perfect and that some cops needed to change with the times. He believed that individuals created most of the weaknesses in the system.

He reflected about his experiences. The world he saw had not always been of people and situations that were right or wrong. Red wasn't always wrong; he often displayed ingenuity and courage. Tokay showed him that easy women could still have character.

Peggy and Flora had made him question law. He wondered if statutes outlawing abortion made sense. These girls, facing tremendous troubles hadn't seen another way out.

Finally, in this tough job, he hoped he could keep his shit together. Perverse as it might seem, he liked the work.

He knew soon he would work a walking beat downtown. He would be out there among them, at night and alone. That would be another test.

About the Author

Doug Drummond served in the paratroops, entered the Long Beach Police Department in 1959 and retired as a commander at the end of 1988, attended the F.B.I. National Academy (98th Class), has a BA, MPA, and Doctorate in Criminology, and has worked as a part-time faculty member in Criminal Justice for California State University at Long Beach since 1976. After his police retirement he was elected to City Council in Long Beach (1990-1998) and served two four-year terms (with two years as Vice-Mayor). He was also the first Chairman (from 1996 to 1998) of Gateway Cities Council of Government, a 26 city "Council of Government" in Southeast Los Angeles County. Term limits ended his political experience.

Printed in the United States
1375800004B/58-558